SWIMMER

Recent Titles by Graham Masterton available from Severn House

DOORKEEPERS

The Jim Rook Series

ROOK
THE TERROR
TOOTH AND CLAW
SNOWMAN
SWIMMER

Anthologies

FACES OF FEAR
FEELINGS OF FEAR
FORTNIGHT OF FEAR
FLIGHTS OF FEAR

SWIMMER

Graham Masterton

Severn House

This first world edition published in Great Britain 2001 by
SEVERN HOUSE PUBLISHERS LTD of
9–15 High Street, Sutton, Surrey SM1 1DF.
This first world edition published in the USA 2001 by
SEVERN HOUSE PUBLISHERS INC of
595 Madison Avenue, New York, N.Y. 10022.

British Library Cataloguing in Publication Data

Masterton, Graham, 1946–
Swimmer – (Rook : 5)
1. Horror tales
I. Title
823.9′14 [F]

ISBN 0-7278-5697-9

Typeset by Palimpsest Book Production Ltd.,
Polmont, Stirlingshire, Scotland.
Printed and bound in Great Britain by
MPG Books Ltd., Bodmin, Cornwall.

For the International Friends of Tibbles
Vince Fahey, T.C., Bruce Thomas and Gary Johnson

One

'Mikey, honey! Don't splash!' she called, as she tilted her wide-brimmed straw hat on to her head and eased herself down on the sun lounger. Mike, as usual, took no notice whatsoever and continued to chase his younger sister around the pool. 'Mike! If you go on splashing you'll be out of that pool so darn fast!'

'He's wetting my hair!' Tracey protested. 'Mom, he's wetting my hair!'

'All right, young man, out of there!' she said, putting down her John Grisham novel and standing up. But at that moment she heard her mobile phone warbling 'The Bells of St Mary's' from inside the house. 'That's your father – you wait until I tell him what you've been doing!'

She hurried across the hot red-brick patio and into the sunroom. Mike was still splashing and Tracey was still screaming. Mike had always been a handful, ever since he was old enough to crawl around the room and pull tablecloths down on to the floor, along with framed photographs, vases of flowers and lamps. Now he was nine he was even worse, and Jennie found him almost impossible to control.

She found her phone under one of the floral cushions in the living-room.

'Doug, is that you?'

'Hi, sweetheart. I just wanted to let you know that this financial forecasting meeting is going on a whole lot longer than we expected. I'll probably grab a bite to eat with George and Sandos, and I'll see you later.'

Tracey was screaming even more loudly than ever. 'Mommy! Mommy! Come quick! *Mommy, come quick!*'

Jennie cupped her hand over the phone and shouted, 'Mike! You're going to be in such trouble when I get back out there!'

'What's that?' asked Doug. 'Mike playing up again?'

'Well, what do you expect when you're never home, and even when you are you always spoil him so much?'

'Oh, come on, Jennie, I'm working my fingers to the bone. How do you think we can afford a pool and two automobiles *and* a skiing vacation every winter?'

'*Mommy! Mommy! You have to come quick! It's Mike!*'

'I have to go,' said Jennie. 'The kids are raising three kinds of hell out there.'

'Listen . . . before you go, can you make sure you get my tan suit out of the cleaners? And can you call Jeff Adamson down at Ventura Pools and see what's happened to that new filter he was going to fit?'

'Okay, okay. What time do you think you're going to be back?'

'I don't know. There's a possibility that I may have to stay over.'

'Oh yes? What's her name?'

'What do you mean? Whose name?'

'The possibility that you have to stay over.'

'Oh, don't start that again. I may be a workaholic but I'm a *faithful* workaholic.'

'*Mommy! Mommy! Mommy!*'

'For goodness' sake!' Jennie snapped. 'I'm on the phone to Daddy!'

'Well, it sounds like you'd better go, anyhow,' said Doug. 'Listen, I'll call you after we've eaten and let you know what's happening, okay?'

Jennie walked out through the sunroom. It was so dazzlingly bright outside that she wasn't sure what she was looking at. The bushes on the left-hand side of the swimming-pool area abruptly shook, as if somebody had walked through them, although there was nobody there. The surface of the pool itself glittered and sparkled, and it was only when she came out of the sunroom that she saw Tracey right up to her neck in the water, her wet hair plastered over her face like a shining brass mask.

'What's happened?' Jennie screamed at her. 'Where's Mike?'

Tracey pushed back her hair. She was wide-eyed with panic. 'Mommy, I couldn't save him, he went right under.'

With a sick jolt of dread, Jennie ran to the edge of the pool. She couldn't see Mike at first, but then she caught sight of a pale shape right at the bottom of the deep end. 'Tracey!' she screamed. 'Call 911! Tell them to send an ambulance, *fast*!'

Without hesitating, she took a deep breath and dived into the water, her straw hat flying off her head. She plunged under the surface and swam down toward Mike with such power that she felt her shoulder muscles cracking. She had never been a good underwater swimmer, but now she managed to reach Mike with only four or five strokes, and seize his arm. He turned, in an idle swirling motion, and rolled over so that he was staring at her. His eyes were wide and he had an extraordinary expression on his face, as if he were smirking at her.

Jennie swam up toward the surface, dragging him after her. She came splashing out of the shallow end of the pool holding him in her arms, his legs swinging, his head hanging back. She laid him on the side of the pool, and immediately started to give him mouth-to-mouth resuscitation. God, he couldn't be dead. She hadn't been talking on the phone for more than a couple of minutes. How could he have drowned so quickly?

'Come on, Mike,' she begged him. 'Come on, Mike, you have to breathe. Come on, darling, you have to breathe!'

Tracey came out of the house. 'Is he drowned?' she asked in a high, fearful voice.

'Did you call the ambulance?' asked Jennie.

'The lady said they were coming real quick.'

Jennie blew desperately into Mikey's mouth. His lips were so cold, he felt as if he had been dead for hours. As she blew, the tears streamed down her cheeks and dripped on to his face. 'Breathe, darling, you have to breathe!'

It seemed like for ever before she heard the siren warbling in the street outside. Mikey's eyes were still open and unblinking, and he lolled from side to side as she tried to force the water out of his lungs. It still looked as if he were smirking, and she couldn't believe that he was dead. She almost expected him to jump up and start skipping around the pool, laughing at her.

Two paramedics came hurrying across the yard. One of them, a short Hispanic woman with thick black curly hair, gently helped Jennie on to her feet while the other one knelt down beside Mike and checked his vital signs.

'He's going to be all right, isn't he?' asked Jennie, knowing that he wasn't, knowing that he was already dead, but praying that two trained paramedics could work a miracle over him. After all, they did it on *ER*, didn't they? And she'd seen so many news reports of kids who'd been drowned and then brought back to life. In Canada, that busload of kids who went through the ice.

'Why don't you come inside?' the paramedic asked her, taking her arm. 'Come and sit down.'

'That's my son,' Jennie protested. 'That's my only son!'

The other paramedic stood up, and came toward her with the saddest expression she had ever seen. 'I'm so sorry,' he said. 'There was nothing more we could do.'

Jennie twisted her arm free and walked toward Mikey's body on legs that seemed to have no more strength than dry sticks. She knelt slowly down beside him and cradled his head in her lap, a southern Californian *pietà*. On the ridge of the house, four or five quail clustered, and for once they were silent, as if they sensed the dreadful tragedy of what had happened.

And Jennie sensed something, too. A coldness, as if a cloud had passed over the sun. It wasn't just shock. It wasn't just grief. It was something more than these – as if something deeply malevolent had passed through the yard. She looked toward the bushes that she had seen shaking as she came out of the house. There was nobody there, and if there had been she would have easily seen them, because the bushes were so sparsely planted. But as she peered toward them she saw that – in the shadow of the orange tree – there were six or seven wet footprints on the bricks. Adult-sized footprints.

The paramedic came out of the house rolling a trolley. He lowered it next to Mike and said, 'Let's make him more comfortable, shall we?'

Jennie nodded, and lifted Mike on to the sheet. 'Don't cover his face,' she said. 'Not yet, anyhow.' She glanced inside the house and saw that the woman paramedic was taking care of Tracey, and that her neighbor Blanche had just come into the living-room, looking tearful and distressed.

She left Mike and walked around the pool until she came to the footprints. There was no question about it: they were grown-up footprints; and in the shaded corner of the patio they were still wet, although the sun had already dried any others that might have been leading up to them.

Blanche came out, her mouth puckered with grief, and put her arms around her. Now, however, Jennie felt strangely calm. She found herself pressing her cheek against Blanche's dry, sun-bleached hair without any emotion, and burying her chin in Blanche's sleeveless seersucker top. She didn't need sympathy. She needed revenge. Somebody had been here. Somebody had entered their yard and killed her son. She wanted to know who it was. She was determined to know who it was.

Lieutenant Harris circled the pool area, frowning at the pool as if he expected another body to come floating to the surface. He was short and broad-shouldered, built like an over-packed flight bag, with a wayward plume of reddish hair and a bright red scar on his chin. If Columbo had been real, he would have looked like Lieutenant Harris. But unlike Columbo, Lieutenant Harris had no intuitive ideas about who might have killed Mike.

'You saw the bushes move?'

'That's right. I came running out of the house and the bushes were moving.'

'Like what? Like the wind was blowing them?'

'There wasn't any wind.'

'But there could have been a gust. Come on, this is almost Santa Ana season.'

'There wasn't any wind.'

Lieutenant Harris walked over to the oleanders and shaded his eyes to look between them. 'A person couldn't hide here, right?'

'No, not really.'

'So if somebody *was* here, the chances are that you would have seen them, right?'

'I couldn't have missed them. But there were all of these footprints.'

Lieutenant Harris circled around, peering at the bricks. 'Well, sure, if you say so. But they're gone now, right? They've all dried up. They were circumstantial evidence at best; and now we don't even have that.'

Jennie said, 'You don't really believe me, do you?'

Lieutenant Harris took a crumpled restaurant napkin out of his pocket and dabbed at his forehead with it. The day was so hot that it was almost deafening.

'What can I say? Your son drowned and I'm really sorry. But there's no *prima facie* evidence here that anybody else was involved. Those footprints . . . well, they could have been yours, right?'

'I never went over to that side of the pool.'

'Well, you don't *recall* going over to that side of the pool. But, you know . . . when you're in shock, your memory can be pretty deceptive . . .'

'Lieutenant, I never went over to that side of the pool. But there were footprints there. Grown-up-sized footprints. Somebody came into this yard and pushed Mike under the water and I'm sure of it.'

Lieutenant Harris covered his mouth with his hand for a moment, and looked down reflectively into the pool. Then he said, 'I talked to Tracey, as you know.'

'Sure. Tracey always tells the truth.'

'Well, this time Tracey said that she didn't see anybody else in the yard, except for herself and Mike. She agreed that you were gone for only a matter of minutes. Two, maybe three at the most. But Mike went under and she couldn't do anything to save him. It's a tragedy that happens here in Los Angeles every day of the week. You have a pool, you have children, there's always a risk that they're going to drown. But what do you do? Have no pools? Or never have children?'

'Mike could swim like a little fish. He never would've drowned.'

'Well, let me tell you, I'm sorrier for what happened here than words can express. But I think this was a tragic accident, and we're just going to have to accept it as that. I'll leave it to the coroner, of course. It's his decision. But I don't seriously think that we're looking for anybody else.' He paused, and his rumpled brow was glistening with perspiration. 'If you or your husband want to talk to anybody, Mrs Oppenheimer, we can put you in touch with specialist counselors.'

'No,' said Jennie. 'I think I know who I need to talk to.'

Jim was trying to fit a four-foot statue of Hanuman, the Nepalese ape-god, into a cardboard box measuring three feet by ten inches. Hanuman had six arms and six legs and the strained, anguished expression of a chronic constipation sufferer. After twenty minutes of struggling to pack him, Jim's expression was almost the same. He was being watched from the back of the couch by his cat, Tibbles Two, who repeatedly closed her eyes as if she were too exasperated to watch his efforts to achieve the impossible, or she couldn't understand why anybody would want to keep a four-foot statue of Hanuman in the first place.

'Hanuman is lucky, okay?' Jim snapped at her. 'And since I've had about as much luck as Wily Coyote lately, I feel the need to take him along.'

Tibbles Two said nothing, but closed her eyes completely and pretended that she was asleep. Jim was still slightly afraid of her. Since she had appeared in his life, and attached herself to him, he had increasingly felt that she was looking after him, instead of the other way around. He opened the cans of 9 Lives, that was for sure; but it was Tibbles Two who seemed to control his spiritual destiny.

Whenever she looked at him with those agate-yellow eyes he felt that she was waiting for him to take another step into the unknown – waiting for him to follow her to places that she had been but he never had. The unknown zone.

But he was packing up now to take up a new posting with the Department of Education in Washington, D.C., and Tibbles Two would have to remain in this apartment block in Venice with his friend and self-appointed super, Mervyn Brookfeller. He knew that Mervyn woud take almost unnatural care of her: Mervyn took almost unnatural care of everybody and everything. Although he wasn't paid for it, he hoovered the hallways, he dug coffee spoons out of jammed Insinkerators, and he ran errands to Ralph's for the older residents. Jim had even stood at a half-open doorway once and watched Mervyn feeding old Mrs Kaufman with Cream of Wheat, doggedly and patiently, like a caring parent with a small child. Mrs Kaufman was wearing an old green flannel bathrobe and Mervyn was wearing a spangled emerald T-shirt and white stretch tights. It had almost been enough to bring tears to Jim's eyes.

At last Jim admitted defeat and pulled Hanuman and all of his grinning ape-attendants out of the split-open cardboard box. 'You'd think they'd make their religious figures a standard size, for God's sake.'

Tibbles Two turned her head away.

At that moment, Jim's mobile phone rang, and he climbed over the couch and a stack of boxes to find it. Sometimes he really enjoyed TT's company, but most of the time he found her exasperating. She ate, she slept, she stared at him, but she never answered the phone and she never brought him a beer out of the icebox.

'Mr Rook?'

'Yes, it is. Jim Rook here. Who wants him?'

'Well, I don't know whether you'll remember me. Jennie Oppenheimer. Well, Jennie Bauer when I was single. I was in your class in '91.'

'Jennie Bauer . . . Jennie Bauer . . . Hey, yes! Of course I remember you! Sure! I remember all of my students, even the students I'd rather forget. Let me see now . . . *King Lear* . . . when Cordelia weeps over the dying king, and says, "Had you not been their father, these white flakes | Did challenge pity of them" – what did you say? "Does that mean he had dandruff?" Yes, Jennie. I remember you. I remember you *clearly*. Long blond hair. Very cute. Short span of attention, I'm afraid to say.'

'My son's dead.'

Jim didn't know what to say. He very rarely heard from his students after they had left Special Class II at West Grove Community College. They always swore that they would write, and keep in touch, but he always knew they wouldn't. Those who had been saved by his remedial English class from a life of car-washing and dog-walking and other McJobs were always too busy to remember the scruffy teacher who had shown them the difference between Hamlet and ham-and-eggs, and who had brought them to the edge of tears with his recitation of poetry by John Frederick Nims: '*Inference of night wind, a rumor of rain*.'

'I'm very sorry to hear that,' said Jim, thinking, Why is she telling me? I haven't heard from her since the leaving party after her final exams. 'What happened? Was it an accident?'

'He drowned. It happened yesterday morning. Mike and his sister were playing in the pool and I left them alone for only a moment, but he drowned.'

'I'm so sorry. That's a tragedy. How old was he?'

'Nine, and he was such a good swimmer.'

'I don't know what to say, Jennie. My heart goes out to you. Was Mike your only boy?'

'His father's devastated. We can't have any more children and he's blaming me.'

'It's the shock, that's all,' Jim reassured her. 'He'll get over it. An accident is an accident.'

'But this is the point, Mr Rook. This is why I'm calling you.'

'Hey, listen. I think you can call me Jim now. We're not in Special Class II any more.'

'I know . . . But you do still have that ability, don't you?'

'Ability?'

'You can still see – well, you can still see ghosts and things like that?'

Jim didn't say anything, but he thought, Uh-oh, what's coming now? So many people who found out that he could see spirits and other supernatural presences wanted him to help them with all kinds of other-worldly problems. Either they wanted him to summon up their late Uncle Charlie to find out what he'd done with all of his rare Civil War coins, or else they wanted to discover if a chilly presence in their kitchen was the cause of all of their rotten luck. They never seemed to accept that supernatural manifestations walk among us all the time, with their own tragic problems and their own complicated agendas, and spirits are hardly ever interested either in contacting the still-living or helping them, and especially not in harming them. They were benign, most of them – benign and slightly stunned, like the victims of a bus crash.

But Jennie didn't say what he expected her to say. 'Listen, Mr Rook, I came out of the house and I was sure that somebody had just pushed their way through the bushes. Then – when I was trying to save Mike – I saw wet footprints on the bricks around the side of the pool. They weren't a child's footprints – they weren't Mikey's or Tracey's – but there was nobody else there. Tracey tells me that she didn't see anybody, and by the time the police arrived the footprints had all dried up. The detective told me I was in shock. Well, I *was* in shock. Of course I was in shock. But I know what I saw.'

'So . . . uh . . . what do you want *me* to do?'

'I want you to find out who murdered Mike, Mr Rook. I want to find out who pushed him under the water, and why.' She was crying now, and she was so grief-stricken and exhausted that her voice acquired a deep throaty undertone, as if she were starting to sing an aria in a tragic opera.

'Jennie, I'd love to be able to help you. But this sounds like police business to me.'

'I told you. The police don't believe me. They're going to say it was an accident, or parental neglect, or whatever.'

Jim sat down on the arm of his couch. Outside the window, the sun was gradually sinking over Venice and the evening sky was the color of boysenberry jelly. 'Jennie, I'm packing up to leave. I've been offered a job with the Department of Education in Washington, D.C.'

'You're *leaving*? What about Special Class II?'

'Well, we all have to move on. This is going to give me the chance to help students all over the country, not just LA.'

'When are you going? Do you think we could meet?'

Jim looked toward Tibbles Two, but all she could do was yawn and dig her claws into the cushions. Either she was provoking him into making a decision, or else she was trying to tell him that he was wasting his time. She was only a cat, for sure, but he had seen what she could do before. Her nose was more finely tuned for fortune-telling cards than any of the so-called 'psychic sensitives' that he had ever met.

The day before he had been offered his new job in Washington, she had scratched out of his Grimaud pack the eight of diamonds, signifying 'delay', and the ace of diamonds, which represented 'a wicked woman'. Then – haughtily – she had stalked back to the couch, curled herself up and sat there watching him to see what his reaction would be.

Jim said, 'I'm packing now, as a matter of fact. I'm supposed to be flying out Wednesday morning.'

'Mr Rook – I'm sorry, Jim – I know this is an imposition. But I know that Mike didn't drown by accident, and I don't have any other way of proving it.'

Jim raked his fingers through his tousled hair. In the mirror on the other side of his apartment, another Jim Rook, with his face back to front, did the same thing. The Jim Rook in the mirror was thinking, When you take on a student, when you teach her how to write and how to talk, and how to make her own impression on the world around her, when does your responsibility end? All of that poetry you taught her, all of those plays, all of those hours struggling with Shakespeare and Emily Dickinson and Kenneth Patchen: 'Have you wondered why all the windows in heaven were broken?'

The trouble was, he knew what the truth was; and the truth was that a teacher's responsibility never ends, any more than a parent's or a priest's.

'Okay,' he said. 'Do you know the Café del Rey, on Admiralty Way? I can meet you there at – what, maybe eight o'clock?'

'I'm sorry,' Jennie told him, and he could tell that she was crying. 'I'm so frightened – I'm so scared – and I couldn't think of anybody else to turn to.'

After she had hung up, Jim sat on the edge of the couch with his head bowed. He had promised himself that he would never again answer an appeal for help from anybody who was troubled by supernatural events – or seemingly supernatural events, anyhow. He had nearly died from pneumonia at the age of nine, the same age as Mike, and ever since then he had seen faces and people and things that he didn't want to think of, ever again. Shadows, ghosts. Demons running through the streets, and screaming at him out of closets. Dead people, standing outside supermarkets. Sad and bewildered faces, reflected in windows, when there was nobody there.

He couldn't take any more of it. People didn't seem to understand that he found his psychic ability even more frightening than they did. He had no choice about what he saw. If he went to visit a friend, and his friend's dead grandfather was sitting in the corner of the room, and only Jim could see him, what could he do about it? What was he supposed to say?

As he sat there, Tibbles Two dropped off the couch on to the floor. She padded across to the coffee table, where Jim had stacked all his various decks of mystical cards. She stood up on her hind legs and tipped the Grimaud deck on to the floor, so that the cards were scattered out of their box.

'Thanks, TT,' said Jim. 'It's nice to know that there's somebody even messier than me.'

He knelt down to pick up the cards, but while he was shuffling them back into order, TT picked one out of the deck between her teeth and walked off into the kitchen with it.

'The hell—' said Jim, and followed her.

TT was standing over her water bowl. With great care she dropped the Grimaud card into the water, and watched it as it sank.

'Great move,' said Jim. He knelt down and picked the card out of the water, and shook it. It was the death card, the card of the empty-eyed skeleton, the nine of clubs, wrapped in a dark gray sheet with a scythe over his shoulder and an hourglass in his hand.

'What's this?' Jim asked her, holding up the dripping card. 'All of a sudden you're playing boats?'

TT stared at him as if she couldn't believe how stupid he was.

'What, then?' he demanded.

She came up to him and flicked the card out of his hand with her paw. Then she picked it up in her mouth and dropped it back in the water bowl.

'Death in the water,' said Jim. 'That's what you're telling me, isn't it? Death by drowning. And more than one death.'

He fished the card out of the water bowl and shook it. 'Listen . . . I'm going to see Jennie and try to find out what happened. But I can't do anything more than that. I'm still leaving for Washington Wednesday, and when I'm gone, I'm gone for good. And nobody else in the world is ever going to discover that I can see their recently deceased nephew playing ball on their lawn.'

Two

Jennie looked smaller and much more pale than he remembered her – as if the laughing, suntanned, provocative girl that he had taught in Special Class II all those years ago had died, and this was her ghost. She was sitting in the corner of the café with a glass of mineral water, staring out of the window, and it was only when Jim walked right up to her table that she lifted her eyes, and focused them, and gave him the faintest suggestion of a smile.

'Well, well. Jennie Bauer.'

'Jennie Oppenheimer these days.'

Jim sat down, and ordered a Coors. 'What happened to your son . . . that was terrible. I had some friends in San Fernando who lost their daughter in their pool. Tragic.'

'You mean that she was deliberately drowned, like Mikey?'

Jim sat back in his chair and looked at her in just the same narrow-eyed way that he looked at all of his students when they flew off on some over-imaginative tangent. 'You saw the bushes move, and you saw some wet footprints beside the pool?'

'Somebody was there, Mr Rook. Somebody or something. I could feel it. It was cold. It was very evil. And I swear to God I'm not making this up.'

Jim's Coors arrived, in a ridiculously tall, frosted glass. Personally, he preferred it straight out of the can. All the same, he scooped up a handful of pretzels, chewed them until they were mush, and then sluiced them down with a cheek-bulging mouthful of cold beer.

'Let me tell you this, Jennie. In my experience, spirits are not half as interested in our world, the physical world, as we are in theirs. They've lived their lives, okay? They're gone. They're too busy worrying about ridiculous little undone details, like Why didn't I tell my father I loved him when I had the chance? They don't threaten us – not very often, anyhow. And they very seldom try to hurt us. Most of the time, they can't. They don't have the . . . whatdyacallit? . . . *substance*.'

'But somebody drowned Mike, I swear to God.'

Jim laid a hand on her arm. 'I don't know what to say. You saw the bushes move. You saw some wet footprints beside the pool. You had the weird feeling that somebody had walked through your yard. But none of that amounts to any kind of real evidence, does it? I mean, let's be serious about this.'

Jennie stared at him. He remembered her eyes: they were such an extraordinary blue, like the windows of heaven before they broke.

'My son drowned. You don't think I'm serious?'

'I don't know . . . You're making me feel guilty. I always used to give you guys in my class the general idea that there's a mystical explanation for everything that happens. But maybe there isn't. Maybe life is just life, and accidents are accidents.'

'You don't believe that, do you?'

Jim shrugged, and looked away. Across the crowded, brightly lit café, a pretty young girl with short blond hair was throwing her head back in laughter, and he had a sudden pang for the life that he had never lived, accidents or no accidents.

'I don't know what to say to you, Jennie. When they *do* harm us, spirits almost always do it for a very good reason . . . in my experience, anyhow. Usually they harm us out of revenge. I can't think what a nine-year-old boy could have done for a spirit to want to drown him.'

'So that's it?'

'That's it, I'm afraid. What you saw, what you felt . . . maybe it was some kind of spiritual manifestation. But there's no evidence that it had anything to do with Mikey's death. And think about it: if there *was* a spirit there, it could have been trying to rescue him, not drown him. Every child has a spirit watching out for him: what some people like to think of as a guardian angel. Maybe Mikey's couldn't do anything to save him.'

Tears were sliding freely down Jennie's cheeks. 'Is there any way to tell?'

'Well . . . I've heard that some mediums can do something they call a "spirit-trace". It's a way of, like, sniffing out a spirit's scent. That would tell you for sure if there *was* a spirit there, and it might give you some idea if the spirit meant to do Mike any harm. But apart from that, I don't think that spirit-traces are very specific.'

'Can you do one? I could pay you for your time.'

'A spirit-trace?' Jim shook his head. 'Way beyond my expertise, I'm afraid. I just see things, by accident. You need a real full-blown mystic for that kind of thing.'

'Do you know any full-blown mystics?'

'I used to. But that was long, long ago, in a galaxy far, far away.'

Jennie reached across the table and took hold of both of his hands. 'Mr Rook – Jim – please help me. I have to know how Mike died.'

'Well, there's a psychic fair in De Longpre Park tomorrow. Maybe somebody there will be able to help you.'

'Will you come with me?'

'I don't know, Jennie. I'm not sure that this is really the right way to go.' Jim didn't really like having anything to do with full-time professional mystics, who always made him feel as if he was a charlatan – in spite of the fact that his psychic talent was probably far more potent than theirs.

Apart from that, he had been planning on taking his fellow teacher Karen Goudemark up the coast for the day, to Captain Flynn's Famous Seafood Shack, followed by a romantic walk on the shore. He was intent on trying to persuade her to quit her job at West Grove and come with him to Washington. Karen was the most delectable woman he had ever met. Soft, warm, feminine, funny. She had cheekbones like Garbo, with honey poured over her head for hair.

'Please, Jim. I'll do anything.'

Jim picked up his napkin and dabbed away the tears on her face. 'Okay. How about twelve o'clock?'

Jennie lifted his hands and kissed his knuckles. 'You don't know what this means to me. I've been feeling like I'm going crazy.'

'Sure,' said Jim. 'Happens to me all the time.'

'A psychic fair?' Karen repeated in disbelief.

'We don't have to stay for long. I just have to find somebody who can do this special kind of spirit thing.'

'Jim . . . you know I don't have any time for all of that hippie-mystical stuff.'

'Yes, I know. But I promised. It's Jennie Bauer. She used to be in my class, about seven years ago. Her kid drowned.' He told her all about the moving bushes and the footprints, and Jennie's feeling that 'somebody was there . . . It was cold. It was very evil.'

'When did this happen?'

'Two days ago. The poor girl's still in shock.'

'Two days ago? And you're taking her to see a *psychic*? For God's sake, Jim, she needs a fully qualified counselor.'

'But she's convinced that what she saw was real, and nobody else believes her. Not even her husband.'

'And you think that somebody at a psychic fair can do that for her? Come on, Jim, you know yourself that all of this seance business is a scam. She's going to end up even more broken-hearted than she is now. And probably poorer, too.'

Jim shrugged. 'I don't know. She's so totally sure that some evil presence came into her yard. What worries me is that if *I* don't help her, she'll go looking on her own for somebody else who will. And then – yes, I agree, there really *will* be a danger that she gets ripped off.'

Karen shook her head slowly from side to side, so that her blond hair swung across her forehead. 'You're impossible, you know that, don't you? You seem to think it's your personal responsibility to cure the whole world of illiteracy, dyslexia, cultural alienation, lack of appreciation of Longfellow, acne and poor self-image – as well as every supernatural manifestation from Angels to Zombies.'

'That's not true. I never said I could cure acne.'

Karen said, 'All right, then. I'll come along to this psychic shindig. But only on one condition: that we still make it up the coast in time for lunch at Captain Flynn's.'

'Deal. Done. Absolutely. And I love you for it.'

He led her out of her house and opened the door of his saddle-bronze Eldorado convertible with a flourish. 'You won't regret this,' he told her. 'Some of these psychic fairs . . . well, you can pick up some terrific bargains. Knitwear, pottery. Magic crystals.'

'Let's just do it, shall we?' said Karen.

Jennie looked even paler today than she had yesterday, especially since she was wearing a black linen dress and a black chiffon scarf around her hair. She acknowledged Karen with a wan, distracted smile, and sat in the back of the car saying nothing at all as Jim drove them to De Longpre Park.

'You heard any more from Lieutenant Harris?' Jim coaxed her.

'Nothing. Not a word. He probably thinks I'm hysterical.'

'You're not hysterical. If you saw something, you saw something.'

'But that's the point. I didn't see anything, and neither did Tracey. That's why I want you to try this – whatever you call it, this spirit-trace.'

'*Spirit-trace?*' asked Karen, with a skeptical lift of her eyebrow.

Jim leaned back in his seat as they swerved on soft, worn-out suspension around the corner from Santa Monica Boulevard into Cherokee Avenue, under the flickering shadows of the yucca trees. 'Sure. It's a thing that professional exorcists do. Like, any spiritual manifestation will always leave some kind of evidence that it was passing by. A vibration in the air. A fragment of ectoplasm. Even a fingerprint, or a footprint. A really good psychic can pick these things up, and tell you if a spirit's been around, and what kind of a spirit it was. That's the theory, anyhow. It's a kind of psychic forensics.'

Karen took a breath, as if she were about to say something, but then she obviously changed her mind. Jim grinned at her. He guessed that she probably didn't trust herself to come out with anything polite.

They found a parking-space on the street two blocks away from De Longpre Park, in between a VW bus decorated with sunflowers and a three-wheeler motorcycle with coonskins hanging from the handlebars. The psychic fair was crowded with bearded men in bandannas and women in kaftans and children with finger-painted faces and long curly hair; as well as earnest-looking types in glasses and crumpled linen suits and Birkenstock sandals. The smell of marijuana and herbal cigarettes wafted between the tents and stalls, and brightly colored balloons bobbed up into the morning sky.

'My God,' said Karen. 'It's the summer of love all over again.'

'How do you know?' asked Jim. 'You weren't even born in 1967.'

'And how old were you? Two?'

'I was an early developer.'

They wandered between the stalls offering crystal healing and palm-readings and i-ching lessons and vegan meditation-burgers. In the far corner of the park, a band was playing Love's old song 'Andmoreagain'. Jim approached a table where an elderly woman with wild gray hair and huge hoop earrings was selling psychic necklaces and dangly gipsy bracelets. 'I'm looking for a medium.'

She took a deep suck on a suspiciously bulky cigarette. 'You came to the right place, captain. We're wall-to-wall mediums here. Wall-to-wall.'

'I'm looking for a special kind of medium. One who can do a spirit-trace.'

'Spirit-trace? Wouldn't know what *that* was if it bit me in the ass. But try some of those tents along the back. How about a psychic necklace before you go? Only a ten-spot. Wear it when you go to sleep tonight, and you'll dream the day when you're going to die. Guaranteed.'

'Guaranteed? So, if I don't die, I can bring it back for a refund?'

'That's right. But be warned, captain. Nobody never came back yet.'

'Okay, I'll take one. Karen, how about you?'

'Forget it, Jim. I know when I'm going to die. In about twenty minutes, if I don't get some lunch.'

Jim handed over $10 and the gray-haired woman gave him a necklace of coins, freshwater pearls and colored beads. As he took it, however, he noticed a young woman in a low-cut black dress staring at him from the end of the next row of stalls. She had feathery black hair, layered and shiny like a raven's wing, and a startlingly white face. She stared at him for a long moment, and then she turned away and disappeared into the crowd.

They walked along the rows of tents together, weaving their way between jugglers and mimes and fire eaters. At last they reached a small tent with a sign outside reading JULIE HOROWITZ, FAMED MYSTIC. TALK TO YOUR DEPARTED LOVED ONES.

'Give me a minute,' said Jim, and ducked his way in through the tent-flap. Inside, in tangerine-colored gloom, a young woman in upswept glasses was sitting at a small card table, with Tarot cards spread out in front of her. She looked more like a secretary from a 1960s comedy show like *The Beverly Hillbillies* than a 'famed mystic', capable of talking to departed loved ones.

'Hi,' said Jim. 'I was wondering if you could possibly help me to track down a spirit.'

'Of course. I can find *anybody,* so long as they've passed over. Who is it – somebody who was very close to you?'

'Actually, I don't know them at all.'

'But you have a name? I have to have a name to call on.'

'Unh-hunh. All I know is that something walked through a woman's back yard a couple of days ago, and it may be responsible for drowning her son.'

'I don't understand how I can help you, I'm afraid.'

'I need you to come to her house and tell me if it really was a spirit, and, if it *was* a spirit, exactly what species of spirit it was.'

Julie Horowitz took off her glasses and stared at Jim solemnly with bulging, unfocused eyes. 'You're talking about something called a spirit-trace. I'm afraid that's way out of my league. I find spirits by connecting the yearning grief of the living with the bitter regret of the recently dead. I don't do random manifestations. Especially random manifestations that might be irritated at being interfered with.'

'Do you know somebody who does?'

'I'm sorry . . . I don't think you'll find anybody like that here. We're not ghost hunters, we're more like an encounter group between the living and the passed-over.'

'I see. Well, thanks for your time, anyhow.'

'You're welcome. But if you *do* manage to find somebody to do a spirit-trace for you, you should be very, very careful. I heard about a medium in Bel Air who tried to trace the spirit in some movie producer's house, and she hasn't been able to stop screaming ever since. Literally.'

'Great, thanks for the advice.' Jim pushed his way out of the tent and back into the sunlight. 'No luck, I'm afraid,' he said. 'These people can let you talk to your dead Aunt Rhoda, but that's about as far as it goes.'

'Maybe we can go for lunch now?' asked Karen.

'Sure,' Jim agreed. 'Jennie, how about I run you home? I'll have another try tomorrow. I know a couple of people who might be able to help me.'

'All right,' said Jennie. Her disappointment was hidden behind her large dark sunglasses, but Jim could hear it in her voice. He took her arm and led her through the crowds toward the park entrance.

They were passing a stall hung with hundreds of different mirrors when Jim saw the white-faced young woman in black reflected in almost every one of them. She was looking at him out of mirrors with gilded frames, mirrors surrounded by seashells, hand mirrors with brass fairies for handles, distorting mirrors and mirrors with strangely tinted glass. Beside her stood a mime in a baggy white Pierrot outfit, with a face as cement-white as hers, and a black-painted slash for a mouth.

Jim turned around – while Karen and Jennie, not realizing that he had stopped, continued walking toward the entrance. The young woman stayed where she was, but she kept on staring at him with the faintest of smiles, her lips as white as the rest of her face. She had a broad forehead, and wide-apart eyes that were gray as a winter sky. Her dress was shiny black silk, with a close-fitting bodice and a full skirt, almost medieval. She was very full-breasted, with a large silver cross in her cleavage.

Jim walked up to her. The mime moved closer to her, as if he were protecting her.

'Excuse me,' Jim asked her. 'But do you *know* me?'

'No,' she smiled. 'But I know what you want.'

'Oh, yes? Is that why you've been following me?'

'I wasn't following you. I was waiting for you to find me.'

'Okay then, it looks like I have. My name's Jim Rook.'

She held out her hand. It was very soft, long-fingered and surprisingly cold. 'Susan Silverstone,' she said. 'And this is my friend Medlar Tree.'

Jim gave the mime an army-style salute. 'Nice to meet you, Mr Tree.'

'Medlar Tree is his whole name,' said Susan Silverstone. 'The medlar tree is the least known of all the magic trees. You can't eat its fruit until it looks as if it's rotten, but it's a strong charm against devils and all kinds of black mischief.'

'I see,' said Jim, turned back to Medlar Tree and said, 'Sorry.' The mime gave him a sweeping bow. Jim had always detested mimes. As a language teacher, he thought that their deliberate refusal to talk was the worst kind of social arrogance.

'So what do you think I'm looking for?' he asked Susan Silverstone.

'The same thing as most people: reassurance. But you want

a very special kind of reassurance, don't you? You want to find out if something *wicked* has come this way.'

'How do you know that?'

She touched her temples with her fingertips, and gave him the most extraordinary look that any woman had ever given him in his life. It was like tilting your head back and staring up at the sky at night and seeing that all the stars had gone out.

'I know because I'm a sensitive, and you're looking for a sensitive, aren't you? I know because I can feel your anxiety from fifty feet away. I know because the woman you're with has just been bereaved, and she's trying to find a reason why.'

Jim took off his sunglasses. 'Are you trying to pull something here?'

'Of course not,' said Susan Silverstone. 'You can ask anybody here. I'm renowned for my interpretation of other people's auras.' Behind her, Medlar Tree pulled his mouth downward like a theatrical mask, and disapprovingly waggled his head from side to side.

Jim said, 'The way I've been walking around asking people questions, it isn't hard to work out that I'm looking for something, especially since I'm not exactly dressed like Jimi Hendrix. And it isn't hard to guess that this lady has been recently bereaved. Who else walks around totally dressed in black on a hot day like this? Apart from you.'

'Then let me impress you a little more. Your anxiety has something to do with water, doesn't it?'

Jim said nothing, but Medlar Tree began to perform a breaststroke in mid-air, and blow out his cheeks as if he were swimming. For the first time in a long time, Jim felt like gratuitously punching a person in the nose.

'More exactly, your anxiety has something to do with somebody drowning.'

Karen and Jennie had realized that Jim was no longer walking alongside, and Jennie had turned back. 'Jim?' she said, looking at Susan Silverstone in apprehension. 'Is everything all right?'

'This lady seems to know what we're here for,' said Jim. 'Can she do a spirit-trace?'

'Of course,' said Susan Silverstone. 'Spirit-tracing is one of my specialties.'

'How much do you charge?'

'You've just lost your child. You don't think I'd ask you for money, do you?'

'How do you know about that?' said Jennie. 'Did you tell her that, Jim?'

Susan Silverstone laid a hand on Jennie's sleeve. She had silver rings on every finger and on her thumb. Beside her, Medlar Tree rubbed his eyes as if he were sobbing in grief. Jim gave him his famous death-stare, but all he did was pout and flounce.

Susan Silverstone said, gently, 'I didn't need to be told. Mothers who have lost their children have a special look about them . . . the saddest look that you can ever imagine.'

'Then you'll help me? I'm sure there was somebody there when Mike went under the water.'

'I'll take a look for you,' Susan Silverstone reassured her. 'If there was anything there, then believe me, I'll know.'

Karen came up and joined them. She pulled a face at Jim and tapped her wristwatch. 'Come on, Jim, if we're going to make it up the coast before twelve . . .'

'If I'm going to do a spirit-trace for you, it'll have to be now,' said Susan Silverstone. 'I'm going to Bakersfield this afternoon, for orchard counseling.'

'*Orchard counseling?*' asked Karen.

'Of course. Trees can get stressed too, you know, just like people. Sometimes scores of them can be seriously traumatized. You can sense it, the minute you walk into the orchard. It's a bad, bad feeling, like there's an electric storm brewing. It unsettles the farm workers and it can have a totally devastating effect on fruit production.'

'Now I've heard everything,' said Karen. 'My lunch is canceled because an orange grove has the heebie-jeebies.'

'I'm really sorry, Karen,' Jim told her. 'How about we go for dinner instead? I can book a table at the Palm.'

'Well, I'm sorry, too, Jim. Especially since this is the last day we're going to be able to spend together.'

'Wait up a minute,' Jim asked Jennie and Susan Silverstone. He took Karen aside, next to a wholefood stall. 'Listen,' he said, 'I can't just turn my back on this. Jennie asked me for help and this is the only way I know how.'

'That's a pretty pathetic excuse for spending the rest of the day with some busty mystic in a low-cut dress.'

'What are you talking about? I didn't even notice her dress.'

'So you're blind as well as unreliable?'

'Look, okay, I noticed the dress but I don't care about the dress. I care about you. I was going to wait until later to ask you this, but the reason why I wanted to take you up the coast today was to find out if you'd consider coming to Washington with me.'

'When?'

'On Wednesday, when I leave. Or maybe join me in a week or two, when you've had the chance to pack up your things.'

'You mean you want me to come to Washington *permanently*? To *live* with you?'

'Is that such a terrible idea?'

'Nuts?' asked the woman behind the wholefood stall. 'Pulses?'

Karen laid her hand on Jim's shoulder. 'Jim . . . I'm really fond of you. I almost love you. But can you see us *living* together? I'm fanatical about neatness, you know that. My sweaters are all folded away by color. My shoes all have shoe-trees. You can call me anally retentive if you like. But you – well, all I can say is that your closet is the nearest thing I've ever seen to a one-man rummage sale and your sock drawer looks like the snakepit in *Indiana Jones*. And your *bathroom*. Who else do you know who keeps half a bicycle and a set of golf clubs in their *bathroom*? Apart from that, we're so mentally different. I believe in facts and figures and empirical proof, but what do you believe in? Spirits, and demons, and weird things that nobody else can see. I like Mozart and you like Hootie and the Blowfish. I like step aerobics and you like slouching on the couch. I like brown rice and you like cheeseburgers. Jim – you make me laugh a lot. Sometimes you even inspire me. But if we tried to live together, we'd end up murdering each other, I promise you.'

Jim frowned at her for a long time, still holding her hands in his. Eventually he said, 'Is that a no?'

Three

By the time they drove up to Jennie's house in Jim's bruised old Eldorado, the midday heat had turned the sky an eerie cadmium yellow, as if the end of the world was only a few hours away. In the yard there was no wind at all, none. Heat rippled up from the bricks and the surface of the swimming pool was so glassy that the pool appeared to be empty.

'Your husband not home?' asked Susan Silverstone, stalking around the pool, looking sharply from side to side. She was wearing tiny gold-rimmed sunglasses with red lenses. Medlar Tree made himself comfortable on one of the sunbeds and started to roll a ping-pong ball between his fingers.

Jennie said, 'Doug's spending a few days with his brother in San Luis Capistrano.'

'He didn't stay to support you?'

'He doesn't believe I experienced anything. He thinks I'm making it up, because it was my fault that Mike was drowned. He always wanted a son more than anything.'

'Sounds like a regular guy.'

'I can't blame him. He's absolutely shattered.'

'And you're not, I suppose?'

Susan Silverstone walked around the pool again and again, her hands raised in front of her face as if she were praying. After about the tenth or eleventh circuit, she stopped by the oleanders on the far side of the pool, away from the house. She frowned, and then she said, 'There was something here. It left the yard by way of these bushes.'

'You're right,' said Jennie, breathlessly. 'I saw the bushes move right where you're standing, and the footprints were—'

Susan Silverstone raised her hand. 'Don't tell me where the footprints were. Don't tell me anything. The spirit-trace has to be pure, without any prejudice whatsoever.'

She came back around the pool and picked up a cushion from one of the sunbeds. She laid it down on the brick patio and knelt on it, spreading her dress all around her like a black convolvulus flower.

Out of a black woven bag she produced a large diamond-shaped crystal, and something which looked like a shiny white ashtray. She set the ashtray down on the ground in front of her, and then she balanced the crystal in the center of it, on one of its points. Jim stared at it and said, 'How does she *do* that?' Medlar Tree responded by balancing his ping-pong ball on the tip of his nose and rolling his eyes. Jim instantly snatched the ball and crushed it in his fist. 'Don't you understand that somebody died here, you cretin?'

Susan Silverstone glanced briefly at him, and he was sure he caught the faintest suggestion of a smile. Then she said, 'Whatever walked here, it deflected light and air and it disturbed the aura that always surrounds every house. That disturbance can be traced many weeks after its passing, especially if there was emotional distress here, and something tragic happened. The crystal will show us what it was and what it did.'

Jim took hold of Jennie's hand and squeezed it. 'I don't know what we're going to see here,' he told her. 'But try not to be frightened, won't you? Some of these manifestations can be pretty scary.'

'I just want to know what happened to Mike,' said Jennie.

Medlar Tree had gone into a deep sulk and was sitting on his sunbed with his arms folded and his mouth puckered into a realistic simulation of a horse's rear end. Susan took hold of the top of the crystal and spun it with a single sharp twist of her wrist. It revolved like a glittering gyroscope, still balanced on one of its points, and as it revolved it caught the sunshine and filled the yard with dancing diamonds of yellow, orange, green and blue light.

Susan Silverstone knelt up straight-backed and lifted her

arms wide. The diamonds of light flew across her face and made her look as if she were acting in a flickery old movie. 'I'm bringing back together the spectrum of light that was split by the spirit who walked here,' she said, although it sounded more like an incantation than an explanation. 'I'm looking for the wake of sentience that was left behind it as it walked through the aura of your house and home. I'm looking for its senses, and its feelings. I'm trying to breathe its breath.'

Instead of slowing down, the crystal appeared to spin faster and faster, until the yard was filled with a blizzard of light. Jim had the strangest feeling that they weren't quite *there*, and not quite *then*, as if they were a split second behind time, and several miles distant. Jennie held Jim's hand tighter, and whispered, 'This is very peculiar . . . it's almost like we're not really here at all. It's like this is last week, before all of this happened. I don't know why, but I feel like Mikey's still alive.'

'I think you've hit it,' said Jim. 'This is your yard the way it was last Thursday. What we're looking at . . . it's kind of a living movie of what happened here.'

Susan Silverstone leaned her head right back. The light from the crystal grew brighter and brighter, until it was dazzling. And it was then that Jim saw the faint, wavering outlines of two small children. One was dancing or skipping on the opposite side of the pool, while the other was splashing in the water. They were very indistinct, and sometimes it was impossible to say if they were children at all, or nothing more than sparkling fragments of light. But the surface of the pool was actually being churned up, as if there were a real child playing in it.

'What is it?' asked Jennie breathlessly, clutching at Jim's arm. 'What is it? What's happening? What can you see?'

'Jennie – I think I can see Mikey.'

'Where? Where is he? Why can't I see him?'

'He's here, Jennie. He's splashing in the pool, just like he was on the day that he drowned. Susan's trying to recreate what happened . . . like an action replay.'

'Oh God, show me where he is. Please, Jim! Maybe I can feel him, even if I can't see him!'

'No, Jennie . . . you're better off staying here. This isn't finished yet.'

'But he's my child, Jim, and I've lost him! If I could hold him in my arms just one last time!'

'Wait,' Jim cautioned her. Very faintly he could hear children's voices, as if they were calling out from the end of a very long tunnel. Echoing and distorted, so that it was impossible to tell if they were laughing or screaming.

'I can hear him,' he told Jennie. 'I can't hear exactly what he's saying, but I can definitely hear him.'

'Oh, Mike!' sobbed Jennie, and tried to pull her hand away. But Jim wouldn't let her go. A thick tension was growing in the air, like the heavy static that builds up before a thunderstorm or an earth temblor. The light from the crystal suddenly grew even more brilliant, until it was sparkling as intensely as an oxyacetylene flashlight.

The yard grew so bright that Jim had to shield his eyes with his hand, and he could barely see from one side of the pool to the other.

Without warning, a figure climbed over the fence on the right-hand side of the yard. Actually, it almost *poured* over rather than climbed over, because it was watery and semi-transparent and Jim couldn't even make out if it was a man or a woman.

Susan Silverstone turned her head toward Jim and said, sharply, 'It's here. The spirit is walking among us! I can feel it!'

'You can feel it?' said Jim. 'I can *see* it!'

'What?' She looked around her, the bells around her headscarf jingling. 'You can *see* it? Where?'

Jim nodded his head toward the figure as it crossed the patio. He didn't want to make it obvious to the spirit that he was pointing it out. Some spirits became frightened or angry if they realized that they could be seen – and he didn't yet know what this figure was or what it was capable of doing.

It crossed the sunbaked patio very quickly, as if it were

barefooted. Occasionally the brilliant white light from the crystal caught its face or its arms or its shoulders, and split into its component colors, and Jim glimpsed an iridescent detail of what it looked like.

Jennie was clutching him so tightly that her fingernails were digging into the palm of his hand. 'Where is it?' she whispered. 'What's it doing now?'

'I think it's a woman,' Jim told her. 'A woman or a teenage girl. I can't see it very clearly. It's almost like it's made out of water.'

The apparition made its way to the side of the pool, where Mikey's image was still splashing in the water. It hesitated for a split second, and then it dived in, as fluidly as if it had been emptied out of a jug.

'You won't let it hurt him?' Jennie begged. 'Please, Jim, don't let it hurt him.'

'I'm sorry, Jennie; if it's going to do him any harm, I can't do anything about it. What I can see here today, it's already happened. It's only an image, that's all.'

'Why can't *I* see Mike? I'm his mother! Why can't *I* see him?'

But Jim didn't answer. The surface of the pool was being churned up in a strong circular motion, around and around the place where the image of Mike was splashing, almost as if a huge shark were circling around him. Susan Silverstone rose to her feet and approached the edge of the pool, her hands raised in rigid horror. Even Medlar Tree stood up, clutching at his ears in distress and shaking his head from side to side.

The feeling of sheer dread was overwhelming. It was obvious that even Jennie could sense it: her eyes widened and she clamped her hand over her mouth. The pool was filled with furious thrashing and splashing, and Jim could hear a small girl's voice screaming, '*Mike! Mike! Mommy, come quick!*'

'What's happening?' said Jennie. 'Tell me what's happening!'

Jim didn't know what to answer. All he knew was that he

had to hold on to Jennie's hand as tight as he could and not let her go.

'Can you see it now?' asked Susan. 'Jim – can you see it now?' In the pool, the water was frothing and splashing, and right in the center of this turmoil Jim could see the flickering outline of little Mike, struggling and screaming. Out of the water rose a pair of arms – a pair of arms that were formed out of the water itself. They seized Mike in a tight, almost loving embrace, and dragged him under the surface.

The surface of the pool slopped and slapped and gradually settled. Susan stood over it and took off her little red-lensed sunglasses. 'I saw something,' she said. 'I swear to God that I saw *arms*.'

'I did too,' said Jennie, and she was trembling like a frightened deer. 'Just for a second . . . a pair of arms.'

But Jim wasn't listening to her. His attention was fixed on the far end of the pool, the deep end. A watery figure was climbing up the ladder, gradually disintegrating as it did so. It turned its head and looked toward him, and for a split second he thought he recognized its face. A girl's face, beautiful but haunted. And he knew that she had seen him, and recognized that *he* could see *her*.

Then her face simply dropped away, and her arms and her shoulders dropped too, and scattered lightly across the surface of the pool, because she was made only of water, like the pool was. Wet footprints crossed the bricks at the side of the pool, the bushes shuddered, and then she was gone.

Jennie said, 'You saw it, Jim? You really saw it?'

Jim nodded. 'I don't have any idea what it was. A girl. I could see right through her. It was like she was made out of water.'

Susan came over. She was looking serious. 'It used the water to take on physical shape . . . to give it the strength to pull your son under the water. I've heard of spirits using all kinds of things to give themselves leverage in the real world: dust, mud, hair, even trash. Six years ago they found an old man strangled in his cellar in Encino . . . the door was locked from the inside and there was no other access. In one corner of the cellar, though, there was a heap of old sacking and newspapers and rope and other garbage.

'The cops called in David DuQuesne. He's an expert in all kinds of urban legends. It was his belief that the sacking and the newspapers took on some kind of physical form. The old man didn't have any living enemies that anybody knew of, but it was David's theory that he had a dead one. A spirit who wanted his revenge.'

'What do you think, Jim?' asked Jennie. 'You saw it, after all.'

'I don't know what to think. I've never seen anything like it, and I've seen some pretty weird things, believe me.'

'What I don't understand is why this spirit should want to hurt Mike.'

'Well,' said Jim, 'I think we're going to have to do some more research on this. Do you want to tell me where Mike went to school? He didn't have any problems with classmates, did he?'

'What are you asking me that for? He was lively, for sure. Well, he was more than lively. He could be real trouble sometimes. But I don't think that he was having any problems with any of his schoolfriends. Or any other friends, for that matter.'

'I'm just wondering if he was bullying anybody, that's all. Maybe some dead relative decided to teach him a lesson.'

'That sounds pretty far-fetched,' said Susan; and behind her Medlar Tree spun his finger around the top of his head as if to suggest that Jim was stupid.

'Maybe it is, but being pulled under the water by a girl made out of nothing but water . . . being strangled by your own garbage . . . you don't think *that's* far-fetched?'

Jim drove Susan back to her house on Franklin Avenue. Medlar Tree sat in the back, grinning and waving at the passengers of other cars whenever they stopped for a red signal.

'I don't know how you tolerate that guy,' said Jim. 'It must be like living with Marcel Marceau.'

'Medlar Tree isn't what he seems to be,' Susan replied.

'He saved my life once, and it cost him a higher price than most people pay for anything.'

'I'm sorry. But that doesn't make him any less of a pain in the rear end.'

They reached Franklin Avenue and Jim pulled over to the side of the road. 'I don't really know what to do next,' he said. 'I can hardly go to the police and tell them that young Mike was drowned by a water spirit. They already think I'm nine-tenths crazy as it is.'

'It doesn't really make any difference, does it?' Susan replied. 'The coroner's going to say that it was an accident; but at least Jennie will know what happened, and that it wasn't her fault that Mike died.'

'The trouble is, her husband's not going to believe that, is he?'

'Jim – when you're a sensitive, all you can do is tell people what you feel. You can't change their lives for them too. You can *see* things as well as feel them, and that's a strange and wonderful gift. But it doesn't mean that you have to be a detective and a marriage guidance counselor and a psychiatrist and a teacher, all rolled into one.'

'You're beginning to sound like Karen.'

'Well, if that's what she's been telling you, it doesn't surprise me.'

'Okay . . . I guess I'll just have to be happy with what we've managed to do today.'

'Come inside for a drink,' Susan suggested. 'I can show you my collection of spiders.'

Susan lived on the top floor of a narrow Spanish-style house, heavily shaded by trees. There was a small damp yard in the back, with a mossy wall all around it, and statues of naked Greek athletes, and a small circular fountain. Susan's two-bedroom apartment was richly decorated with arts-and-crafts wallpaper, and hung with dark velvet drapes. All of the furniture was old and eccentric, especially a huge armchair with two grotesque faces on the arms, their eyes bulging and their tongues lolling out; and there was a smell of stale incense everywhere.

'This is pretty much for show,' said Susan, kicking off her silver sandals and lying back on a gilt chaise-longue. 'Personally I prefer the minimalist look. Walls painted cream, no chairs, and futons in the bedroom. But when people come to talk to a sensitive . . . well, they expect gothic.'

Medlar Tree went to the kitchen and came back with a large chilled bottle of Chilean Sauvignon. He poured them each an enormous glassful and then lifted his own glass in a silent toast.

'What are we supposed to be drinking to, Medlar Tree?' asked Jim.

Medlar Tree put down his glass. He mimed that he was swimming. Then he mimed that he was thrashing around and drowning. He stood still, with his eyes closed, as if he were dead. He stood like that for almost thirty seconds and Jim said, 'What—' but Susan shushed him.

Eventually, Medlar Tree lifted up both hands so that they covered his face. Jim thought: Where have I seen this before? Then, very slowly, Medlar Tree opened his face, like a book opening. For one moment, so brief that Jim couldn't be sure if he had really seen it or not, Medlar Tree's face looked exactly like that of the spirit-girl that he had seen climbing out of the pool. The hairs on the back of Jim's neck fizzed with shock.

'Clever, isn't it?' laughed Susan. 'But it's only a party trick. Hypnotic suggestion. He's very good at it, aren't you, my dearest Medlar Tree?'

Jim raised his glass. 'Okay . . . I'll drink to that particular trick. And I'll drink to you, Susan. At least you showed Jennie that she wasn't imagining things.'

They spent over an hour together, before Susan had to go off for her orchard-therapy session. They talked and drank wine and laughed. Medlar Tree still brought him close to committing mimicide, but Susan seemed to think so much of him that it was hard for Jim to be openly hostile. It took strength, though, especially when Medlar Tree scowled at him from behind Susan's back, and pushed his fingers up his nostrils to make himself look like Lon Chaney in *The Phantom of the Opera*.

'When did you first realize you were sensitive?' he asked Susan.

'When I was six. I was walking with my mom along Hollywood Boulevard when I heard this woman screaming. I looked around, and there she was, a middle-aged woman in a beige flowery dress, standing by the side of the road, screaming. Except that her face looked completely calm and her mouth was closed.

'About two seconds later, she stepped out into the road, right in front of a bus. It hit her and she went flying through the air like she was showing everybody how good she was at cartwheels. She was dead, of course.

'At first I couldn't understand why nobody had heard her screaming. It was only two or three years later that I had a similar experience and I realized that nobody had heard her because she hadn't made a sound. The only person who had heard her was me.'

She hesitated for a moment, and then she looked at him with narrowed eyes. In this light she was really quite beautiful, in a strangely dated way. Black hair, white face, like a publicity photograph for a 1940s movie star.

'You believe me, don't you?' she said. 'And you're relieved, too, that somebody else has to carry a burden like yours. You're not alone, Jim; and now you never will be.'

Medlar Tree looked daggers at him, the kind of daggers with decorated handles that come out of people's eyes in cartoons. Jim sniffed, and smiled, and said, 'How about another glass of that Sauvignon, Mr Tree?'

Four

That night, after his shower, Jim hung the psychic necklace around his neck, along with the silver St Christopher medal that his mother had given him only two hours before she died. He didn't really know why he wanted to wear it. Maybe he wanted to step just a little nearer to the edge. Maybe he wanted to look into the darkness, face to face.

'I hope you realize this isn't going to work,' he told his reflection in the bathroom mirror. His reflection looked oddly unimpressed. 'I hope you also realize that you don't *want* it to work. Supposing it tells you you're going to meet your maker at lunchtime tomorrow, choking on a cheese and alfalfa sandwich?'

In truth, he didn't seriously believe that the necklace would reveal the exact date he was going to die. But ever since he had discovered that he could see almost every kind of spirit that walked through the world of the living, he had become fascinated by occult paraphernalia such as crystal balls and Ouija boards and Tarot cards, as well as voodoo fetishes and Native American sundolls. After all, they were all attempts by mystics of varying cultures to see through to the other side – and, if he could ever find one that actually worked, he would be able to share his visions with other people. He could show them that spirits are everywhere, close beside us. He could show them that their dead relatives are still close at hand. More than that, he wouldn't feel so different, so alone.

Before he went to bed, he sat on the couch with his scraped-clean spaghetti plate still on the coffee table in front of him, and called up Karen.

'Karen – it's Jim. I want you to know that I'm deeply, deeply sorry about today. Deeper than deeply. Bathyscaphically.'

'That's okay, Jim. You're forgiven. And it was all in a good cause, wasn't it?'

'Well, yes it was. The spirit-trace worked, believe it or not. It worked! We saw the spirit! Well, *I* saw the spirit. And at least Jennie doesn't blame herself for Mikey's death any more.'

'So she came through? The busty mystic in the low-cut dress?'

'Susan? She's interesting. A very interesting young woman. And very, genuinely sensitive. And interesting.'

'And busty.'

'Yes, busty. Okay. That's a natural attribute. But that's not what makes her interesting.'

'All the same, you like her.'

'Sure I like her. I'm not going to deny it. I like lots of women. No, I didn't say that right. I like lots of women, not *lots* of women. For God's sake. But I still want you to come to Washington with me. I mean, this is why I'm calling. This is a genuine repeat offer for a limited time only. I've thought very seriously about your color-coded sweaters and I've thought about your step aerobics and your logical mind and your tofu; and I've come to the conclusion that I could easily adapt. Easily. Do you know what I did this evening, when I came home? *I rearranged my spice rack.* It's all in alphabetical order, starting with Allspice and ending with Wasabi. Then I tidied my sock drawer. I swear to God. All of my socks are matching and they're all rolled together and they're all in rows. They look like a passing-out parade at West Point. Well, except for seven or eight of them that don't seem to have a friend.'

'Maybe your busty mystic in the low-cut dress could help. If she can do orchard therapy I'm sure she can manage sock treatment.'

'Karen, it's *you* I'm asking to come to Washington. Nobody else. Marry me.'

'No, Jim. I'm sorry. What we have together . . . it's good. Occasionally it's nearly wonderful. But it's not enough.'

'It's not enough?'

'I'm sorry.'

'*You're* sorry. How do you think I feel?'

'I don't want to hurt you, Jim. But it could never work out, alphabetical spices or not.'

'I see. Well, I guess I can take a hint.'

'I'll see you tomorrow, at college.'

'Sure.'

'Don't be angry, Jim. You know it wouldn't work. There's more to marriage than a tidy sock drawer.'

From where he was sitting on the couch, Jim caught sight of a pair of shorts that he had kicked under the armchair about five days ago. Candy-striped, faded and crumpled. He was beginning to feel very sorry for himself, but he dropped his head in mock-resignation, like a marionette with its strings cut.

He fell asleep within five or ten minutes, which was unusual after a day in which he had been involved in so much psychic activity. Most days, a supernatural experience would leave him nervy and sweating, and he would roll about in bed for hour after hour while all kinds of mysterious images danced and flickered in his head like black-and-white movies. Pale, featureless faces, staring, half hidden behind misted-up windows. Monk-like figures in hoods and habits, rushing silently around corners before he could reach them. Sometimes he heard music, somebody playing a discordant piano in an echoing upstairs room. Sometimes he heard women weeping, '*Don't, don't, don't . . .*' over and over.

But tonight he slid down that long dark shelf into unconsciousness almost immediately, and when he opened his eyes he was caught up in a dream so sharp and detailed that it was even more realistic than life itself.

He was walking along a wide gray seashore, with the wind fluffing in his ears. The sky was overcast, and the beach was so flat that the waves were only inches deep. The waves poured over the sides of his shoes and soaked his socks, and then retreated.

As he walked along, he became aware that somebody was walking far up ahead of him – a woman, it looked like, with her hair streaming in the wind and her shoulders bowed. He tried to walk faster, to catch her up, but she always seemed to remain out of reach. He had the urgent feeling that he needed to talk to her, or else something was going to go seriously wrong. The wind was rising now, and very much colder, and the waves began to splash against the legs of his pants, soaking him up to his knees.

Without warning he was hit by a huge, overwhelming wave. It was freezing cold, and it dropped on top of him like a ton of wet cement, forcing him down to his knees. He tried to stand up, but the undertow dragged his feet away from him, and the next thing he knew he was floundering in nine or ten feet of salty water, his arms waving and his legs thrashing, completely helpless.

Desperately, he tried to swim to the surface. But no matter how hard he kicked his legs and paddled his arms, he couldn't seem to rise any higher. There was something clutching his ankle . . . something dragging him back down again.

Bursting for breath, he twisted himself around to see what it was. With a cold shock of recognition, he saw that it was the same liquid figure he had seen climbing out of Jennie's pool – a sinuous shape with long, fluent hair, fashioned entirely out of water. Her skin rippled like a fast-flowing current, and her eyes gleamed like glass, without pupils or irises. Her expression alone was enough to terrify him: she was furious-faced, and obviously intent on drowning him.

He kicked and kicked, but he couldn't break her grip. His lungs felt as if they were just about to detonate. His head throbbed and it took every ounce of strength not to open his mouth and breathe in a huge lungful of icy cold seawater. He heaved himself around, and gave a desperate double kick with both feet. The figure seemed to scatter apart, like beads of liquid mercury. He kicked again, and again, propelling himself upward.

He broke the surface, screaming for air. '*Hah! Hah! Hah!*' He thrashed his arms, trying to keep himself afloat. And then looked around the ocean, and found that it wasn't an ocean at all, but a bedroom, with a bedside clock, and a bureau, and a pair of khaki Dockers hanging over the back of a basketwork chair. He was still lying on his bed, his sheets twisted like the Indian rope trick and his T-shirt soaked in icy cold sweat. He sat up, wiped his face with his hands, and drank a large mouthful of tepid water. Outside his apartment, he could hear distant samba music and the sound of automobiles swishing along the street. He checked his bedside clock. It read 13:06:01.

This was ridiculous. It wasn't six minutes past one in the afternoon: it was more like quarter past two in the morning. He picked up the clock and stared at it. Last year's class had given it to him, and on the back were engraved the words: JIM ROOK, BECAUSE HE OPENED OUR EYES.

It was then that TT padded into the room, and let out the faintest mewling sound.

'What? What is it now?'

TT jumped up on to the bed beside him and nuzzled the clock.

'What are you trying to say to me, you witch of darkness? My alarm clock's gone on the fritz, that's all. Probably a brown-out.'

But TT mewled again, and almost head-butted the clock, and then laid her paw on top of it.

'You're trying to tell me something, right? I know. But you obviously don't understand that you're trying to communicate with a higher species of vastly superior intellect. When cats start writing rhyming couplets and sending each other e-mails, then I'll worry. But right now, all of this mewling and scratching and head-banging . . . I'm sorry, you've lost me.'

TT didn't give up. She jumped off the bed, trotted into the living-room and jumped up on the back of the chair in front of the calendar. Jim followed her, and stared at her uncomprehendingly for a very long time. Impatient, she jumped up and swatted at the calendar with her paw.

‘I don’t get it,’ said Jim. But then TT ran back to the bedroom and nuzzled the clock.

‘Clock . . . calendar. Calendar . . . clock. What’s going on here, TT?’

TT came back, and again she was carrying the Grimaud death card in between her teeth. She dropped it in front of Jim’s feet and stood there staring at him, almost willing him to understand.

‘Clock – calendar – death card. Oh, hold up a minute. This is beginning to make sense. The clock is wrong, right? So these numbers on the clock . . . these aren’t the *time*, they’re the *date* . . . thirteen, six, oh one. The thirteenth of June 2001. Which is . . . let’s take a look . . . precisely nine days from now.’

Jim slowly reached up and felt the psychic necklace that was dangling on his chest. *Wear it when you go to sleep tonight, and you’ll dream the day you’re going to die*.

‘No way, José,’ he told TT. ‘I believe in seeing the past, but I don’t believe in seeing the future. It hasn’t happened yet. How can anybody know?’ TT remained where she was, staring at him implacably. ‘How can anybody know, TT? Especially a cat? Just because the Egyptians thought the sun shone out of your litter trays.’

All the same, he went back into the bedroom and looked at the clock lying on the bed, and it was still reading 13:06:01. He had a cold, helpless feeling, like Ebenezer Scrooge must have felt when the Ghost of Christmas Yet to Come showed him his own tombstone.

He went into the kitchen, put on the kettle and made himself a mug of hot chocolate. He had been putting on a little weight lately – not much, but Karen had always told him that he looked underfed, ‘like a refugee from something that the rest of us don’t even want to think about’.

It was 2.25 a.m. Jim was still sitting at the kitchen table finishing his chocolate when the doorbell chimed, making him start. He shuffled into the hallway and peered through the spyhole. It was Mervyn, his face covered in a livid green mudpack and his bleached-blond hair in curlers. Jim said, 'Shit,' under his breath, and reluctantly opened the door.

'Hey, Jim! I saw your light was still burning and thought you could use some company.' Mervyn was wrapped in a shiny pink silk kimono with huge black chrysanthemums on it, and he was wearing extraordinary Japanese clogs that made him teeter around the room with all his weight tilted forward, like a huge chicken. 'If I'm disturbing you, you can throw me out. In *these* shoes, I'll probably throw *myself* out. What do you think of them? A Japanese businessman gave them to me for singing "Hello, Dolly" in Japanese, or should I say "Herro Dorry". I was sensational.'

'You're always sensational, Mervyn. Come on in, make yourself at home. I couldn't sleep. Well, I did sleep, but I had one hell of a nightmare.'

'You know *why*, don't you?' said Mervyn, collapsing into one of the kitchen chairs. 'You're emotionally disturbed about going to Washington. Leaving LA behind, leaving your Special Class II behind, leaving TT behind. You're bound to be feeling anxious.'

Jim said, 'I'm not stressed at all. Not about leaving West Grove, anyhow. Dr Friendly's been riding me every day for the past semester. And Special Class II . . . well, next year there'll be a new Special Class II, all fresh faces. I won't miss students I've never met. As for TT . . . Well, she's decorative for sure, but she's about as useful as an overstuffed cushion.'

'Oh, don't be so negative,' said Mervyn. 'You're going to miss all of us, sorely. Even those students you've never met. By the way, I love your necklace. Very New Age.'

Jim took it off and handed it to him. 'It's supposed to possess powers of clairvoyance. Ten bucks, at the psychic fair. It predicts the exact day you're going to die.'

'Oh, get out of here. You don't believe that, do you?'

'I don't know. But this is the point. I was wearing it tonight, when I had this nightmare. I dreamed that I was being drowned. Somebody was holding my ankle, a girl, and she was pulling me under the ocean. I woke up, and this is what my clock said.'

Mervyn stared at the clock, uncomprehendingly. 'It's a great little clock, isn't it? Does it have a snooze facility? I love a clock with a snooze facility. Just the word, "*snooze*", isn't that wonderful? You can just lie there, and sort your life out before you have to climb out of bed and sort it out for real. Don't you think real life is so depressing? I could spend the rest of my life in bed.'

'Mervyn . . . look what the clock says.'

Mervyn squinted at it, and then he said, 'It's *wrong*, isn't it? This is either yesterday or tomorrow. By the way, did you ever hear me singing "Yesterday"? It brings tears to people's eyes. It brings tears to *my* eyes, too. Especially the high notes.'

'Mervyn . . . I woke up out of that nightmare and the clock said thirteen, six, oh one and it hasn't moved since. This isn't the *time* here, for God's sake. This is the day that I'm going to shuffle off the mortal coil.'

'The what?'

'The mortal coil. That's Shakespeare talk for buying the farm. This bedside alarm clock has just told me that I have nine days to live.'

'Oh, that's ridiculous.'

'You think so?' said Jim, and told him all about Jennie's plea for help, and Susan Silverstone, and the watery figure that had risen out of the pool when Susan had set up her spirit-trace. For once, Meryvn looked serious. 'Maybe you shouldn't go to Washington, Jim. Maybe you're cracking up.'

'But this little nine-year-old kid was drowned, and his mother asked me to find out who did it. And then I had specific warning that something bad was going to happen to me. Something to do with water, too.'

'A warning? Who from? You should tell the police.'

'I can't. They wouldn't believe me, would they? The warning . . . well, it came from the cards.'

'Oh, the *cards*. Well, you know what I think about those. They're for menopausal women and lonely widows and middle-aged gays.'

'So what? Just because they appeal to vulnerable people,

that doesn't make them any less accurate. They're real, Mervyn. They tell the truth. And there's nothing wrong in being menopausal or lonely. Or middle-aged. Or gay, for that matter.'

'Hunh! You should try it sometime! I think I'm every one of those.'

Jim said, 'For God's sake, Mervyn, I'm trying to tell you that I'm going to die in nine days from now. I think I'm going to be drowned.'

'In that case, you should stay away from water. I'm not just talking about pools, or the ocean. I mean, don't even have a glass of water on your nightstand.'

'Get out of here.'

'I'm kidding around with you, Jim. I'm trying to make you see sense. That poor little Mike was dragged down under the water, but it was an accident, most likely. Faulty pump. Missing safety grille. The number of little children who get their hair all tangled up in swimming-pool filters, you wouldn't believe. Those filters, they scalp more people than the Oglala Sioux. I know, I used to work for Valley Pool Pumps. The stories I could tell you. We found a guy who got his pony-tail tangled in his hot tub and he sat there for seventeen days, simmering. By the time we found him, he was guy broth.'

'Well, let's leave those horror stories for now, Mervyn. What I need to know is, did you ever hear anybody else mention a water creature, a person all made out of water?'

'Oh, come on, Jim, I don't think so. You're just trying to spook me out. I guess the nearest we had was two of our operatives who worked on a pool in Sherman Oaks. They were refilling it, after somebody's daughter drowned in it. And when the pool was almost full, one of our operatives pushed the other one in – you know, just for a joke. But that guy came out that pool in a total panic. He said that somebody had tried to pull him under, and drown him. But who, or what? There was nobody else there. The other guy could testify to that. And there was a neighbor leaning over the fence, and the neighbor didn't see nothing, neither.'

'That sounds distinctly similar,' said Jim. 'That figure I saw . . . she was made out of nothing but water, I swear it. But she had arms that could drag you down below the surface. And she had such an expression on her face. Scowls weren't in it. She gave me the feeling that she would kill me, as soon as she could lay hands on me.'

'Hm. You're sure it wasn't my mother? When she's mad, boy, the looks she gives you. They could turn cheese.'

Jim said, 'I feel like I'm losing it, Mervyn. I feel like I don't know the difference between one side of reality and the other.'

Mervyn held his hand, and gripped it tight. 'You're a good man, Jim. You're better than you know. But you should allow yourself to be selfish sometimes. You should do what *you* want to do. I clean up around here, and unblock toilets, and run errands for the old folks. But that's not charity. That's not martyrdom. I do it because I love it. And if you feel the same way about the things that *you* do . . . about those young people you teach how to read and write and appreciate poetry . . . you do it because it's your lifeblood. You do it because what's the point of getting up in the morning if you *don't*?'

Jim said, 'Maybe you're right, Mervyn. I don't know.'

'You're scared, aren't you?'

Jim looked up at Mervyn, with his khaki mudpack and his bright pink curlers, like the chief of a primitive tribe, and said, 'You're damn right I'm scared. If this is real, I'd hate to see the supernatural.'

'How about a drink?' Mervyn suggested. 'A piña colada with a pink beach umbrella would do.'

'How about a cup of coffee?'

'For sure . . . if you insist.'

Jim went into the kitchen and switched on the light. As he approached the stainless-steel sink, he suddenly became aware of *scurrying* on the draining board, like dozens of cockroaches scuttling for shelter. But then he realized that it wasn't cockroaches. It was drops of water, hurrying off the draining board and into the sink, and flying *upward* into the faucet. He stood stock-still and watched in horrified fascination as drop after drop flew upward, totally defying gravity, and disappeared from sight.

It was just as though he had caught them out, these drops of water, and they were running away from him, and hiding.

Very cautiously he approached the sink. He put his hand on the faucet, and wondered if he ought to fill the percolator or not.

In the end, he went back into the living-room and said, 'I'm sorry, Mervyn. I'm bushed. Why don't we call it a night? Or a day, rather. Look, it's growing light.'

'No coffee?' asked Mervyn plaintively.

Jim shook his head. 'Not now. It always gives me nightmares.'

Five

He walked into class the following morning and his students were all chatting and laughing and throwing rolled-up gum wrappers and propping their Nike trainers up on the desks. He couldn't blame them: there were only two days to go before the end of the summer semester, the end of the year and the end of their time in Special Class II. If they hadn't learned anything about self-expression by now, they never would.

He hung up his crumpled blue linen jacket and sat down at his desk. He opened his copy of *New American Poets* and began to thumb through it very slowly, licking his thumb with every page that he turned. Gradually, Special Class II began to settle down. At the very back, Nestor Fawkes sat down first, frowning expectantly. Nestor was wearing a washed-out T-shirt and grubby jeans and trainers that were worn through right to the soles. His cheekbones were bruised, and there was a livid scratch on his forehead.

Out of everybody in Special Class II, Nestor was the one student that Jim was most reluctant to leave. Nestor still needed his help, both emotional and educational, but he was going to have to leave him behind. What else could he do? He couldn't shoulder responsibility for the whole world. For one thing, he didn't have the time. *You should allow yourself to be selfish sometimes*, that's what Mervyn had said.

Stella Kopalski kept on chattering. She had blond, piled-up hair, and eyes as green as spearmint, and today she was wearing an ultra-tight white T-shirt and an extra-short blue denim skirt, and white high-heeled ankle boots. 'You know what I'm thinking of doing this summer?' she was saying.

'I'm going to work in this topless bar, Jugg's, on Sunset. I'll bet you I'll land me a part in a movie by September.'

Jim didn't say anything, but continued to leaf through his poetry book. He and his students had only six more hours together, and then he was going off to Washington to work for the government's Literacy Action Force. If he hadn't managed to change their lives by now, he never would. Stella Kopalski had written one of the saddest and most eloquent poems that he had read this year, but, if she felt it was her destiny to work in a topless bar on Sunset, there was nothing he could do about it.

> Whenever I open up my closet doors,
> My clothes, on hangers, remind me of the days I've spent
> With friends, with dearest friends; with people who have loved me good and true.
> With people who are dead, or disappeared.
> I bury my face in the soft forest of cotton and wool, and cry and cry for all of you.

And there was Tarquin, arch-rapper, tall, gangly and black, with his Sony headphones on his ears, listening to some macho music about bitches and blowing people away. And Washington Freeman III, still leaning back in his chair and pontificating that society owed him a living, no matter what he did. 'I didn't ax to be born, now did I?' And Laura Killmeyer, who had grown out of her witch phase, with the deathly-white make-up and the arched eyebrows, and who was dressed in Gap now, tight black T-shirts and big flappy canvas pants, and short-cropped crimson hair. And Dottie Osias, who had stopped slavishly following Laura Killmeyer and was making her own fashion statement, which was principally baggy and orange.

Jim loved them all; and if they had ever guessed how much he loved them they would have been deeply embarrassed, even though they loved him too. Joyce Capistrano, Randy Relling Jr and Linda Starewsky, with her bouncing red curls and her arms and legs like a newborn giraffe. Waylon Price and Christophe l'Ouverture, who came from Haiti and was deeply interested in voodoo. Every year, Jim's remedial English class had presented him with new challenges – but more than that, it presented him with new faces, and fresh chances, and startling new opinions.

'Okay . . .' he said at last, looking up from his book. 'You and I have two more days together. After that, I'm going off to Washington, D.C., to develop a literacy program for the federal government. And you . . . well, you're all going off to do whatever it is that young people do when they finish community college. Take over General Motors; open up a peanut stand; dance; sing; go to Hollywood.'

'You ever coming back, man?' asked Tarquin.

'To West Grove? No, I don't think so.'

'What about the kids coming here in September? Kids who can't read and write too good?'

'They'll be well taken care of. Ms Schaumberg is taking over Special Class II, and believe me she knows what she's doing. You should hear Ms Schaumberg reciting the Gettysburg Address. Enough to send shivers down your back.'

'Just *lookin'* at Ms Schaumberg, that's enough to send shivers down anyone's back! Like, *Night of the Living Dead*, or what?'

'You behave yourself, Tarquin. Ms Schaumberg is a lady, and one of the best remedial English teachers in the county.'

'You the man, Mr Rook.'

'Well, I appreciate your saying so. Now, shall we get on?'

'You don't understand. You the *man*. My kid brother coming here next year. Who's he going to turn to? Ms Schaumberg, I don't think so. Maybe she teach English good, I'm not saying she don't. But what we learned here in this class with you, Mr Rook, that weren't just English, that was like how to live our lives and stuff.'

'For Christ's sake, Tarquin. I'm only a teacher.'

'No, Mr Rook. You the beacon. You taught me all kinds

of shit I didn't even want to listen to. Walt Whitman, some stupid white faggot. William Shakespeare, about a thousand years old, from England, who cares? And then you taught me Theodore Spencer and stuff like that and you open up my eyes like I was blind before.'

Tarquin jabbed his finger in the air and he was so emotional that he was almost crying. 'I was *blind* before, like Stevie Wonder, only poor as well. So before you go let me quote you this Theodore Spencer poem that you quoted to us.

> 'She was a high-class bitch and a dandy
> Prancing man was he and a dandy
> Man he was with that tall lady.
>
> 'I should have known that a bitch and a dandy
> Dancing man – and Oh, what a dandy! –
> Would with a prance of a dapper dandy
> Dance into grass: and to grass that lady.
>
> 'Bitch as she was – and he was a dandy
> Prancing man – it makes me angry
> That those dance people should stagger and bend.
> I think of that dandy and bitch and am angry
>
> 'That over that bitch and over that dandy
> Dancing man – and Oh, what a dandy
> Man he was with tall lady! –
> Only crass grass should dance in the end.'

'Hey,' said Jim, very impressed. 'That must be the first poem you ever learned by heart.'

'I learned it to show you,' said Tarquin, defiantly. 'I always understood that poem, but I never knew why. It clicked with something inside of my head. And that's what you did for all of us, Mr Rook. You clicked with something inside of our heads. And that's the biggest compliment that I ever paid to anybody, ever.'

It was then that Dr Friendly rapped on the classroom door, and opened it. 'Mr Rook . . . A word, please.'

'Sure,' said Jim. 'Meanwhile, class, you can read John Ciardi's "Elegy", page two hundred and twenty-one in your *Twentieth-Century American Poets* and tell me what you think if it by the time I come back. And I'm looking for some really original ideas. You've finished all of your exams now. I want you to think for yourselves . . . because that's what you're going to have to do, now that you're going out into the big, wide, distressingly expensive world.'

Outside in the corridor, Dr Friendly immediately put his arm around Jim's shoulders and propelled him over to the far side of the corridor. 'James . . . Jim – I know you prefer it if I call you Jim – we've just had some very serious news.'

'Go on,' said Jim. He had never seen Dr Friendly like this before. Usually he made a point of making Jim feel that he was only half listening to what he was saying, and he hardly ever missed an opportunity to tell him what a criminal waste of time and public resources he considered it to be, trying to teach literature to the underclass. He was a tall, gangly, overpowering man, with a shock of wiry white hair and bulbous eyes. A respected teacher who had been brought into West Grove Community College last year to produce a far better educational average. But sometimes improving the average meant quietly abandoning the slowest and the neediest, and those who were incapable of passing any exams at all.

'Jim . . . it's Dennis Pease. We had a call from LAPD about twenty minutes ago.'

'What's happened? Is he hurt?'

'I'm afraid it's worse than that, James. He's been drowned. He went surfing last night off Will Rogers State Beach, with a bunch of friends. They reported him missing around one a.m. His body was washed up this morning, just after six.'

'Oh, God. Tell me it's not true.'

'I'm sorry, James. His mother identified him about an hour ago.'

'Oh, God.' Jim felt so shaky that he had to lean against the door. Dennis Pease had been one of his most promising and sensitive students – a boy who had worked painfully hard, not just to overcome his severe reading difficulties, but also the scathing nagging of his alcoholic mother. She had done everything she could to make him feel that he was letting her down by going to college, when he could have been making $8 an hour working in a car wash or packing bags in a supermarket. How could he love his mother if he never gave her money to pay for her vodka?

Dr Friendly said, 'If you want to dismiss your class for the day, James, I'll quite understand. Of course we'll be holding two minutes' silence and saying a special memorial prayer at tomorrow's final assembly.'

Jim shook his head. 'No . . . this is something my students and I need to talk over together. I'm not just sending them all home in a state of shock.'

'Well, please yourself. But go easy on the mush, won't you?'

'Go easy on the mush? The *mush*? A friend and a fellow student has drowned, a young guy not even twenty-one years old, and you're asking me to go easy on the *mush*?'

Dr Friendly gave an awkward shrug, as if he had accidentally left his coat hanger in his jacket. 'It's just that . . . well, I know that your methods of teaching tend to be a little on the emotional side.'

'Of course they're on the "emotional side",' Jim retorted. 'I'm teaching these young people to express their feelings. I'm teaching them to tell the world what they really think. What do you want me to do? Go back in that room and say, "Dennis Pease is dead, guys, get on with your work"?'

Dr Friendly laid a hand on Jim's shoulder. His voice tasted like the oil being poured out of a freshly opened sardine can. 'Do you know what I've always liked about you, James? Your single-mindedness. You don't meet many single-minded people any more. But you . . . you support that class of dummies like they're candidates for Princeton. Don't get me wrong, I'm not waxing sentimental here, but I'll kind of miss you when you're gone. Like waking up one morning and realizing that you don't have a cold any more.'

Jim said, 'You'll excuse me, won't you? I have some bad news to tell my dummies.'

Dr Friendly nodded and smiled, and said, 'Of course. And be sure to tell them that Dr Ehrlichman and I . . . we both join them in their sense of loss.'

Jim hesitated. In his mind, he formed the most blistering retort he could think of, couched in the kind of street language that he was always telling Washington Freeman III not to use. But then he thought: No. That won't do you any good; and Dr Friendly will only think that you're being hostile and out of control; and more than that, it's an insult to Dennis, who is dead.

'Thank you,' he said. 'I don't know what they're going to carve on Dennis's headstone; but I know what they're going to carve on yours.'

'Come on, James. Let's be mature.'

'Of course. You're right. But it's a pity that Dennis never got the chance to be mature.'

Dr Friendly frowned at him. He opened his mouth and then he closed it again. He obviously didn't understand what Jim was talking about, and didn't want to understand, either.

'I'll catch you later, in the staff room,' he said, and went squelching off along the highly waxed corridor in his rubber-soled shoes. At the corner, however, he stopped and called back, 'Go on, then, tell me. What *will* they carve on my headstone?'

'"George Friendly . . . Misnomer",' said Jim, and went back to Special Class II.

The grief was very hard for him to take. Special Class II sat in silence while he gave them the news; then Stella Kopalski started to sob, and Laura Killmeyer too, and even the boys were sitting with their heads bowed and tears dripping on to their *Twentieth-Century American Poets*.

Jim walked slowly down the aisle between the desks, laying his hand on every shoulder. 'Dennis was a quiet guy,' he said. 'He had his own struggles, but he fought them hard, and he never gave in. His mother, as most of you know, had a drink problem, and she made his life very miserable for most of the time. But Dennis never said a single word against her. He understood that she was sick – and that she was just as much of a victim of her illness as he was.

'I guess the saddest thing is that Dennis was about to graduate with very good marks, with a chance of finding himself a job doing what he loved the most, which was working with sick and disabled people. And he wasn't lonely or isolated any longer. He had friends . . . not just here in Special Class II, but outside of college too. It's very hard to understand why somebody like Dennis gets taken away from us. We almost blame them for hurting us so much. But let's try to think of all those moments when he made us laugh, and when he made us feel better, just because he was alive.'

It was then that Nestor Fawkes stood up, with his poetry book in his hand, and said hesitantly, 'That poem you gave us to read, Mr Rook . . . there's a verse in it I'd like to say out loud, for Dennis.'

Washington Freeman III groaned, said, '*Man* . . .' and shook his head, but Jim said, 'Go ahead, Nestor. It's an elegy, after all.'

Nestor cleared his throat.

> 'Ah, love has followed them and tears attest
> They stood as slim as grass, they moved like fish
> Into the silent oceans where they rest
> Dark as the squid. Like trees they held their wish
> A season on the leaf, and cannot perish.'

Nestor could barely manage to finish the last line because his voice was so choked. The sheer sorrow that filled the class was overwhelming, and Jim said, 'Let's have a few moments of quiet now, to think about Dennis. But after that, I think we ought to share a few memories, and then we ought to go home. This has been a very sad way to end this year, but I hope you'll all leave here tomorrow with hope for the future, as well as regrets for the past.'

He sat at his desk and watched the morning go by. The class

talked quietly amongst themselves, and he heard fragments of their conversations. 'Do you remember the time I'm carrying my lunch tray and Dennis trips me up? Like, corned beef and mashed potato goes flying everywhere, and Dottie gets a broccoli tiara. Like, it was the first antisocial thing he'd ever done in his entire life. And I'm just about to rip his head off. But he's like, "I'm so sorry, man, I don't know why I did that." But the reason he did it was because he didn't want to be scared of nobody no more.'

'How about that time he came in dressed like a girl, with a blond wig and high heels and everything, because Ray had called him a faggot?'

Jim closed his eyes. He was listening to young people who had come to his class only a year ago as children, both emotionally and educationally, and were now capable of analyzing other people's behavior and their own, and expressing how they felt. He was proud of them all, but right now he could only think that another precious light had winked out, long before morning.

He was walking across the parking-lot when he was hailed by Lieutenant Harris. It was almost midday and the temperature was up in the high nineties. Lieutenant Harris was carrying his bronze coat over his arm, and his yellow-striped tie was loosened to half-mast. 'Jim! Talk to you for a moment?'

'Sure. I was on my way home.'

'What did you do, dismiss the class?'

'We had a discussion first, then I let them go. Dennis Pease was a very popular student. Friends with everybody, poor guy.'

'That was what I was going to ask you about. Did he have any enemies at college? Any run-ins with anybody? Maybe not from your class, but other classes?'

Jim shook his head. 'Dennis was as mild as milk. I don't remember him having a run-in with anybody, ever.' He paused, took off his sunglasses and said, 'Why?'

'He never had trouble with girls? Or one particular girl?'

'No way. I think he'd dated a couple of times, but there was nobody serious.'

'You know that for certain?'

'Listen, lieutenant . . . I teach remedial English. Poetry, drama, expressive literature. I equip my students to put their deepest feelings into words. If any one of them has any kind of romantic trouble, believe me, I'm the first to know it.'

Lieutenant Harris took out a crumpled handkerchief and dabbed at the reddened furrows on his forehead. 'Anybody else I should talk to? Who was his closest buddy?'

'Is there something *wrong* here, lieutenant? I thought that Dennis was drowned when he went out surfing.'

'He was. Except that the medical examiner has told me that there was bruising on his ankles which suggests that he was pulled down under the water . . . and pulled down with considerable force.'

'What are you saying? That somebody *murdered* him?'

'The positioning of the fingermarks sure makes it look like a possibility, yes. To have inflicted similar bruising on dry land, somebody would have had to drag him on his stomach along the ground, which would have caused some knee and elbow bruising too, which he didn't have. Or maybe somebody pulled him down from the top of the parallel bars in the college gymnasium.'

'You can count that out. Dennis hated phys ed with a passion.'

Lieutenant Harris looked around the sunlit campus, with its flags flying and its students playing basketball and sitting out on the grass, and let out a sigh. 'The age of no responsibility, huh?'

'Oh, they all have their problems. Are my grades going to be good enough? What am I going to do when I leave college? Why doesn't the captain of football ever notice me?'

'I wonder what Dennis's problem was? And with who?'

'With *whom*? I don't know. But it seems like a pretty difficult way to kill somebody, doesn't it – *pulling* them under the ocean by their ankles? How do you do that, without drowning yourself?'

'I guess you could do it if you catch your intended victim unawares, so that he instantly breathes in a whole lungful of water. Or if you're capable of holding your breath for very long periods of time. Or if you have an aqualung.'

'So what kind of a person are you looking for, lieutenant?'

'No doubt about it. I think we're looking for a swimmer.'

'Oh, come on, lieutenant. That must include eighty per cent of the population of greater Los Angeles.'

'This swimmer was a very strong swimmer. And, judging by the bruises on Dennis Pease's ankles, this swimmer was a woman.'

Mervyn was running himself a bath. After his morning chores around the apartment building, and shopping for the elderly residents at Ralph's, he was more than ready for a good long soak while he listened to *Cole Porter's Greatest Hits* on his CD player and ate a whole family-size raspberry Danish.

In the evenings he sang satirical songs at the Slant Club, under the stage name of Chet Sideways. But in the afternoons he liked to be serious, and alone with himself. Very few people realized that his outrageous clothes and camp behavior were nothing more than a way of protecting his vulnerability, of keeping the real Mervyn safe. He had been orphaned at the age of three and spent a miserable childhood in the care of foster-parents.

He wasn't even sure that he was gay; but the only people who had ever accepted him and shown him any affection were homosexual men, while his early experiences with women had been with cold and overbearing foster-mothers who ignored him when he wept and hadn't even kissed him good-night.

While the tub gradually filled up, he went to the bathroom mirror and tidied up his eyebrows with tweezers – he favored the Joan Crawford arch. He blew himself a kiss and said, 'You gorgeous devil, you!' although he was worried that lines had started to appear at the sides of his eyes, and that the stubble on his chin was turning gray.

He was still plucking his eyebrows when he heard a strange wallowing sound in the bath behind him. He turned around, frowning. The surface of the water was slopping from end to end, as if somebody had been stirring it with their hand, but that was all. Maybe it had been disturbed by a minor earthquake that he hadn't even noticed. Or an air bubble. He finished off his eyebrows, humming along with 'Night and Day'.

Eventually he unwound his bright satin bathrobe and hung it on the peg on the back of the door. He noticed that the door was slightly ajar, which it hadn't been before. He didn't bother to close it. He wasn't expecting anybody.

Before he climbed into the bath, he weighed himself. Two hundred eighty-four pounds, three pounds lighter than last week. He was quite pleased with himself, and he gave his stomach a brisk wobbly slap of approval. Only another sixty-four pounds to go, and he would have reached his target weight. Watch out, Rupert Everett!

He placed his raspberry Danish on a plate beside his bottles of bath oil and skin exfoliants. Then he eased himself into the water, grunting in satisfaction and relief. This was the only hour of the day in which he could lie back and dream. He didn't have to worry about his job, or his errands, or wiping up the turkey-flavored sick that Mrs Laksa's Pekinese had left in the hallway.

'Night and day . . .' he breathed, 'You are a part of me . . .'

He splashed his face with water, and used a washcloth to scrub his neck and behind his ears. His foster-mother had sent him to school without any lunch if he didn't wash behind his ears, and so he never failed to do it, twice a day. Even now, he remembered the misery of going through a whole school day without anything to eat.

Now he could twist himself around and break off a large chunk of raspberry Danish. But as he took the first bite, he felt something stirring in the water, down below the foam. It was something slippery, and muscular, and his first horrified thought was that it was a snake. Jesus –

a huge snake had slid into the tub when he wasn't looking! He let out a shriek of terror, and pastry exploded from his mouth. He gripped the handrail and tried to heave himself out of the water, but he slipped and fell back again, with a splash that sent water all across the bathroom floor.

It wasn't a snake. It was more than a snake, it was two snakes! It was something even bigger than two snakes! Frantically he groped under the water, trying to find it, trying to get a grip on it so that he could throw it out of the bath.

At the same time, he saw that all of the water that he had splashed across the room was sliding back across the tiles, back toward the tub, almost as if it were magnetized. He gripped the handrail again, but before he could pull himself upward, the bathwater churned right in front of him, and a *figure* rose out of it, a figure that seemed to be made out of nothing but hot, transparent water, with steam rising from it.

Mervyn dropped back into the tub, his heart clutched by a seizure of complete terror. The figure rose above him, and he could see that it was a young woman, although he could see right through her, he could see the pink-tiled wall behind her, and the sun shining through the slatted blinds.

'Holy shit,' he said, with Danish crumbs all around his mouth. 'Tell me I'm dreaming.'

But the figure rose even higher, and leaned toward him, and he knew that he wasn't dreaming. He wasn't even having a nightmare. Through the steam that curled around it, Mervyn could see its face. Its glassy eyes were staring at him and its mouth was dragged downward in absolute hatred.

Again he tried to clamber to his feet, but the figure pushed him back. The impact was so strong that Mervyn felt as if he had been hit by a giant wave. He rolled around and attempted to get on to his knees, but the figure knocked him down again, and then again. Then it gripped hold of his neck and forced his face right under the water.

'*No!*' Mervyn bubbled, and reared his head up, gasping for

air. But the figure pushed him down again, so hard that his nose was pressed against the bottom of the bath. He struggled and kicked and tried to roll round on to his back again, but the figure was sitting astride him now, clenching his body between its thighs, and he was so fat that he was wedged.

His eyes were open. He could see the bubbles blurting out of his mouth. He saw his nailbrush slowly sinking past him, and then tumbling away. He made one last supreme effort to lift himself up on his hands and knees, and for a few straining seconds he thought he was going to make it. He grunted and spluttered as his face came out of the water. But then the figure gripped his throat like a lock-wrench, and smashed his head back down under the foam, breaking his nose. The bath grew cloudy with blood.

Mervyn's lungs couldn't take any more. He knew that he was going to have to breathe in camellia-scented bathwater. He couldn't believe that he was going to die like this. His ears were aching and his nose felt as if it had been crushed into a hundred grating fragments of bone.

'*Abbggbblllrrhhhh!*' he shouted in panic and desperation, and the last bubbles rushed out of his lungs.

Six

Jim came struggling along the corridor of his apartment building with his dog-eared brown-leather briefcase under one arm and two sacks of shopping under the other. He hadn't bought any food – he had no appetite after hearing about Dennis – but he had needed some Whiskas for Tibbles Two and some kitchen-cleaning spray so that he could leave his work surfaces looking slightly less gummy when he left on Wednesday and flew off to Washington.

He still wasn't sure what he was going to do with his car. It was nearly fourteen years old and it needed new shocks and a head gasket, but he didn't want to part with it. It came from the era when cars weren't cars, they were ocean liners. Eight-point-two-liter, twenty-one feet long. Maybe Mervyn could look after it for him. Mervyn was ostentatious enough.

As he passed Mervyn's apartment, he saw that the front door was half open. He hesitated, then set down his briefcase, went back and knocked on it. 'Mervyn? You in there?' He knew that Mervyn liked to spend his afternoons in seclusion, playing music, and it was very unusual for him to leave his door ajar.

'Mervyn? It's Jim.'

He set down his shopping and cautiously stepped into Mervyn's apartment. It was furnished with a leopard-print three-piece suite and its walls were decorated with circus posters, Barnum and Bailey, Pindar and Bouglione, Forepaugh and Sells. Acrobats, clowns, and buxom ladies with ostrich feathers in their hair riding equally buxom horses. On the bureau stood a framed photograph of a woman in a straw hat who bore a very strong resemblance to Mervyn, with the same sad eyes.

From the bathroom came the sound of Cole Porter music . . . somebody singing 'You'd Be So Nice To Come Home To'. Jim listened outside the door, but there was no sound of Mervyn singing along, which he usually did. Jim gave him a quick postman's knock. 'Meryvn? . . . Hope I'm not intruding. Your front door was open and I just wanted to check that you were okay.'

No answer. He waited for a moment, and then he knocked again.

'Mervyn? Are you in there? You haven't drowned or anything, have you?'

Still no answer. He eased the door open and peered inside, hoping against hope that he wouldn't catch Mervyn in the tub or – worse still – sitting on the john. At first it looked as if the bathroom was unoccupied. But when Jim took two or three steps inside, he saw the white whale-like curve of Mervyn's backside in the bathtub.

'Mervyn!' he called out. 'Mervyn! What the hell's happened?'

Mervyn was lying face-down. The bathtub was empty, and he was clutching the plug in his hand. There were streaks of blood running from his nostrils and down the drain, and his lips were blue.

Jim tried to turn him over on to his side, but he was still slippery and he was far too heavy to lift. He pressed his fingertips against Mervyn's carotid artery but he couldn't feel a pulse.

'Mervyn!' he said, shaking him. 'Mervyn, can you hear me? It's Jim!'

Jesus, he thought, *Jesus*. This is all I need. He went back to the living-room and picked up the Madame Pompadour-style phone with shaking hands. 'Ambulance? I've got a guy here who's drowned in his bathtub. Well, I really don't know. I'm just a neighbor. Yes, I've tried to put him into the recovery position but he weighs nearly three hundred pounds.'

‘Hold on,’ said a nasal voice at the other end of the phone. ‘A paramedic team will be right with you.’

Then all he could do was pace around the bathroom, glancing now and again at Mervyn’s huge, flabby, inert body; and wonder how he could have drowned in an empty bathtub.

He was just about to call 911 for a second time when Mervyn gave a thick, phlegmy cough. He coughed again, and let out a deep, sonorous sigh, as if he had been disturbed during a particularly happy dream. Then he coughed again, and lifted up one hand, so that his fingers squeaked against the side of the bathtub. Jim knelt down beside him and helped him to lift up his head. His nose was enormously swollen, like a clown’s, and his eyes were puffy.

‘Mervyn, it’s Jim. Are you okay?’

‘Jim . . . hi. Am I dead?’

‘No, you’re not dead. You’re lying in the bath. What happened?’

‘That water-woman. The same water-woman we were talking about last night. She was going to kill me. She came right out of the water and she was going to kill me.’

‘You’re kidding me.’

‘Do I look like I’m kidding? At first I thought she was a snake but she wasn’t a snake and she grabbed hold of my throat and she tried to drown me.’

‘Come on, Mervyn, we have to get you out of there. It looks like your nose has been broken.’

‘Tell me about it. She smashed my beezer on the bottom of the bath.’

Gradually, groaning and puffing, Mervyn managed to turn around and lift himself out of the bath. Jim was waiting for him with a Turkish towel held out wide and his eyes averted. ‘You’re an angel, Jim. An angel from heaven. I don’t know what I’m going to do without you.’

‘You’ll manage. I called the paramedics . . . they should be here in a minute.’

‘You’re an angel. You should be sitting at God’s right hand.’

'Well, not just yet, Mervyn. Here, come and sit down. You're shivering.'

'You'd be shivering if you saw what I saw. She came right out of the bath, *whoosh!* And, just like you said, she was all made out of water. Hot water, too.'

'Can I get you something to drink?'

'No thanks. I already drank half the bath. Jesus, I thought I was dead, for sure. If I hadn't have pulled out the plug . . .'

'Something seriously weird is going down here,' said Jim. 'First there was that little Mikey, drowned last week. Then the cops came round to the college today to tell me that one of my students was deliberately drowned in the ocean. Now you.'

'It's this water-woman,' coughed Mervyn. 'She's like a . . . serial drowner.'

'It looks that way, doesn't it? But why Mikey? And why you? I don't know for sure that she had anything to do with Donald Pease drowning, but from what the cops told me, it sure sounds like it.'

At that moment, there was a brisk knock on the door and two paramedics came in. 'Somebody drowned?' asked one of them, a big swarthy man with a heavy black mustache.

'Nearly, but not quite,' said Mervyn, dabbing his nose.

'I can see. Your nose is some kind of a mess, ain't it? What happened?'

'I – ah – I slipped on the soap. Cracked my nose right on the edge of the tub.' Mervyn glanced at Jim as if to say, 'Let's not make this any more complicated than it already is.' He didn't care for the Los Angeles police very much, and he certainly didn't want them trampling all over his apartment, looking for evidence of a woman whose material appearance had simply poured away down the drain.

The paramedic sat on the couch, pinched the end of Mervyn's nose between finger and thumb and wiggled it. 'That hurt?'

'Ow! What the hell do you think? I just broke it in fifty-eight places!'

'Hit your head at all? Any black-out? Any concussion?'

'I don't know . . . I may have been unconscious for a minute or two.'

'Okay . . . whyn't you get yourself dressed and we'll wheel you round to the ER.'

Jim gave Mervyn a helping hand, and Mervyn rose unsteadily on to his feet. 'Do you want me to come with you?' Jim asked.

'No, no. I'll be fine. Really. This handsome young paramedic can take care of me, can't you?' He peered closer at the paramedic and said, 'You were never in Village People, were you? No, maybe not. Before your time.'

Before he left, Mervyn laid a hand on Jim's arm and spoke confidentially into his ear. 'You realize what the connection is, don't you, between what happened to me today, and that student of yours, and young Mikey?'

Jim knew what he was going to say. 'It could be nothing more than a coincidence.'

'Maybe you're right. But if I were you I'd go around to every single person I cared for, and tell them to start wearing life-jackets, even in the shower.'

He called round at Susan Silverstone's house on Franklin. Nobody answered when he rang the doorbell, but he heard voices around the back, so he pushed his way through the dense sub-tropical plants until he reached the courtyard where the fountain was splashing.

Susan was dressed in tight black satin jeans, a scoop-neck black-silk sweater and strappy black sandals. She was potting a row of ferns, and talking to them while she did so. 'There, my frondy little friend . . . how does this nice little blue ceramic number suit you?'

A young man in jeans and a Nirvana T-shirt was sitting on the garden swing with a can of beer held between his thighs. The canopy above the swing was overgrown with ivy so that Jim couldn't see his face. He was idly kicking himself backward and forward with one bare foot.

'Susan?' said Jim. 'Hope I'm not interrupting anything.

I tried reaching you on your mobile phone but it was switched off.'

'I do that,' said Susan, standing up. Her raven-black hair was tied with a white satin bow. 'It's enough of a nuisance communicating with the dead, let alone the living.'

'It's come back,' Jim told her. 'The water spirit, whatever you like to call it.' He told her about Mervyn, and about Lieutenant Harris's suspicions that Dennis Pease had been deliberately drowned.

'Did you know that ferns were hermaphrodites?' said Susan, in a matter-of-fact tone, easing another one out of its pot. 'Whenever they want more ferns, they have sex with themselves. Don't you think that's far less messy than the way we do it? And cheaper. You don't have to take a fern to the movies.'

She paused, and then said very seriously, 'It's looking for revenge.'

'Revenge? What kind of revenge? Revenge for what?'

'I'm sorry, Jim. I may be clairvoyant but I don't have any idea. The only way to find out what any spirit wants is to ask it – which could be very dangerous, considering how malevolent it is. But if it's drowning people, one after another, it's doing it for a reason. Spirits hardly ever commit random acts of destruction. Even poltergeists throw plates around for a reason . . . not that it's ever very easy to discover what it is.'

'Will you help me? You see, the thing is that, even if I didn't know young Mikey, I knew Mikey's mother; and Dennis Pease was a student of mine; and Mervyn's been like a brother to me. Well – more like a sister, but very close.'

'What are you saying?' asked Susan, turning around. In the shadows of the courtyard her face shone luminously pale.

From underneath the swing canopy the young man said, 'He's saying that all three incidents involved somebody he knew; which is leading him to worry that the next time it happens, if there *is* a next time, somebody else he knows will come to a watery finish, which is something he is very anxious to avoid.'

'I know that voice,' said Jim. He walked over to the garden swing and lifted the canopy. Underneath it was sitting a good-looking young man with a spiky blond haircut and mischievous blue eyes. 'Michael Tosca, class of '95. Mr Verbal Diarrhoea himself. Do you know something, Susan, this guy used to sit in the front of my class and never stop talking from nine o'clock in the morning till four thirty in the afternoon. What are you doing here, Michael?'

'I work for Miss Silverstone these days, Mr Rook. Secretary, personal assistant, driver, bodyguard, diary planner, tofu gofer, cook, cleaner of Oriental rugs and burnisher of crystal balls.'

'I thought you were going to go into politics.'

'I was. But I couldn't stand the chiseling and the bribery and the pork-barreling and the general hypocrisy. It didn't pay, either. No money in it. Then I met Susan at a party one weekend and . . . well—'

'And well what? I'm waiting with bated breath.'

'It's another story, that's all,' Susan put in. 'Besides, Michael has found a way to control his talking these days, haven't you, Michael?'

'That's right. Once in a while I spend a whole day saying nothing at all. It's very refreshing for the spirit, and it allows you to express yourself in ways you wouldn't normally dare to.'

Jim pointed his finger at him. 'Don't tell me. *You're* that obnoxious mime artist – whatever your name is, Medlar Tree.'

Michael lifted his beer can in salute. 'Right first time, Mr Rook. Nobody could ever pull the wool over your eyes, could they?'

'I hate mimes. Why do you think humans have the power of speech? If we don't speak to each other, we might as well be monkeys.'

'Monkeys are cool.'

'Sure they're cool. But you wouldn't want to spend the evening talking to a roomful of orang-utans, would you?'

'I don't know. You should meet some of my friends.'

Susan came up to Jim and linked arms with him. 'I'll tell you something, Jim. Michael helped to save my life when nobody else around me cared anything at all. I don't know what you taught him when he was in college, but he's always been so considerate. And gentle, too.'

'Well, you amaze me,' said Jim. 'I always had him down as a grade-A smartass.'

'He even wrote that on my report,' said Michael, with a grin.

Susan said, 'You know, we should try another spirit-trace on the beach where this other boy drowned. What was his name? Dennis? If we do that, at least we'll know what happened for sure.'

'Well . . . it's up to you. But I don't want to put you in any danger.'

'I think I can handle a water spirit,' said Susan. 'We were all sent into this world to help each other, weren't we? And to protect each other from the next world, too.'

Jim checked his watch. 'It's still light; maybe we should start off by the beach.'

Jim drove them down to Will Rogers State Beach, and they parked and walked across the sand. The sun was shining in their eyes, and the afternoon was windy and warm. 'He drowned right out there,' said Jim. 'According to his friends, he was fit and raring to go and he hadn't had anything more to drink than a couple of beers.'

Susan stood still for a moment with her eyes closed. Then she took off her sandals, handed them to Michael, and walked right down to the edge of the surf. Jim followed her, and stood beside her while she stared out over the glittering ocean.

'There's still something here . . . some redolence. I can feel it.'

'I can't feel anything.'

'Yes you can. You're a sensitive, just like me. Look at the light. Listen to the seagulls. They're calling out to you, telling you that something happened here, something tragic.'

The way the seagulls were wheeling and keening, it was easy to believe that Susan was right. Although children were still running along the shoreline and laughing, and dogs were still barking, there was a sense of loss in the air, a sense of tragedy. Maybe it was nothing more than the end of another day. But Dennis Pease had drowned here, late last night, and he was never coming back.

Michael opened the bag that he was carrying on his back, and Susan took out her crystal. She knelt down, set it on its stand and started to spin it. It caught the sunlight, and multi-colored diamonds danced across the sand. A small girl stopped in her tracks and stared at it, entranced, and a dachshund that had been yipping and snapping and chasing its tail stopped right beside her, and stared at it too with black beady eyes.

Jim couldn't be sure. Maybe it was nothing more than the sun going down. But the afternoon seemed to darken, and the color of the sky grew more intense. The sound of the surf rasped ever more sharply in his ears, like sandpaper. Above his head the gulls continued to circle and cry, around and around, as if they couldn't leave the flickering light around the crystal, no matter what.

Down by the shoreline Jim saw six or seven boys, their images jumping and fading like a worn-out movie. They were laughing and tumbling, and kicking water at each other. Then two of them picked up surfboards and rushed into the waves. One of them had lanky hair, tied back with a bandanna, and a large, triangular nose. Even though he was only intermittently visible, Jim recognized him at once as Dennis Pease.

'*Don't do it, Dennis*,' he said, under his breath, although he knew how futile it was. If there was only a way to turn the clock back to yesterday night. But Dennis's carefree image went on bounding into the water, and Jim could even hear the faintest echoes of his voice, whooping and laughing. He had always been such a bright, wild, enthusiastic boy, ready for anything.

Michael said, 'I can never get used to these spirit-traces, they're so weird. Look at it: that happened last night, that really happened, and there they are, doing it all over. Makes you wonder if you ever get any rest, even when you're dead, or whether you spend the rest of eternity acting your life out again and again, like some kind of never-ending loop.'

'I don't know,' said Jim, peering out across the ocean. The waves seemed to be almost black, like a glistening, restless sea of Indian ink. He could see Dennis rising up on one foamy crest after another as he paddled further and further away from the shore. *Don't do it, Dennis.* But Dennis had already done it, and his drowned body was already lying in the West Grove Mortuary.

Susan arched her head back so that she was staring up at the sky. 'Show yourself!' she demanded. 'I know you're here! Why don't you show yourself?'

The wind began to rise; flecks of spume began to fly off the tops of the waves. But Dennis and his friends kept on plowing out into the ocean, and Jim could hear them calling and whistling to each other as they went.

'Maybe it was just an accident,' he said. 'Anybody could drown in a surf like that.'

But Susan turned to him, her white face lit up in harlequin colors by her rapidly spinning crystal. 'Wait,' she said. 'There's a presence here. I can feel it. It's coming toward us, from the north-east, and it's coming very quickly.'

'You can *feel* it?'

'It's just like the wind. Hold my hand, Jim, it's almost here. I want you to tell me everything you see.'

When the apparition appeared, however, Jim was speechless. It came running over the sand, so light and fast that he could barely see it. A young woman, almost completely transparent, running toward the ocean with her hair streaming behind her.

'She's there!' he told Susan, tugging at her sleeve. 'For Christ's sake, can't we stop her?'

Susan unexpectedly gripped his hand, and very tightly. Michael glanced at them; and there was an odd, possessive look in his eyes. But when he saw Jim looking at him he immediately turned his head away and stared out over the surf.

Dennis had paddled so far out that Jim could see only the tip of his red metallic-flake surfboard; and occasionally his head, with the red bandanna tied around it. But he could clearly see the water-woman, swimming toward him. She left a trail in the sea, she lit up the tops of the waves, leaving a ghostly arrow-shaped wake behind her, phosphorescent green and glittering sapphire-blue. She swam as straight as a torpedo, and almost as fast; so that even when she was only a few feet away from Dennis he still hadn't seen her. Why should he? Who expects an invisible woman to come swimming toward them at eighteen knots?

Dennis must have sensed *something*, however, because he turned his head around, gripped his surfboard a little tighter, and shouted out, 'Guys? Is everything okay? What's the matter?'

It was then that the young woman's luminous trail disappeared deep under the water, so that Jim could see only the faintest greeny-blue glow of her. There was a long moment's pause, and then an arm suddenly rose up, an arm made completely out of water, and clamped its hand over Dennis's face. 'Help me!' he screamed out. '*Vinnie, help me, I'm drowning! Help me, Vinnie! Something's pulling me down!*'

His friend turned his head around wildly; but the troughs were so deep and the white spume was blowing as thick as blossom; and he couldn't see anything at all. Jim, on the shoreline, saw only a rapidly dimming radiance, which died away as the spirit dragged Dennis deeper into the ocean. There was a moment's pause, and then Dennis's metallic-red surfboard came flying out of the ocean, almost vertically, like a Polaris missile. Jim kicked off his shoes and started to pull open the buttons on his shirt.

Susan gripped his wrist and stopped him. 'Jim, there's nothing there. It seems like it's real but it's only a trick of the light. Dennis is dead, Jim. If you swim out there now, you won't find anything at all. No Dennis, no spirit. No surfboard.'

She cupped her hand over the crystal to stop it from rotating. Then she picked it up and handed it to Michael, and Michael slipped it back into its black woven bag. Again Jim caught that look in his eyes, almost as if he were warning him off.

Susan said, 'I'm sorry, Jim. I don't think there's any doubt at all. This student of yours was drowned by the same water spirit that drowned Mikey . . . and from everything you've told me, the same spirit tried to drown your friend Mervyn too.'

'So what is it? And what do you think it wants?'

'I don't know. It's not an ethnic manifestation, like a Native American river spirit. Ethnic spirits can be incredibly powerful, and they would flood a whole town rather than drown one poor struggling student. It's not a regular ghost, because a regular ghost wouldn't be able to use the water to take on a physical shape. Like, ghosts are just smoke and mirrors. They're all *suggestion*, rather than physical fact. Cold spots, smells, pictures rearranged . . . that's all ghosts are good for. I mean, they're frightening enough, but they can't do you any real harm.'

'So this is like that heap of rubbish that came alive and strangled that old man in Encino? An urban legend?'

'That's my guess, anyway. It's like the phantom hitch-hiker in the back of the car; or the Blair Witch; or the guy who had himself sewn up inside an armchair so that he could fondle the woman he loved whenever she sat down.

'Let's put it this way. Not all spirits are old. Not all evil influences are ancient, no matter what H. P. Lovecraft had to say about it. There are new spirits being created every day – every time something horrible happens. A homicide, a car smash. Somebody committing suicide. Most of the time they don't do anybody any harm . . . but now and again they want revenge for the way their lives were cut short.'

'So what do we do now? How do we find out what this water spirit is?'

'I think we'll have to pay a visit to David DuQuesne. He's the expert. It'll probably cost you, though.'

'I don't mind that. I just want to find out how I can stop this thing before any more of my class get hurt.'

'Okay, I'll see what I can do. The last I heard, he was living up in Topanga Canyon someplace. I have a couple of friends who should know how to find him.'

Jim dropped Susan and Michael back at Franklin Avenue. Before she left him, Susan took hold of his hand and gave him a kiss on the lips. 'I'll call you later, all right, as soon as I've gotten in contact with David DuQuesne.'

Jim unlatched the passenger seat and folded it forward so that Michael could climb out.

'Something on your mind?' he asked. 'You were giving me some pretty meaningful looks down there on the beach.'

'Nothing in particular,' said Michael. 'I just want you to be careful, okay?'

'Careful about what?'

'You know what I'm talking about. Susan. I'm asking you to keep your relationship on a strictly business level. She's still very breakable.'

'She looks tough enough to me.'

'Hidden fault-lines, Jim.'

'All right. But I wasn't thinking of starting anything with her, believe me. I'm already involved with somebody else.'

'A lot of guys say that. But she's hard to resist.'

Jim started up his engine. 'Maybe you should stick to miming, Michael. Nobody can legislate fate.'

'A word to the wise, that's all. You don't know what you could be getting yourself into.'

Jim drove away, leaving Michael standing on the sidewalk. He couldn't think what Michael was trying to warn him about. Susan was undeniably attractive, in a strange, sensual, other-worldly way. She had a look in her eyes that made him think that she had been to places and thought of things that most girls wouldn't even dare to go to or think of. But it was more like the bright, cold attraction of the moon. His heart still belonged to Karen, even if she wouldn't join him in Washington.

He started to sing Santana's 'Black Magic Woman', but after a couple of blocks the words died away on his lips.

Seven

At college assembly the next morning, Dr Ehrlichman, the principal, led some simple and poignant non-denominational prayers for Dennis and his family, and even Dr Friendly had his handkerchief out.

After prayers, Jim stepped up on to the rostrum and said, 'Whenever we lose somebody close to us, we question the natural justice of the world we live in. Many people believe that there is no natural justice, only fate. They think that all we can do when a friend like Dennis leaves us is to grieve for him, and then pick up the pieces of our own lives and carry on, and, whenever we can, remember him.

'But I don't subscribe to that. I believe that the world has forces of good and forces of evil, and that whenever something tragic occurs, like the premature passing of a fellow student, then the evil that caused it must be found, and faced up to, and destroyed.

'As you know, the police suspect that Dennis may have been deliberately drowned, and they are conducting their own investigation. For my part, I'm going to be doing everything I can to find out what happened to him. But as you leave for your summer vacation, I want you all to promise me one thing – all of you – and this is relevant to what happened to Dennis.

'I want you to be extra vigilant whenever you're swimming or whenever you're anyplace near water. I don't yet know what's happening exactly, but you may be in danger of being drowned, the way Dennis was.'

Dr Ehrlichman came up to him and put his hand over the microphone. 'Jim . . . what the hell are you telling these kids?'

'Dr Ehrlichman, they have to be warned. It may sound screwy, but believe me, every one of these students is at very real risk.'

The assembled students began to murmur and whisper and shuffle their feet. Dr Friendly slowly shook his head from side to side, as if to say, Here we go, another wacky Jim Rook performance,' and to show that he couldn't wait for this last day to end, so that he would never have to suffer Jim's eccentricities, ever again.

Jim said, 'Okay . . . I've said what I needed to say, in any case. Now I want to dedicate a few words to Dennis, if you don't have any objection.'

Dr Ehrlichman gave a theatrical sigh. 'No, Jim. I guess that's your privilege. But whatever you're going to say, I hope it makes some kind of sense.'

'Oh, it does, believe me. It's a poem by Kathleen Raine. It used to be one of Dennis's favorites.'

Jim approached the microphone again, and said simply, 'For Dennis,' and recited:

'Out of hope's eternal spring
Bubbled once my mountain stream
Moss and sundew, fern and fell,
Valley, summer, tree and sun,
All rose up, and all are gone.

'Now by the spring I stand alone
Still are its singing waters flowing;
Oh never thought I here to greet
Shadowy death who comes this way
Where hope's waters rise and play!'

From the balcony at the rear of the auditorium, Dottie Osias let out a loud wail of anguish and collapsed into sobs. Many of the other students were crying openly too. Jim stepped away from the rostrum, and said a silent prayer to himself that he wouldn't ever have to do this again.

* * *

Special Class II was deeply subdued that morning. They were affected not only by the shock of Dennis's death but by the sadness of leaving college and each other after one of the most demanding years that Jim could remember – but one of the most rewarding, too. This year's entry had struggled heroically and often tearfully to overcome their stumbling reading, their catastrophic spelling and their slack-jawed lack of comprehension – not only that, but the sense of social isolation that comes from being so inarticulate. It was no good being as pretty as Stella Kopalski if you didn't know the difference between 'finance' and 'fiancé'. But Jim had given them the greatest single gift that anybody would ever give them: the ability to express themselves, and the power to say exactly what they wanted to say.

Washington Freeman III tilted his chair back and shifted a toothpick from one side of his mouth to the other. 'What was that you saying in the auditorium, Mr Rook? All about staying away from the water, and shit?'

'Washington, this is your last day here. Your last few hours of remedial English. Can you try to make this the very last time that you end a sentence with the words "and shit"?'

'Do what I can, Mr Rook. But you don't know how hard it is when practically everybody else in the known universe keeps on saying "shit" and shit.'

'It don't matter Washington saying that, Mr Rook,' put in Tarquin, who was wearing beetle-like sunglasses and a shiny black T-shirt, which made him look like a cross between Stevie Wonder and a giant insect. 'The only job that Washington's ever going to get is cleaning out the johns at McDonald's . . . so what other words is he ever going to need?'

'I'm going to be a Corvette salesperson, fool,' Washington retorted. 'What I don't know about Corvettes ain't been invented yet.'

'Who cares? All I need to know about Corvettes is that you ain't got one.'

Joyce Capistrano was fiddling with a piece of paper torn out of one of her files. She couldn't sit in class for longer than ten minutes without producing paper flowers or dancing dollies or lacy mats. She wasn't a particularly pretty girl, although she had huge dreamy brown eyes and glossy brown hair, and one of the sweetest personalities that Jim had ever come across in all of his years of teaching. Over the year, Jim had helped her to conquer an almost overwhelming shyness and a hesitancy in her speech which used to have the whole class groaning and banging their heads on their desks to make her hurry up and finish her sentences.

Jim had never run Special Class II with sentimentality. Any student who had a stutter had to fight it out against teasing and imitation. Any student who couldn't tell the difference between D and B had to write the word 'bed' on the chalk-board, again and again, while the rest of the class sarcastically chanted, 'B! E! D!' at the tops of their voices. But there was never any resentment, because every student in Special Class II knew that he or she was no cleverer than any other student: they all had serious problems in communicating, and this was their very last chance to get over them. They also knew from personal experience that nobody in the world outside West Grove Community College would ever make allowances for them, either.

Joyce said, 'You're really worried about something, aren't you, Mr Rook?'

'Yes, Joyce, I am.'

'It's not like all that ice we had in the swimming pool, is it, when Suzie Wintz drowned?'

'Not exactly. But it's something like it. Something very strange, and very dangerous.'

'It'll be okay. The summer vacation starts tomorrow.'

'That's what I'm worried about. Just because college is out, that doesn't necessarily mean that this thing is going to go away.'

'Well, what is it exactly?' asked Christophe l'Ouverture. As usual Christophe was dressed in a short-sleeved designer shirt, strawberry-colored today, with a matching silk tie. Very fastidious about his clothes, Christophe. His hair was plaited in dreadlocks.

'I couldn't say this to the whole college this morning: Dr Ehrlichman thinks I'm halfway nuts as it is. But you all know that I can see things . . . like supernatural manifestations.'

'Ghosts and shit,' put in Washington helpfully.

'That's right, Washington. Ghosts and shit. I've been investigating Dennis's drowning, and also the drowning of a little boy called Mikey . . . the son of one of my former students, Jennie Bauer. Yesterday a neighbor of mine was nearly drowned too. He says he saw a figure come out of his bathwater, a figure made all out of water, and try to push him under. I went to Will Rogers State Beach, where Dennis drowned, and the pool where little Mikey drowned, and I saw the same kind of figure with my own eyes. A water spirit, I guess you could call it. I don't know.'

'A water spirit?' asked Dottie. 'You mean like a mermaid or something?'

'I don't know. Maybe this is how the legends of mermaids originated. But I'm not particularly interested in myths and legends. What really concerns me is that this water spirit seems to be trying to hurt the people who are closest to *me* – my friends and my students. I don't have any idea why, but I know that I love you guys, all of you, and I don't want to see any of you hurt in any way. That's why I'm warning you to be very careful whenever you go near water . . . the ocean, the pool, the bath, anyplace at all. Because it looks to me like the spirit can take on a physical form anyplace and any time, provided it has enough water to give itself shape.'

'Wow,' said Laura Killmeyer. She used to walk around the campus with a black cat on the end of a ribbon, quoting lines from *Faust* and the *Codex Daemonicus*. But she had lost interest in becoming a professional witch after she had tried to work a very complicated love-spell on the captain of the track team. She had discovered the very next morning that he had got engaged to the team's red-headed cheerleader. Laura no longer wore silver Romanian coins around her head or painted her eyelashes to look like hairy black spiders, but she was still fascinated by the occult. 'A *water* spirit! I never heard of anything like that before!'

'To be frank with you, neither did I. But there it was – or there *she* was, because it's a girl for sure. I saw her climbing out of Mikey's pool, and I saw her in the ocean after Dennis was drowned. I can't lie to you. I'm scared for you guys. And the worst thing is, I think it's all my fault, although I don't know why.'

'Hey, don't go blaming yourself, man,' said Tarquin. 'You never let us down, never, specially when Dr Friendly told us we was all irreversible lame-brains. If you say there's a water spirit, then we believe you, there *is* a water spirit, and this vacation we're going to stay away from anything watery, believe me.'

'Oh, come on now,' put in Washington. 'You going to tell me you going to go through the whole summer vacation without taking one single shower?'

'I didn't mean that. Showers is different. You never heard of nobody drowning in a shower, did you?'

'Anybody can drown in less than a half-inch of water,' Jim interrupted them. 'Talk to Nurse Andrews, she'll tell you. When you breathe in water, a froth of mucus bubbles up in your lungs, and that's what makes it so hard for you to breathe.'

'No shit.'

'No, Washington. Just froth. But as I say – be very careful, and if you're not sure if it's going to be safe to swim, then don't. I hope I don't spoil your summer, but it would be even more spoiled if you were drowned.'

He looked around the class. He would miss this room, and all the faces that he had seen in here, staring up at him expectantly. 'There's one last thing I'd like you to do for me before we finish. I'd like each of you to write me a four-line poem. Subject: doesn't matter. Anything that interests you. Anything that sums you up . . . the kind of person you are. Then I'd like you to sign it for me. I'd like to walk away from here today with something a little more than memories.'

He walked down between the rows of desks. 'Where's Dottie? Anybody seen Dottie?'

'She went for her jog,' said Laura. 'She always goes for

a jog before class. Her dietician said it was the only way she was ever going to take control of her weight problem.'

'Weight problem? I never knew Dottie had a weight problem.'

'She *thinks* she has a weight problem. That's as bad as having a real weight problem.'

'Well, she's cutting things close. The semester's officially over in an hour.'

'Want me to go look for her? She's probably hit the showers by now.'

Jim shook his head. 'Don't worry about it. If she doesn't have time to write me a poem, I'll ask her to send me a postcard.'

Silence fell over the room. There was a lot of frowning and a lot of lip-chewing and a lot of head-scratching. Only Nestor Fawkes seemed to be writing steadily, and he was one of the least gifted students in the class. Tarquin kept popping his fingers as if he were writing a rap (which he probably was), and Stella kept on sighing at her sheet of paper like a parent sighing at a disobedient child.

Jim sat at his desk and started writing a letter to Karen – a last-ditch effort to persuade her to change her mind.

> You don't meet soulmates more than once in a lifetime, Karen. As Victor Hugo wrote, 'When two souls, who have sought each other for however long in the throng, have finally found each other, there is then established for ever between them a union, fiery and pure as they themselves are, a union which begins on earth and continues for ever in heaven.' Or, hopefully, in our case, Washington, D.C.

Only five minutes had passed, however, before Jim heard feet loudly slapping along the corridor outside. The classroom door burst open and Clarence the janitor came in, his face sweaty and his eyes wide, holding a mop.

'Clarence? What's wrong?'

'You better come real quick, Mr Rook. Something's going on in the showers.'

'The *showers*? What are you talking about?'

'It's the female showers, Mr Rook. The whole place is full of steam and there's somebody screaming.'

Jim immediately tossed down his pen and crossed the room. 'Stella, get on that mobile phone of yours and call for paramedics – now! Tell them to go to the girls' showers, fast as they can. Tarquin – Eugene – Laura – you come with me!'

They ran together along the corridor until they reached the showers outside the college gymnasium. Clarence was right. Steam was billowing out of the open outer door, and a girl was screaming inside at the top of her voice. A knot of terrified girls were gathered outside, some of them crying.

'What's happening?' asked Jim. 'Who's in there?'

There was another scream, which ended in a high-pitched, agonized wail. 'Oh my God, it's Dottie,' said Laura.

Jim went through to the inner door. It was shut, and when he took hold of the metal doorhandle he burned his hand. Steam was hissing viciously out from underneath the door, and the window was totally fogged up.

He tried kicking the door, but it opened outward, and it was made of solid varnished oak. 'Give me a towel!' he shouted, as Dottie started screaming again. One of the girls passed him a towel, and he made himself a thick glove out of it. He took hold of the doorhandle again and pulled it as hard as he could.

At first he couldn't budge it, but he tugged it again and again, and at last he managed to open it an inch. The steam that came blasting out of the shower room was scalding, and he was already dripping with sweat. The noise, too: it was like standing next to a locomotive.

'Here, Mr Rook!' said Washington, jostling his way through the frightened crowd of students with an aluminum baseball bat. He forced it into the gap that Jim had already managed to open, and between them, grunting, they gradually levered the door wide enough to get in.

'Be careful!' Jim shouted. 'Steam is like boiling water, it can take your skin right off!'

At that moment, Dr Ehrlichman arrived outside. 'Jim? What's going on? What the hell is all of this steam?'

Dottie let out another agonized scream, and Jim said, 'Make sure those paramedics are on the way! Give me another towel! Does anybody have another towel?'

'I'm going in with you, man,' said Washington.

'Don't. This is my responsibility, not yours.'

'What did the Three Musketeers say? "All for all and everyone for everybody else."'

'All right, then,' said Jim, wrapping another towel around his head, like a hood. 'But stay well behind me and watch out for that steam.'

'Jim! Wait for the fire department!' ordered Dr Ehrlichman.

But Jim had already squeezed his way through the gap in the door and entered the showers, with Washington hunched up close behind him.

The steam was so dense that he could hardly see where he was going. It was blasting out of all the shower-heads, and the noise it made was deafening. There was a row of cubicles all along the right-hand wall, each with a reinforced-glass door. Jim went quickly along from shower to shower, checking each one, his towel pulled down to protect his forehead and eyes from the heat.

Dottie screamed again, and this time it sounded as if she was suffering unbearable pain. Jim hurried along to the very last cubicle, and through the steamed-up glass door he could make out a reddish shape, arms flailing, head waving wildly from side to side.

'Dottie!' he yelled. He tried to pull open the door but it was jammed tight. 'Dottie, it's Jim Rook! Push the door open! Try to push the door open!'

But all Dottie did was to thrash her arms even more furiously, as if she were trying to beat something off. The pressurized hissing of the steam was so loud that he couldn't even be sure that she had heard him. He pulled the door again, but it wouldn't budge. Either the heat-expanded frame had clamped it tight, or else somebody had deliberately wedged it.

'Oh God! *Aaaahhhhh!* No! No, don't do that! *Aaaaaaa-hhhhhh*, don't do that!'

Jim turned to Washington and said, 'Give me that bat.' Washington handed it over, and Jim lifted it high behind his head.

'Dottie! I'm going to break the door! Turn your face away! You hear me, Dottie?'

Dottie gave another wail, but Jim wasn't sure what it meant. All the same he swung the bat around and cracked it right into the middle of the door. He made barely any impression – only a small, crystallized crater. He swung again, and again, and again, and only succeeded in pitting the door with even more craters.

'*Aaaaahhhhh!* Please! Oh God, no! *Aaaahhhhhh!*'

Without a word, Washington took the bat from Jim's hands. He stepped back, hefted it up once, twice, and then swung it around and smashed the door into thousands of glittering, tumbling fragments.

So much steam billowed out of the cubicle that in the first few seconds Jim couldn't understand what he was looking at. Then, as it cleared, he saw Dottie right in front of him, jerking in agony like a badly handled marionette. Her face was scalded bright red, and her eyes were so swollen that she couldn't even see. All over her body, her skin was burned and scarlet-blotched and hanging off her in thick, tattered ribbons.

Yet it wasn't poor agonized Dottie who made Jim's hair prickle with fright. It was the figure who was standing in the shower behind her, almost invisible, and thickly clouded with steam. A figure made of nothing more than boiling water, with a surface that rippled and rolled. It was a girl's figure, not much taller than Dottie, but much more slender. It was running its boiling hands over Dottie's shoulders and down her back and forcefully caressing her stomach and her upper thighs, and every time it did so, Dottie screamed and shivered and flinched. She must have felt as if she were having kettlefuls of boiling water poured slowly over her, over and over, until her skin shriveled and her nerve-ends shrank. And all the time

Jim could hear a low, underlying bubbling sound – just like the sound of a saucepan of water when it boils.

He hesitated for a split second and took a deep, steadying breath. Then he threw himself forward and tried to snatch Dottie out of the shower. But the figure instantly swung its arm out, and lashed his face with boiling water. He staggered back against the wall, feeling as if his cheeks were on fire.

Washington yelled out, 'Let her go, you mother!' and tried to grab Dottie too – but this time the figure retaliated with a huge, scalding splash, and Washington screamed out, 'Shit! You burned me, you bitch!'

As if to enrage them even more, the figure took hold of Dottie in a tight embrace, and slid its steaming, watery arms all the way down her, so that she let out a high, penetrating shriek of pain.

Coughing, wincing, Jim looked down and saw that the shower tray was filled ankle-deep with steaming hot water, because the drain was blocked with a sodden blue towel. He suddenly remembered what had happened to Mervyn, and how Mervyn had escaped drowning – by pulling out the plug. He dropped to his knees in front of the shower, covering his face with his hands.

'Mr Rook!' said Washington, in panic. 'You all right, Mr Rook?'

Dottie screamed yet again – but as she did so, Jim lunged forward and plunged his hand into the nearly boiling water in the bottom of the shower. He seized the sodden towel that was blocking the drain and heaved it out, tossing it across the room. It landed with a thick slap against the opposite wall and then dropped to the floor.

With a sharp, enthusiastic gurgle, the water in the shower tray began to drain away. As it did so, the figure began to drain away too. It stood still for a moment, its surface still. Then it shuddered a deep and appalling shudder. Its ankles were drawn down the drain, faster and faster, and then its lower legs, and then its knees, and in seconds it had been sucked away completely, bubbling and boiling, leaving nothing but a glutinous froth. The last that Jim saw of it was a curl of transparent hair, as liquid as a memory, and a waft of steam; and then they too slipped into the drain and disappeared.

For a fraction of a second, he saw the spirit standing in the shower cubicle, staring at him hollow-eyed. Then she turned and vanished straight into the tiled wall.

Dottie collapsed in the shower, amid the broken glass. She had stopped screaming now, but she was shivering violently with pain and shock. Jim didn't want to touch her, in case he made her burns even worse, but he tugged the towel off his head, went over to the washbasins and soaked it in cold water. Then he carefully draped it over her.

Laura came into the shower room, white with distress. 'Dottie . . . oh my God, is she going to be all right?'

Washington leaned close to Jim and said, 'Was that the thing you was warning us about? The water spirit? Jesus! You didn't tell us it was a *hot*-water spirit!'

'Paramedics coming through!' somebody shouted, and three paramedics came bustling into the shower room, one of them wheeling a trolley.

'What happened here?' one of them asked Jim as his partners knelt down beside Dottie and examined her.

'I don't know. Some kind of failure in the plumbing system. Maybe the thermostat jammed.'

'I want a drip set up right away and I want morphine, *now*!' said another paramedic. 'She's losing fluid fast!'

Jim laid his hand on Laura's shoulder. 'Come on, Laura. There's nothing more we can do for her, except pray. Washington – you don't know how glad I am that you were here. If Dottie makes it then, believe me, all of the credit for saving her life goes to you.'

'I wouldn't have thought of pulling that towel out, Mr Rook. I wouldn't have believed that something like that could even *exist*.'

Laura was in tears. Jim led her away and Washington followed. Dr Ehrlichman was waiting for them outside in the corridor, twisting his handkerchief in agitation.

'What happened in there, Jim? Is Dottie going to be all right?'

'I don't know. She was pretty badly scalded.'

'God, this is terrible. On her very last day of college, too.'

Jim walked slowly back along the corridor. The college was milling with excited students, all of whom had come pouring out of their home rooms as soon as they heard the ambulance sirens. Some of them jostled against him, but Jim ignored them. He was too upset by what had happened to Dottie, especially since he believed that the water spirit – for whatever reason – was trying to take its revenge on *him*.

He went through the large double doors at the end of the corridor and stood outside on the steps for a moment, breathing deeply to steady himself. After a few minutes Dr Friendly came out too. 'James – Jim – this is terrible! What are we going to say to Dottie's parents?'

'It's all right, I'll take care of Mr and Mrs Osias. I need to say a few words to my class first.'

'Jesus, this is going to give us such bad publicity! Who's going to send their children to West Grove if they can never be sure that they're going to come home alive?'

'Dr Friendly . . . I'll talk to you about our public image later, okay? Right now I have some very distraught young people to deal with.'

'I'm not talking about public image, Jim. I'm talking about *you*. You're a jinx on this place, if you ask me. Trouble seems to follow you around like a junkyard dog.'

'Well, you're officially rid of me as of today, so don't worry about it.'

'I wish I could be one hundred per cent confident of that.'

Jim said, 'Pardon me, won't you?' and opened his classroom door. The room was completely deserted. Chairs and desks had been left askew, crumpled sheets of notepaper were strewn all over the floor. Stacks of books had been left on his desk – dog-eared copies of *Twentieth-Century American Poets*, *Hamlet* and *Look Homeward, Angel*. On the chalkboard somebody had scrawled, *Happy New Life, Mr Rook*, and he wouldn't have been surprised if it was meant ironically.

He sat down at his desk and opened one drawer after another, taking out his pens, his dictionaries and a take-away chow mein that he had forgotten about for almost three weeks. He prodded it with a pencil but apart from one hairy-looking prawn it looked pretty much inert.

He was still sitting there when there was a cautious knock at the door. It was Nestor Fawkes, wearing a washed-out gray T-shirt and a baggy pair of combat pants with holes in the knees.

'Nestor,' he said. 'What did you do, forget something?'

Nestor approached his desk. He was a scrawny, undernourished boy who often turned up on Monday mornings with black eyes or bruises. His father didn't believe in poetry or drama or classical music or any entertainment that didn't involve beer, gambling and car crashes. Jim had always admired Nestor's persistence in staying at college in spite of constant derision and countless beatings. But Nestor knew that education was the only thing that was going to save him from ending up like his father – stupid and narrow-minded and almost ludicrously violent.

Nestor cleared his throat. 'There was going to be kind of a surprise. We were going to have you called away, and deck out the classroom with balloons and stuff. We even had a cake and a bottle of champagne.'

'Well, under the circumstances . . .' said Jim.

Nestor nodded. 'Everybody's totally blown away, what with Dennis drowning and now this. So we're all going home now, but we didn't want you to think that we didn't care about everything you did for us.'

'That's all right, Nestor. It's my job.'

'You never made it seem that way. You always treated us special. Not "special" like in "backward", neither. But *special*.'

'I didn't treat you special. You *are* special. You arrived here reading Pokémon comics. Now you read Oscar Wilde. I couldn't have taught you to do that unless you already had the intelligence. Fixing literacy problems isn't like fixing automobiles. Fixing literacy problems is finding out what a person needs to say, and showing that person how to say it.'

'Well, whatever,' said Nestor. 'But we didn't want you to think that we'd left without saying goodbye, and thanks.'

Jim stood up and took hold of Nestor's hand. 'Tell them goodbye back. Tell them I wish them all the happiness their hearts can find.'

Nestor said, 'Yes, sir,' in a husky voice, turned around and left the classroom. Jim stood there for a while, staring at the open door. Then he gathered up the rest of his belongings and stowed them into a cardboard cat-food box.

He looked around one last time, and then he walked out of the classroom and along the corridor toward the main doors. The corridor was deserted now, and his footsteps echoed. He almost believed that Dr Friendly was right, and that trouble dogged his footsteps wherever he went.

He met Clarence, who was sweeping up outside Dr Ehrlichman's office.

'Guess this is where you and me reach the end of the trail, Clarence,' said Jim.

'Sad way to go,' said Clarence. 'That poor Dottie . . . she was one of the nicest kids we ever had here.'

Jim left the building without saying goodbye to anybody else. He climbed into his car and drove down the avenue of rustling maples that led to the main gate, and out into the world, the same way his students now had to go.

Back home he called the hospital to see if they had any news of Dottie, but a nurse told him that it was far too early to say how serious her burns might be.

Depressed and guilty, he finished packing up the last of his books. Then he went out on to the balcony, where Tibbles Two was lying asleep in the sun. She opened one eye when he sat down beside her, as if she were irritated at being disturbed.

'Well, TT, that's it,' said Jim. 'As Scarlett O'Hara said, tomorrow is another day. You wouldn't like to try telling my fortune again, would you?'

TT stretched herself and yawned.

'I know,' said Jim. 'Too darned lazy.'

He poured himself a beer and took a long, icy mouthful. It

was then that his mobile phone warbled. He dragged it out of his pants pocket and burped straight into it.

'What was that?' asked Karen.

'Interference. We get a lot of it in Venice. Something to do with the power-lines.'

'I heard what happened to Dottie Osias. It's just awful.'

'I know. What a great way to finish up the year. I called the hospital but they can't tell me anything yet. I'm praying. That's all I can do.'

'I'm really sorry, Jim. Dottie was one of your favorites, wasn't she?'

'I'll tell you, Karen, I'm glad to be going. I never seemed to bring those kids anything but grief.'

'You can't blame yourself, Jim. It was an accident. From what I heard, you saved her life.'

What could he say? That Dottie would never have been at risk if she hadn't been one of his favorites? That everybody he liked and loved was in serious jeopardy, simply because they meant something to him? He had done his best to warn them, but who was going to believe that they were going to be drowned or suffocated or scalded by a figure made out of nothing but water? It sounded completely insane.

'Jim . . . I don't want you to go to Washington without seeing you one more time.'

'It's only Washington. It's not Mongo. I can get back to LA for weekends.'

'All the same . . . you're going to be pretty busy, aren't you, and so am I.'

'Meaning what? That it's all over between us?'

'Meaning nothing except that I want to see you before you leave, that's all. How about you come round to my place this evening and I'll cook your absolute favorite for you. *Rigatoni alla napolitana*. With a bottle of Barolo. And tiramisu to follow.'

'I don't know, Karen. This has really shaken me up. I don't think I'd have much of an appetite.'

'Then come round anyhow and have a glass of wine. I need to talk to you. I want us to work out where we're going to go from here. I don't want to lose you, Jim, stray socks or not.'

'Okay, it's a deal. I'll see you at eight.'

'I'm looking forward to it.'

He had just managed to push his phone back into his pants pocket when it rang again.

It was Michael. 'Susan's managed to get in touch with David DuQuesne. He didn't want to talk to her at first. He's, like, famously reclusive. But she told him all about the water spirit and what it had been doing, and in the end he agreed to see her. Well, us.'

'That sounds promising. When and where?'

'If you can come to Franklin Avenue around seven thirty to pick us up, that would be great.'

'Seven thirty? I have a dinner engagement at eight.'

'I'm sorry, Jim, that's the only time he could make it.'

'What about tomorrow? I could always postpone my flight to Washington.'

'I don't think so. Susan said something about him flying off to Europe tomorrow.'

'All right, then, if there's absolutely no alternative. I'll see you at seven thirty.'

He stared at the phone for a long time, with his index finger poised. TT roused herself and looked at him, and he could have sworn that she was smiling. 'Do you find this funny?' he demanded. TT turned away.

He punched out Karen's number and waited.

'Yes?' said Karen, at last. She was out of breath, as if she were jogging.

'Karen, it's Jim. Listen, Karen, it's about tonight.'

He was wearing a crumpled black jacket, a black short-sleeved shirt and off-white chinos that he had rescued from the laundry basket. He had pasted his hair flat with water because it kept sticking up at the back, so he looked rather like a 1920s silent-movie star, Rudolf Valentino in glasses. He came out of his apartment building and walked around the corner to the parking-lot. The first thing he saw was that there were two people sitting in his car, a black man and a woman in a headscarf.

He approached them cautiously. As he came up to them, however, he recognized them: Washington Freeman III and Laura Killmeyer.

'Hi, you two,' he said. 'Something I can help you with?'

'Hi, Mr Rook. Yeah, there is. We couldn't stand sitting on our duffs no more, so we came to see if there was anything we could do.'

'Well, that's very thoughtful of you. I'm on my way to Topanga Canyon to see a guy right now – somebody who may be able to help us.'

Washington said, 'I told Laura what I saw in the shower, Mr Rook. That water-thingy. I didn't tell nobody else, not even the cops, but I had to tell Laura. Dottie's her best friend, right?, she's entitled to know. And not only that, she believes in this shit, man, whereas almost nobody else does.'

'We have to find this water spirit, Mr Rook, don't we?' said Laura. 'I mean, like, *urgent*.'

Jim nodded. 'Yes, Laura, we do. I don't want any more of you hurt. I don't know whether this guy I'm going to see tonight will be able to tell us anything more about the water spirit, but he's supposed to be the world's expert on urban manifestations.'

'Mind if we tag along?' asked Washington.

'No reason why you shouldn't. The more heads we put to this problem, the better.'

'By the way,' said Laura. 'I just heard from Dottie's mother. She's still critical. But they think she's going to make it.'

Jim climbed into the driver's seat and started the engine. 'I can promise you one thing. If anything happens to Dottie, I'm going to find that water spirit and I'm going to empty it down the nearest sewer.'

Eight

Susan Silverstone came out wearing a tight black turtle-neck, tight black satin pants and high-heeled boots. 'Who are these people?' she wanted to know. 'David DuQuesne is a very private man. We can't walk in with an *army*.'

'Washington and Laura were Dottie's closest friends. They were friends of Dennis Pease, too. If anybody deserves to come along, they do. And – besides that – they could be really helpful. Laura's very well versed in witchcraft and natural magic, and she's something of a sensitive too.'

'And *him*?' she said, nodding at Washington.

'He's a very useful young man to have around in times of trouble, believe me.'

Michael appeared, dressed in a shiny scarlet shirt and black flappy pants. He looked as if he were about to burst into a flamenco dance at any moment. 'We'd better get moving, Susan. David DuQuesne said eight sharp, remember?'

'All right,' said Susan. 'But tell these two students of yours to keep a low profile, okay? David DuQuesne is the master. I don't want to show him any disrespect.'

'Don't worry. Laura's a very well-mannered young lady, and Washington is a global authority on every conceivable form of disrespect.'

They left the house and climbed into the car, Susan sitting in the front passenger seat and Michael sharing the back seat with Washington and Laura. Jim turned around on groaning suspension and headed toward Sunset.

Washington turned to Michael and gave him a 150-watt grin. 'Mr Rook tells me you was in Special Class II one time.'

'Yes – yes, I was,' Michael replied, uncomfortably.

'What kind of problem was you having? Dis-lecksher? Or just plain stupid?'

Michael opened and closed his mouth; but Washington put his arm around him, gave him a friendly squeeze and said, 'I'm only ribbing you, man, because whatever it was you ain't got it now. That's Mr Rook for you. He works the miracle. He says, "Pick up your book and read."'

They sped up Coldwater Canyon with bald tires squealing on every curve. Susan directed Jim almost to the top, to Hidden Valley, where they turned off left and drove around a twisting private track between the trees. It was cool and breezy up here, and the sky was the color of tarnished brass. Birds fluttered and whistled all around them, and as they rounded the very last bend they startled a young deer, which went springing into the undergrowth as if its legs were pogo-sticks. Eventually they reached a pair of black iron gates, with an intercom positioned on the verge.

Jim pressed the buzzer and said, 'Susan Silverstone and friends for Mr DuQuesne.'

There was no reply, but after a short pause the gates began to shudder open. Jim looked at Susan and said, 'This reminds me of a movie I saw. Nobody came out alive.'

They drove up a tightly winding track until they reached a large, single-story house set amongst a stand of sugar pines. The house was brand-new, very geometric, with huge picture windows and verandahs all around it. There were three cars parked outside it: a silver Jeep, a Volvo station wagon and a classic red Corvette. Washington's eyes immediately widened. 'Look at that 'Vette, man! That's a '62, last of the real Corvettes. Three hundert sixty horsepower with Rochester fuel injection! How much *money* does this dude make?'

As they parked, a tall man with an iron-gray crewcut appeared on the front verandah, restraining two slavering Dobermanns. He was very tanned, with deep-set eyes like Kris Kristofferson. He wore an impeccable pink shirt, light gray permanent-press slacks, and sandals. 'Ms Silverstone? I see you've brought an entourage!'

'I'm sorry, Mr DuQuesne,' said Susan, as she climbed the steps. 'But Jim here insisted on bringing two of his college students . . . they were friends of the boy who drowned.'

Jim came up behind her, and immediately the Dobermanns started snarling and straining at their chains. Their claws clattered on the oak decking, and they were so keen to jump on Jim and tear his throat out that David DuQuesne could hardly hold them back.

'They smell something on you,' said David DuQuesne, clinging on to the handrail to stop himself being dragged across the verandah.

'Guess it's my cat.'

'Your *cat*?' said David DuQuesne, as if he couldn't believe that a grown man could do anything so effete as to keep a cat.

'Yes, I have a – cat. Quite an intelligent cat, as a matter of fact. Bit of a fortune teller.'

'You'd better go inside. I'll put these brutes back in their kennel.'

While David DuQuesne took the dogs away, the five of them wandered into his living-room. It had mountain views on two sides through floor-to-ceiling windows, and it was so sunny and light that it was almost like being outside. The floors were highly polished oak, with Persian scatter-rugs, and the furniture was all white leather, and huge, so that they felt as if they had strayed into an episode of *Land of the Giants*. On the walls hung vast abstract paintings in smeary grays and blacks with occasional red spots on them.

They were still looking out of the windows when David DuQuesne came briskly back in, extending his hand. 'Sorry to have kept you. I'm David . . . you're Susan, and this must be Jim.'

'This is Laura and Washington,' said Jim.

'And Michael,' said Michael, when nobody else introduced him.

'Please, sit down,' David told them. 'Would you care for a drink? I have some very good Chardonnay.'

Susan said, 'Mineral water for me, thanks. Alcohol plays havoc with my aura.'

'Umm . . . you wouldn't have a *beer*, would you?' asked Jim.

An unsmiling Chinese woman in black silk pajamas brought them drinks and nuts.

Once they were settled, David sat back and said, 'I don't usually get myself involved in personal consultations any more. But I was very intrigued by what Susan told me on the phone. If what she told me was right, then this is the first reappearance since the 1950s of an extremely dangerous urban manifestation.'

Jim said, 'I gather Susan has filled you in on what's happened so far . . . little Mikey drowning, and then Dennis Pease, and Mervyn nearly being drowned in his bathtub?'

'That's right, she has. She also told me about her spirit-trace, too. Very brave of you, to try a spirit-trace with this particular bogey-person.'

'Ignorant, more than brave,' Jim admitted. 'And I'm afraid to say that there was another incident this morning. One of my female students was trapped in the shower. The water was boiling hot, and she was very severely scalded. In fact we don't even know if she's going to pull through.'

'You witnessed this incident?'

Jim nodded. 'I saw the figure again, too. The water spirit.'

'And it was *boiling*? I never came across that before. That's extraordinary.'

'All I need to know is: what is it, what does it want, and what can I do to get rid of it?'

David DuQuesne said, 'The reason I agreed to see you was because what Susan described to me sounded like a rare but very potent urban legend.'

'What's that, urban legend?' asked Washington. Michael frowned, but David DuQuesne didn't seem to be irritated in the least. 'I'll give you a well-known example. There's a story that went around every high school in America. A girl and her boyfriend drove out to the woods one night. They ran out of gas, so the boyfriend told the girl to stay in the car while he walked to the highway and filled up a can. He told her to lock all the doors, which she did. But about twenty minutes later, she heard somebody banging on the roof of the car. Then this guy appeared, smiling at her through the windshield. He lifted something up in his hand, and it was her boyfriend's severed head. She screamed and covered her eyes. But then he knocked on the window again, and this time he wasn't just holding up her boyfriend's severed head, he was dangling his car keys, too.'

'Yeah, I heard a story like that,' said Washington. 'Only the knocking on the top of the car was the boyfriend's feet, hanging from a tree right over the car.'

'There are dozens of legends like that. Some of them are obvious hoaxes, like the South American bush spider that was supposed to be hiding under public-toilet seats, and biting women whenever they sat down. Or the family guard-dog that was found choking when its owners returned home, and when it was taken to the vet they found a burglar's finger stuck down its throat. We *need* stories like that, just like we used to need stories about devils and vampires. They help us face up to our fears. They're a kind of updated superstition.'

'But they ain't all just superstition, are they?' Washington interrupted. 'Some of them must be real . . . like that boiling-water person we saw today.'

David DuQuesne poured himself another glass of white wine. 'No, Washington, they're not all superstition. I personally believe that, when certain specific tragedies happen within our modern society, new demons can be . . . created, for want of a better word. These aren't demons from ancient cultures. Not Astaroth or Beelzebub or Loki, or even Native American demons like Coyote and Big Monster. These are demons of modern American civilization – products of our own special terrors. The Hitch-hiker . . . Mary Worth . . . the Ant Boy, whose friends covered him with molasses and tied him up naked next to a fire-ants' nest.

'In almost every one of these urban legends, somebody dies and comes back to take their revenge on the people who hurt them. Did you ever read about Black River Falls, Wisconsin?

In 1897, they had a plague of homicides and suicides and people going mad. In fact, they used to happen so often that the local newspaper scarcely thought them worth putting into print. One woman deliberately drowned herself head-first in a water-butt, and farmers were always cutting their throats or hanging themselves or throwing themselves into the river. One guy even blew his own head off with dynamite – filled a hole in the ground with explosive, leaned right over it and lit it. Said, "Here I go, and the Lord goes with me."

'The story went that – less than a month before this happened – Black River Falls was visited by a traveling carnival . . . with clowns, and mimes, and bareback riders, and a freak show. And that carnival changed the whole town for ever. Once it had left, those who survived spoke of terrible apparitions: dead babies crying in the night; lunatic screaming in people's attics when there was nobody there; hunchbacks running through people's back yards. And on the anniversary of that guy blowing his head off – every year, eleven o'clock in the morning on the dot – they'd hear this massive bang from the back of his house. People said you could set your watch by it.'

'I'm not sure what you're trying to tell us,' said Jim.

David DuQuesne stood up and glided over to the window. 'I'm trying to explain to you that modern American legends aren't all campfire stories or internet hoaxes. What happened in Black River Falls is true. There are photographs to prove it. And, what's more, after the carnival had left, a private detective called A. P. Moran went to look for it, because one of the townswomen complained that she had been raped and robbed by one of its owners, Douglas Shade.'

'Did he have any luck?'

'Oh, yes. If you can call it luck. Three years later Moran found the remains of the Shade & O'Bryan Traveling Carnival in a long-forgotten railroad spur, way up high in the Rockies. It seems as if their railroad had been overtaken by severe winter weather, and they had decided to hole up until the snowstorms died down.

'They were dead from typhoid fever, most of them, and the

ones who hadn't died from typhoid had succumbed to hunger and hypothermia. They had tried to eat their show-horses and even one of their lions, but it looked as if the weather had bested them in the end, and somebody had put up a cross in the snow which said nothing but CARNIVAL. Pretty appropriate, since "carnival" means "feast of flesh".'

'But what does this have to do with this water spirit?' asked Laura.

'Nothing, really. Nothing and everything. It just goes to show that the so-called supernatural can be just as real as you and me. The Shade & O'Bryan Traveling Carnival had contracted typhoid fever during a visit to Black River Falls in 1894. They had made it as far as the Rockies, but no further.'

'But you said they visited Black River Falls in 1897,' said Laura. 'How could they have done that, when they all died three years earlier?'

'Maybe the new carnival was nothing but impostors, using their name,' suggested Jim.

David shook his head. 'I have original nineteenth-century photographs of most of the carnival troupe, and I can assure you that the showpeople who arrived at Black River Falls in 1897 weren't impostors. They were *the exact same people.* You can pick out the same clowns, the same trapeze artists, the same girl selling the cotton candy, even.'

'What's your point, man?' Washington wanted to know. 'Maybe they got froze to death and maybe they thawed out and came alive again.'

'Impossible . . . even if it were possible. Most of their bodies were mutilated and half desiccated.'

'So how do you explain it?' asked Jim. 'Are you saying that the showpeople who arrived at Black River Falls . . . they weren't real? Were they ghosts? Or were they some kind of delusion? Some kind of hysterical mass-suggestion?'

'I don't know, Jim, to be frank. But whatever they were, they still managed to drive the population half mad. All I'm trying to explain to you is that people have been known to appear long after they were supposed to be dead, and that they can take some pretty unpleasant revenge.'

'You think this water spirit is somebody who died?'

'That's my guess. After Susan had called me, I remembered a very similar manifestation in the nineteen-fifties. I checked through my archives and found it. There were several reports in the *Los Angeles Times* as well as a feature article in *Time* magazine. In the summer of 1954, seven children between the ages of nine and eleven were drowned in the Sherman Oaks area. Nobody really took any notice until Jo-Anne Millar drowned – she was the daughter of Gary Millar, who used to play Randy in *Wagon Train*. Then there was a whole mess of publicity, and a huge police investigation, but that didn't stop three more children from drowning.

'All seven children were members of a synchronized-swimming team from St Bernadette's Elementary School in Stone Canyon Avenue. They were one of the attractions at the school's July fourth celebrations that year. Apparently there was a cook-out, and fireworks, and a swing band, and then the girls gave a floodlit swimming show.

'The next morning, however, when he was clearing the streamers and the paper cups out of the pool, the school janitor saw a body floating at the bottom. It was Esther Jordache, nine years old, the youngest member of the swimming team. The coroner said that she must have gone under sometime during the swimming display, and what with the water being churned up, and all the other girls' legs thrashing around, she hadn't stood a chance.

'Her mother hadn't worried when she didn't come home because she was supposed to be sleeping over with a friend. And her *friend* wasn't worried because Esther was always kind of a quiet, introspective girl, and so she assumed that Esther had decided not to sleep over after all and simply gone home.

'But only a month after that, another member of the synchronized swimming team was drowned, and two more followed. There were witnesses to all three drownings, and all of them said that the girls looked like they were pulled right under, straight down, they didn't even struggle. Two witnesses said that they saw arms coming out of the pool and dragging the girls down, even though there was nobody else in the pool.

'The coroner decided that these witnesses were suffering from shock, and that they simply imagined what they saw. But a well-known historian called Harold Bronsky said the drownings bore a striking similarity to an incident that occurred during the Civil War, when a young Yankee soldier called Stephen Andrews was drowned while crossing the Mattaponi River under fire. Seven of his fellow soldiers were wading across the river close by, but none of them made any attempt to save him because they were afraid of being picked off by Confederate snipers. During the course of the next two months, however, every one of his fellow soldiers died by drowning. Two while they were fishing in a boat; another in a flooded shell-hole; another while he was swimming in a lake; and three more while they were crossing Dismal Swamp under cover of darkness, with full backpacks and rifles, and waded straight into a deep pool that none of them could see.

'In five of these cases, witnesses said that they saw hands coming out of the water and pulling the men to their death; and in one case a cavalry sergeant said he actually saw a figure "all made out of water, so it looked like it was glass". They called the figure the Swimmer, and for a long while many soldiers refused to ford river crossings or go bathing in streams, in case the Swimmer got them too.

'After the seven died, however, no more soldiers were lost, which led to the story going around that the Swimmer must have been Stephen Andrews' spirit, back from his watery grave, come to take revenge on the so-called friends who had left him to drown.'

'And you think that the girls who drowned in the fifties were victims of Esther Jordache?' asked Jim.

'No question at all, except that I never told anybody about it. I would have been accused of having a very sick imagination and causing the parents even more grief than they'd suffered already. I make my money out of writing about modern myths and legends, Jim, and everybody enjoys a good spooky story. But nobody really wants to believe that they're true – especially when young children are involved.'

'So what you telling us, man?' asked Washington. 'You saying that Dennis and Dottie and this little Mikey guy were all attacked by some Swimmer, too?'

'It certainly seems like it. Especially since you and Jim here have actually seen some kind of watery figure for yourselves. It's a young woman, you think?'

'No doubt about it,' said Jim. 'It was impossible to tell for sure, but I'd guess nineteen or twenty.'

'In that case, who do you know of that age who has recently drowned?'

'Nobody recently.'

'How about a year ago? Or two or three years ago? Or longer?'

'The only one I can think of was nearly eleven years ago, my first year at West Grove College. It happened right in the middle of the annual swimming gala. After the formal races there was a kind of free-for-all in the pool – high spirits, that's all. But a young girl dived off the top board and struck her head on the bottom of the pool. There were so many students in the pool that nobody noticed her until it was too late. What was her name? Jane Something. Jane Tullett, I think.'

'Were you there when this happened?' asked David DuQuesne.

'Oh, sure. Practically the whole college was there.'

'And she was in your class?'

'That's right. She was suffering from dyslexia, but I was trying out a new reading technique with her – covering up one eye to stabilize her vision – and she was responding very well.'

'So she might very well have regarded you as something of a father figure? Somebody who was supposed to take care of her?'

'Well, only in a very general sense . . . just like any teacher. But she was a very affectionate girl, I remember. Very enthusiastic in class. Very keen to learn.'

David DuQuesne said, 'I think you should start by having Susan here try to contact Jane Tullett, to see if her spirit is still accessible. If it is, you should ask her if she's responsible for these drownings . . . and if she admits that she is, you should ask her why she's doing it. You should try to find out if there is anything that you can do to put her at rest.'

'We could try, for sure,' said Susan. 'But it can be incredibly dangerous, trying to contact somebody who's out to get their revenge on you.'

'I don't know what else to suggest. It's equally dangerous to let a spirit like this go unchallenged. Spirits can get a taste for killing, like serial murderers. It gives them a sense of power . . . of still having some influence in the physical world. You just don't know who she's going to drown next and when she's ever going to stop. She may try to get her own back on *everybody* who was there that day.'

'My God,' said Jim. 'There were hundreds.'

Michael had been unusually silent while David spoke, but now he gave an emphatic shake of his head and said, 'No. Absolutely not.'

'Absolutely not what?'

'I am absolutely not going to allow Susan to contact this Swimmer. It's far too much of a risk. She could be injured, or driven out of her mind, or even killed. She doesn't have the psychological strength for it. It's taken her over a year to recover from the last experience – a whole year of nightmares and delusions and terrors that nobody else can even begin to imagine. So the answer is no – and nothing that you can say is going to change my mind.'

David DuQuesne looked sober. 'If Susan doesn't do it, then you'll have to find somebody else who will.'

'Isn't there any other way of stopping it?' asked Laura. 'Some kind of exorcism, or a spell, or something like that?'

'As far as I can tell, a Swimmer isn't susceptible to the usual kind of sanctions that affect the demons of heaven and hell. A Swimmer is a purely modern phenomenon. After Jo-Anne Millar died, all of the parents of the synchronized-swimming team held a church service and prayed that the spirit of Esther Jordache should find eternal peace. They even had Cardinal

O'Heenan to give a special blessing. But the drownings went on regardless.'

'That's our only hope, then – negotiation?'

'There's no other way of stopping a Swimmer, except for depriving it of water until it loses its strength altogether, and that's pretty much impossible. There's water just about everywhere – swimming pools, lakes, ornamental fountains . . . even lawn sprinklers and domestic faucets. A Swimmer needs less than seven gallons of water to take on a physical shape; that's what the human body displaces.

'No . . . your best answer is to contact this girl's spirit and try to find out why she's suddenly acting so vengeful. You may be able to satisfy her with some form of atonement, or an apology, even. Even the dead can be reasonable, if they realize that you really care about them.'

'You sound like you've been involved in this kind of thing before,' Jim remarked.

David DuQuesne gave him an odd, complicated smile. 'As I told you, Jim, I'm a dealer in myths and legends. But just like everything else in this world, some of those myths aren't completely mythical and some of those legends aren't totally legendary.'

'I'm still not letting Susan contact this Swimmer,' Michael insisted.

'All right, then. Do you know anybody who can contact the other side as successfully as Susan? Somebody who's psychically sensitive, but mentally strong?'

'No, I don't,' Michael admitted. 'But I'll find somebody, I promise you. There's no way that I'm going to let Susan have anything more to do with this. No way at all.'

'Susan?' asked Jim; but Susan reached out for Michael's hand and said nothing.

'All right,' said Jim. 'Nobody's forcing anybody to do anything. But Dottie's in intensive care and there could be dozens of people's lives at risk, so if we're going to find a sensitive to contact the Swimmer we'd better get our shit together.'

Washington stared at him, wide-eyed.

'*Act*,' Jim corrected himself.

Nine

On the way back down the steps, David DuQuesne laid his hand on Jim's shoulder and said, 'I wish you luck with this, Jim You're going to need it. It's fortunate that only a few people ever get to find out what's really going on in this world of ours.'

'Tell me what really happened to you,' said Jim. 'Something must have led you into this business.'

'Oh . . . It was a long time ago, when I was a kid. We lived in Pennsylvania then, not far from a railroad track. When we went to school in the morning, my brother and I could either cycle to the nearest grade crossing, or else we could go through this drainage pipe that went right under the railroad embankment. The tunnel was dark and dripping and real scary, especially in the winter, and you had to crouch down to go through it, but it saved us almost a mile.'

'Jim? You coming?' asked Michael impatiently. 'Susan's feeling cold.'

'Be right with you.'

'I won't hold you up,' said David DuQuesne. 'Maybe we can talk another time.'

'No, no – just tell me what happened in the tunnel.'

'The local kids used to say that years ago a man had gone shack-wacky and murdered his wife and three babies, ripped them apart with a skinning-hook. The sheriff sent out a search party, but he hid in the tunnel under the railroad. Anybody who went in looking for him was torn into pieces: dogs, deputies, you name it. He literally dismembered them, and ate their livers, raw. Forget about Hannibal Lecter: this guy was the real thing.

'They never found him, and the story went that he lived rough in the woods for years – but now and then, when he was hungry, he would go back to the tunnel and lie in wait for anybody who used it as a short cut. Mad Frank Butler, that was what they called him.'

David DuQuesne was silent for a while, his eyes so narrow that he looked almost as if he were blind.

'What happened?' asked Jim.

'It was February. I was off school with the measles. My brother Philip went to school alone. Four o'clock came, then five, then six. My mother called the school to find out if Philip was staying late for drama class. The principal told her that he hadn't been at school all day . . . and they had naturally imagined he was sick too.

'It took the search parties three days to find all of him – or most of him. They found his bicycle in the tunnel, and his books all torn up and bloody and strewn through the undergrowth. His body . . . well, they didn't tell me then, but I read about it later. He was literally torn to shreds. They never found his feet. Can you imagine that? They searched an area of four square miles and they never found his feet.'

'Did they ever discover who did it?'

David DuQuesne shook his head. 'Maybe it was Mad Frank Butler . . . maybe it was some maniac pretending to be him. But you can understand now why I developed a serious interest in urban legends. There are things happening in our cities and our towns that defy all rational explanation. But that doesn't mean they're not happening, and that doesn't mean that innocent people are not being killed or seriously injured.

'You have to find the Swimmer, Jim. Susan's right, it's going to be very dangerous. But what's the alternative? More of your students being scalded? More of your friends being drowned in their bathtubs? She's taking her revenge out on *you*, Jim, no question about it, as well as other people who were there when she went under. And what's the most painful form of revenge? Not drowning Jennie, or you, but drowning the people you care for the most. She won't stop, Jim, I can promise you that. She won't stop until you've lost everybody you love.'

'Jim!' called Michael.

'I'm coming,' said Jim. He took hold of David DuQuesne's hand and squeezed it. 'You've been a great help, David. From the way that Susan was talking about you, I had the impression you were going to be kind of – well, *aloof*.'

'Oh, I can be aloof. I can be *very* aloof, especially with all the fruitcakes and loony-tunes who try to get in touch with me. If I hear one more alien abduction story, I'm going to retire to a monastery. But when Susan called me and told me about the Swimmer, I knew you had a genuine problem – and there's no justification for being aloof when people are in mortal danger.'

Jim went down the steps and climbed into his car. As they drove away, he turned back and saw David DuQuesne standing stiff and straight on the verandah, like the captain of a sinking liner. Jim felt a sharp pang of sympathy for him. Just like Jim, he had come into contact with the demons of this world, only to find himself burdened with a dread responsibility – a responsibility which he could never escape, no matter how much terror it brought him.

He returned to his apartment building feeling fractured. As he walked along the corridor, he smelled a pungent aroma of garlic, onions and soy sauce. Mervyn's door was ajar – and, as he passed, Mervyn suddenly appeared in a turquoise silk kimono with his hair drawn up in a Japanese-style bun on top of his head. His chubby cheeks were white with rice powder, and he had used black eye-pencil to make his eyes look slanted. 'Jim! I've been expecting you!'

'Hi, Mervyn. You're looking very geisha.'

'Gay, yes. Not so sure about the sha. You're back late. I was beginning to fret.'

'We had an accident at college today. One of my students was scalded in the showers. She's at Sisters of Mercy, in intensive care. Then I had some other business to take care of.'

'You haven't forgotten, I hope?'

'Sorry, forgotten what?'

'I'm cooking you a special farewell supper on a Japanese theme.'

'Oh, yes. Sure you are.' Mervyn had invited him weeks ago, and what with packing everything up, and the prospect of losing Karen, and most of all the Swimmer, it had completely slipped his mind. 'Give me a couple of minutes to straighten myself out and I'll be right with you.'

'Listen – if you don't want to do this, I won't be upset.'

'For God's sake, of course you'll be upset. Look at all the trouble you've gone to.'

'Don't forget to give me that list of TT's dietary requirements, will you? And Her Majesty's food bowl.'

'Sure thing. I'll give you the vet's number, too. Just in case she needs worming or anything disgusting like that.'

'Jim . . . I've cooked you a wonderful ethnic meal, complete with rice crackers, warm sake, vegetable tempura and *koto* music. Don't let's start talking about worming.'

'Mervyn . . . you really shouldn't have done this.' He was almost glad that his visit to David DuQuesne had obliged him to turn down Karen's invitation to dinner. Mervyn would have been desperately hurt if he hadn't showed.

Mervyn flapped a pale, plump hand. 'Don't be ridiculous. We've been friends for how long now? If I can't give you a modest *sayonara*, then for God's sake.'

Jim took hold of his hand. 'You're right. And I really appreciate it. Just give me a moment to go to the bathroom.'

'You can use mine if you like. There's a wonderful poster of Jim Morrison on the wall, in those skin-tight leather pants.'

'It's okay, I'll, uh – use my own. I was never a Doors fan, personally.'

Jim went back to his apartment and splashed his face six or seven times with icy cold water. He changed his shirt and rolled on some more Contradiction deodorant. He stared at his face in the mirror for a while and thought he looked haggard. It was no good. Ever since he had come out of hospital at the age of nine and seen dead people hurrying through the streets, he had known that he would never escape from his near-death experience. Death had touched his shoulder, *Tag, you're it*, and let him know that it was always close by.

Tibbles Two came up to him and rubbed her head against his leg, purring thickly.

'Come on, TT, give me a break. You'll be living with Mervyn from tomorrow. Don't start getting affectionate now. You know you hate me.'

TT loped into the living-room. She jumped up on to the table and nudged his pack of Grimaud cards with her nose.

'Come on, TT, I don't want you telling my fortune.'

TT nudged the cards again, but Jim said, 'Forget it, TT, what do cats know? This is just a charade, isn't it? All you want is attention. I'm going to be giving you away to a transvestite torch singer, okay? But he's a great guy and he's going to take care of you better than me. So forget the cards. This is where you and me part company.'

All the same, TT tapped the deck of cards with her paw, again and again, until they all spilled on to the carpet. Then she dropped down from the table and nudged out the three of clubs, hope, showing a woman standing by the ocean.

'Well . . . that's the most optimistic card you've ever picked. Hope, huh?'

TT looked up at him with baleful yellow eyes. Then she nudged out another card, the nine of spades. Card number 44, death, in his tattered gray shroud.

'Well, thank you for making my day. Hope, and death. I feel better already.'

TT slowly rose up on her hind legs. He had never seen a cat do that before – not balanced on its own in the center of the room. Her ears were folded right back and her eyes were slitted so that she looked more like a snake than a cat. As she reached her full height, Jim heard a sudden sharp clattering sound in the kitchen.

'The *hell*?' He hurried into the kitchen and found that both of the faucets were turned on full, and that water was blasting into the sink and spraying across the draining board. He turned the faucets off and then went back to the living-room, dabbing at the front of his shirt with a towel. TT was still standing erect, staring at him.

'How did that happen?' he demanded. 'Did you do that?'

TT slowly sank down, but she didn't take her slitty little eyes off him.

'You're warning me, aren't you? You're really warning me.'

But TT stayed where she was, watching him, unmoving; and he knew that, ultimately, the decision to hunt down the Swimmer was his alone.

He went back to Mervyn's apartment with a chilled bottle of Cuvée Napa sparkling wine, which he had been saving for his last night with Karen. It had only cost $12.98, but Mervyn fluttered his eyelashes and said, 'Champagne, *pour moi*?' and opened it up with the softest of exhalations, like an expert. 'Do you know what sommeliers call that sound, when they open up a bottle of champagne? *Le pet d'un ange.* An angel's fart.'

'You have hidden depths, Mervyn.'

'I know, and I've tried so many diets.'

They sat cross-legged on the floor in Mervyn's living-room and Mervyn brought in little lacquered bowls of braised lotus root and tuna salad with a bean-paste dressing and crisply fried pieces of chicken and green peppers. The room was illuminated by paper lanterns, and Mervyn played a CD of traditional Japanese *ongaku* music, soft and plangent and almost hypnotic. They drank cups of warm sake and after a while Jim began to feel more relaxed than he had since Sunday morning, just before Jennie had called him.

'I have to admit, Mervyn, I'm enjoying this.'

'Well, I shall miss you, dearest Jim, when you're gone. You're one of the few people I know who treat me like I really am, rather than what I look like.'

'Just as well, I guess. At the moment you look like a low-budget production of *The Mikado*, with you playing all of the parts.'

‘Have some more *takenoko kimpira*. I love Gilbert and Sullivan. “We are not shy; we’re very wide awake, the moon and I!” You were telling me about this David DuQuesne. I think I’ve heard of him. Hasn’t he been on the television?’

‘Yes, he used to have a show called *Modern Mysteries*. Kind of an *X-Files*, only true.’

‘Oh, yes. I think I remember. The bloodied bedsheet that came to life, that was one, wasn’t it? Ugh! That gave me nightmares for *weeks*.’

‘You’ve got it. He says we need to find a really top-class medium and try to confront this Swimmer face to face.’

‘I thought you already had a medium. This Susan Silversocks, whatever her name is.’

‘Her minder won’t let her do it. I have the impression that she had a seriously bad experience not long ago, getting in touch with some malicious spirit, and she still hasn’t got over it yet.’

‘Don’t you love this lotus root? It’s supposed to work wonders for your sex life. Either that or your catarrh, I forget which. You ought to try my friend Gabriel Dragonard – well, his real name is Rooney – *he’s* a medium. He runs a weekly ad in the *Hollywood Reporter*. “Talk to the loved ones you’ve lost.” Woooooh!’

‘Is he any good? I’m not being rude, but we can’t risk having any amateurs on this job. They could get themselves hurt, or worse.’

‘Oh no, Gabriel’s *wonderful*, I swear it. He got in touch with James Dean once. Dean had borrowed a copy of this guy’s screenplay to read and it was the only copy he had and after Dean was killed nobody could find it. But Gabriel talked to James Dean and found out that he had left it by accident in the men’s room at the Beverly Wilshire . . . and that’s where they found it. And that’s a true authenticated story.’

‘Where can I find this friend of yours?’

‘I’ll call him myself, if you like. Let’s put it this way . . . he tends to be way over the top when he’s dealing with the general public. Well, they expect it. The moody music. The incense. You don’t want any of that, do you?’

'Not unless it genuinely helps.'

'I shouldn't think so. It's part of the showmanship, that's all – and that's what Gabriel does. He's a showman. But he knows what he's doing, too.'

'I hope so. This could be seriously dangerous.'

Mervyn sucked soy sauce from his fingers and picked up his mobile phone. He punched out Gabriel Dragonard's number and waited while it rang. 'You should hear *his* phone. It plays "Danny Boy". He has terrible taste. In fact, unlike *moi*, he has no taste at all.'

Eventually he said, 'Gabriel! How are you? It's Mervyn! Yes, I know I did, but I got so tied up. No, not like that, you cheeky boy. Listen, Gabriel . . . a very dear friend of mine needs to communicate with the spirits. Not an ancestor, no. A young girl who's been giving him some trouble. Yes, he knows her name. Yes, he can probably find you a picture. But it could be risky. She's a very vengeful spirit, this young girl. I know. All women are the same, aren't they?' He cupped his hand over the receiver and said to Jim, 'He'd like to talk to you personally, if that's all right.'

Jim took the phone. 'Jim Rook here, Mr Dragonard . . . I hope this isn't asking too much.'

Gabriel Dragonard sounded distinctly Irish. 'It depends what you expect me to do. And whatever it is – even if you're a friend of Mervyn's – I'm afraid I can't do it for free. Even a medium has to pay the rent.'

'That's okay, I'm sure we can come to some kind of arrangement. I need you to get in touch with the spirit of a young girl who died about ten years ago in a drowning accident.'

'What sort of trouble is she giving you?'

'Serious trouble. She's already drowned a nine-year-old boy and a student of mine; and she tried to drown Mervyn, too.'

Gabriel was silent for a moment, and he was obviously thinking hard. 'This is heavy stuff now, isn't it? This isn't just a bit of *craíc* with your dead grandpa.'

'No . . . I'll admit that it's probably going to be dangerous.

But unless I can get in touch with her she's going to drown more people, no doubt about it.'

'Well, I always relish a challenge. Most of the spirits I'm called on to contact are tedious old seniors who don't want to talk about anything but golf. I haven't had to deal with any genuinely difficult spirits since I was called in to exorcize a house in Malibu.'

'You carried out an exorcism?'

'Oh yes, about three years ago now. The local priest wouldn't do it. He said that possession by evil spirits was nonsense. Imagine that – a priest who didn't believe in evil spirits! This spirit was a Mexican maid whose fifty-five-year-old employer had made her pregnant, and she hanged herself in the stairwell. Only seventeen, poor kid. But every time her employer tried to sleep in the house he felt that he was being strangled by a rope. Personally I think he deserved it, but it was only fair on the girl to give her some peace. She was a difficult one, very vengeful. She nearly strangled me, too. But if you know what you're doing, the risk is reasonably controled. You have to make the spirits feel that the living still remember them and still care about them. It's the loss of their physicality that enrages them the most. They feel useless and hopeless. You have to give them hope, and then you have to give them death.'

Jim thought of the Grimaud cards that TT had nudged out for him. Hope and death.

'Would you consider holding a seance?' he asked.

'I don't actually call them seances,' said Gabriel, a little sniffily. 'I call them "transmigratory consultations".'

'I see. Well, would you consider holding one of those?'

'I think so. As long as we take certain basic precautions.'

'Such as?'

'For obvious reasons, we don't do this anywhere near water; and you give me two hundred and fifty dollars cash in advance and a further two hundred and fifty if I can successfully contact the spirit. Is that fair? It's less than half my usual fee.'

'Okay,' Jim agreed. He would have to wait a little longer

to buy himself a new tennis racquet, but this was far more urgent. 'What time would be good for you?'

'Tomorrow night, around nine? Nine is a very auspicious time for spirits. Three times three. Twice three is six. Three sixes are six-six-six.'

'Can't you do it tonight? I'm supposed to be flying to Washington tomorrow.'

'I'm sorry, I'm all booked up this evening. Six ladies from Pasadena. It's up to you. But it sounds to me like you've got yourself a very, very serious problem. The sooner you lay this spirit to rest, the better for all concerned.'

'All right. Nine tomorrow. Give me your address.'

He wrote down Gabriel's address in Santa Monica and then hung up. Mervyn raised a thinly penciled eyebrow and asked, 'Everything all right?'

'Sure. It's just that this isn't a farewell dinner after all. I'm going to have to postpone my flight tomorrow.'

'Oh! Tibbles will be delighted. Not.'

Jim tiredly rubbed his eyes. 'Tell me something, Mervyn . . . have you ever felt that you were cursed?'

Ten

The evening was still uncomfortably warm when they parked outside Gabriel Dragonard's single-story house at the more expensive end of Lincoln Boulevard. Laura was wearing a skimpy pink top and a white mini-skirt, and Washington was sporting a pair of wrap-around sunglasses with yellow mirror lenses, so that he looked ineffably cool.

The house looked like an illustration from a Grimm's fairy tale, with leaded windows and a bright red clay-tiled roof and bougainvillaea climbing all around the verandah. The lawn was almost poisonously green and looked as if it had been clipped with nail scissors.

There was hardly any breeze at all, and seagulls circled silently overhead as if they were flying through syrup. Jim hadn't called Susan to tell her what he intended to do. He had the feeling that she would be badly upset if she knew that he had consulted another sensitive – no matter how dangerous it might be for her to try to contact the Swimmer, and no matter how adamant Michael had been that she shouldn't try. After all, she had found Jim, rather than the other way around, so she must have felt the urge to help him from the moment they had first met.

'Looks like the Wicked Witch of the West lives here,' Washington remarked as they climbed out of the car. Outside the front door hung a bronze bell-pull with the face of a serene young woman on it, wearing a hood. Her eyes were closed as if she were sleeping, or dead; and for some reason Jim found her unnervingly creepy. He tugged her, and they heard a long and complicated carillon of bells.

'See what your friend means about the dude's dubious taste.'

It was over a minute before the door opened and a thin bespectacled man appeared. He had a wild overgrown bush of brambly gray hair and three days' growth of prickly white stubble, so that he looked more like a species of wild animal than a man. He was wearing an emerald-green shirt, with a sand-colored linen vest and scrumpled linen pants to match, emerald-green socks, and sandals.

'Jim Rook is it?'

'That's right. Pleased to know you. This is Laura and this is Washington.'

'Come right in. You've, ah, brought the essential?'

Jim handed Gabriel Dragonard a plain white envelope. 'I've brought a picture of Jane Tullett, too.'

'Good,' said Gabriel, holding the photograph at arm's length and peering at it long-sightedly. 'Wrong glasses, as usual. Why don't you follow me?' He led them through a tiled hallway with rough-plastered walls and into a large living-room, also tiled, but painted absolutely white, with white hessian-covered furniture and white lilies in tall white vases. At one end of this room was a large circular table, also white, with white chairs and white cushions.

'Pretty white in here,' said Washington. He walked appreciatively around the room, and then went across to the large sliding doors at the far end, which overlooked a yard filled with terracotta flowerpots, and a swimming pool.

Gabriel looked at his wristwatch. 'It's nearly nine. We should start as soon as possible. I'm not going to attempt to materialize the spirit herself . . . I don't think that's necessary yet. I'm simply going to try to communicate with her by using a little Chinese trick called smoke talking. All the same, I've taken the precaution of locking the doors to the back yard, just in case her spirit does decide to pay us a visit. We don't want her getting access to the water in the pool, and I've locked the kitchen and the bathroom, too.'

'Spirits can pass through doors, can't they?' said Laura.

'Of course. But the only time we need to be concerned about *this* spirit is when it takes on physical shape. Spirits can pass through doors and walls, but a figure made out of several gallons of water can't. In any case, I'm probably being over-careful, but you never know with these vengeful presences. Devious beggars, some of them.'

He walked around the table, drawing out a chair for each of them. Then he sat down himself, and laid his hands flat on the glossy white surface. 'The reason this room is totally white is because it offers the spirits no dark corners to hide themselves in. It's also symbolic of complete spiritual purity, and truth. Spirits can be terrible liars, don't you know. Worst of all, they lie to themselves. They delude themselves into believing that, if it wasn't for the negligence of other people, they would still be alive. Like most people, they find it very difficult to accept responsibility for their own misfortune. It was always somebody else's fault that they died, and somebody else must suffer for it.'

He pulled out a shallow drawer underneath the table, and produced a sheet of white paper and a white ceramic saucer. With a large shiny pair of scissors he cut the paper in half, and wrote the name *Jane Tullett* on one of the pieces in purple ink. He folded it into a triangular pyramid, which he carefully placed in the center of the saucer. 'Three sides, each with three angles. Three threes are nine.'

Washington gave Jim a frown of bewilderment, but Jim lifted his finger to his lips to advise him to stay quiet.

Gabriel took a match out of a plain white box and lit it. He held it up for a moment, so that its flame was reflected in his glasses. Then he said, 'This is the fire that will release your name, Jane Tullett. This is the message that will bring you back to us.' He lit the paper pyramid; it flared up instantly, and vanished into a little heap of soft white ash.

A faint puff of smoke rose over the table and hovered there, twisting and curling. Gabriel said, 'I am calling on Jane Tullett to come across. I am calling on Jane Tullett to step out of the shadows. I want to see her face and hear her voice.'

Laura was biting her lip and looking disturbed; but Jim could see that Washington was completely skeptical. He was slowly shaking his head from side to side as if he couldn't believe that he had agreed to come here and witness all this mumbo-jumbo.

'I am calling on Jane Tullett to leave the world of darkness and walk out into the light. I command you, Jane Tullett. You, the dead, have to answer to the living for your acts of revenge. You have to speak to me, because I command you.'

Gabriel's voice became softer and quieter, until it sounded like tissue paper rustling. At the same time the wisp of smoke over the top of the table began to coil itself into an elaborate knot, weaving in and out of itself and forming strange, constantly changing shapes.

'Can you hear me, Jane Tullett?' Gabriel whispered. 'There's no place for you to hide. You drowned in the pool and the water will never release you unless you allow me to help you.'

Gabriel was speaking so quietly now that Jim couldn't hear him at all, only the occasional clicking of his lips. Washington and Laura were leaning forward, trying to catch what he was saying. But suddenly, in a deafening roar, with spit flying out of his mouth, he shouted out, '*Open up the door of death, Jane Tullett! Step out where we can see you!*'

Washington actually jumped, and clapped his hand over his heart. 'Man, you almost made me have a accident then.'

But right in front of them, the wisp of smoke gradually formed itself into the shape of a girl's face . . . a face that reminded Jim of the bronze doorknocker, sleeping or dead. Her eyes were closed and her hair blew around her forehead as if she were standing in the wind.

Jim stared at the face in disbelief. It was Jane Tullett, no question about it. He recognized her with a deeply unpleasant thrill of shock, like accidentally touching a bare electric wire. She looked exactly as she had on the morning when she had been lifted out of the swimming pool at West Grove College, her eyes closed and her lips slightly parted. The swimming coach had broken her breastbone trying to revive her – Jim had forgotten that, but now he remembered the way it had cracked as vividly as if it had just happened.

Gabriel looked at Jim and said, 'Is this the Jane Tullett you're looking for?'

Jim swallowed and nodded. Laura was staring at the smoky face with her hand clasped over her mouth, and Washington was shaking his head again, but not in mockery.

'Jane Tullett, why can't you rest?' asked Gabriel. 'Why are you trying to hurt those people who tried to save you?'

The smoky head didn't reply, but drifted and shuddered in the wind that none of the living people in the room could feel.

'Jane,' said Jim, his voice hoarse. 'This is Jim Rook here. Do you remember me? I was your teacher in Special Class II.'

The head opened her lips a little wider, as if it wanted to say something, but still no sound came out.

'Jane . . . you drowned Jennie Bauer's little boy. You drowned Dennis Pease. You nearly managed to drown my friend Mervyn. I don't understand why you want to hurt us all so much, Jane. We did everything we could to try and save you that day. Your death was an accident, believe me. Nobody grieved for you more than your friends at West Grove, and they still grieve for you, even today. We loved you then, Jane, and we love you now.'

The head stirred, and partially dissolved, so that it looked as if Jane's face were melting.

'Jane!' snapped Gabriel. 'Are you listening to me, Jane? I command you to answer us! If you don't help us, then by God I'm going to exorcize your spirit if it takes the rest of my life!'

The head took on a slightly more definite form, so that Jim could clearly see the outline of Jane's oval face and her long, straight nose.

'. . . *Can't* . . .' she breathed. Her voice was no louder than a net curtain blowing against a summer window.

'Can't?' Gabriel insisted. 'Can't what? Can't exorcize you? I'll have a damn good try.'

'. . . *Can't rest . . . not ever* . . .'

'That's where you're wrong. You *can* rest. Your mortal

existence is over, Jane. It ended ten years ago when you drowned. All you need to do now is sleep, and dream, for ever.'

'. . . Can't sleep . . .' said the soft, blurry voice.

'You can, Jane. Forget the life you had before you drowned. It's nothing but a memory now. It's all finished, for ever. You can't go on taking revenge on your friends, or on Jim here, and the people he cares about. They weren't responsible for what happened to you. It's all over, Jane, accept it.'

'I ain't seeing this,' said Washington. 'I ain't seeing this and I definitely ain't not hearing it, neither.'

'Ssh,' Laura told him, taking hold of his hand. 'This girl's so *sad*.'

'. . . All have to pay . . .' said the head. '. . . *Everybody . . . they all have to pay . . .*'

'But why now, Jane?' Jim asked her. 'Why does everybody have to pay *now*?'

The smoke began to waver again. Gabriel's hands were trembling and it was clear that he was having to use all his strength to keep the image intact. 'I can't hold this much longer,' he said. 'She might be nothing but a young girl, but she's resisting me with so much strength.'

'Jane, listen to me!' Jim insisted. 'I have to know why you're drowning all of these people! I have to know what you want! Just tell me what it is you're looking for!'

The smoky head said nothing for ten drawn-out seconds. Then she appeared to turn toward Jim, and *open her eyes*. Jim sat back in his chair, seriously alarmed for the first time since this encounter had begun. Her eyes were nothing but dark hollows, yet they gave her an expression of terrifying malice.

'What happened in the pool that day?' she asked him, and her voice gave him a slow, crawling sensation down his back like a hairy spider. 'Don't ask me what I'm looking for. Ask yourself what you should be looking for. *What really happened in the pool that day?*'

'You dived in, Jane. You hit your head. There were too many people in the pool and nobody noticed you. That's all. It was tragic, but it was an accident.'

Without saying anything more, the smoky head gradually disentangled itself and drifted away across the room. In a few seconds it had vanished altogether. Gabriel took off his glasses and his hands were trembling. 'That – without any question at all – was the most difficult transmigratory confrontation I have ever done in my life. Ever.'

Laura said, 'What do you think she meant, when she asked you what really happened in the pool that day?'

'I don't know,' said Jim. 'I personally don't remember seeing anything out of the ordinary, and the coroner was satisfied that it was accidental death.'

Gabriel stood up, dragged a grubby handkerchief out of his pocket and loudly blew his nose. 'As I said before, spirits are very good at deluding themselves about the way they died . . . especially if they were the victims of their own carelessness. Auto-wreck victims, they're the worst. "It wasn't me! The other guy wasn't looking where he was going!"'

'What are we going to do now, Mr Rook?' asked Washington. 'It don't look like the Swimmer's going to stop drowning people, does it?'

'No, it doesn't. I think the next step is to try to find out if anything unusual happened on the day that Jane drowned, although I'm not at all sure how we're going to be able to do that.'

'Aren't you going to Washington, Mr Rook?' asked Laura.

'I can delay it for a couple of days. But I have to report for duty at the Department of Education on Monday morning, eight sharp.'

Gabriel said, 'I could use a drink . . . anybody want to join me?'

'I'll have a diet Coke if that's okay,' said Laura.

'A beer would be good,' said Jim.

At that second, however, Jim heard an extraordinary noise. It was a deep, furious *rushing*, as if a hurricane had risen out of nowhere at all. The whole house began to quiver, and a tall vase of white lilies toppled over sideways and broke.

'Earthquake?' frowned Gabriel.

'This doesn't feel like an earthquake,' said Jim.

'Hope it's not a mudslide,' put in Washington.

'Mudslide? We haven't had rain in over two months.'

Jim looked out through the sliding windows into the back yard. It was almost dark now, but he could see the yuccas thrashing up and down like frenzied dancers; and there was a scattering of dried leaves blown against the glass. But as he approached the window more closely, his hand shading his eyes, he suddenly realized that the rushing sound wasn't the wind, and it wasn't an earthquake either.

There was something glistening and dark in the yard. Something huge. All of the water in the swimming pool was rearing up into an immense tidal wave. It was crashing across the loggia toward them, thousands of gallons of seething water, as fast as an ocean liner. Jim didn't even have time to shout out a comprehensible warning before the wave struck the windows with devastating force, smashing them into a million glittering fragments, and ripping away the frames.

The whole living-room was filled with surging, foaming water. It swept from one end to the other, lifting Jim clear off his feet, and overturning the table and chairs. He saw Laura just before he went under, her eyes wide with panic, but he couldn't see Washington or Gabriel. The next thing he knew, he was under the surface, tumbling helplessly across the carpet and colliding with the coffee table. He could hear distorted shouts and booming echoes, and he saw showers of crackling sparks as the water shorted out the electric plugs.

He was whirled from one end of the living-room to the other, almost into the hallway. He managed to seize the top of the doorframe to steady himself, and it was then that Laura came past him, gasping and paddling and gagging for air. He managed to catch the strap of her suntop and pull her behind the door, where the current wasn't so fierce.

'Where's Washington?' he shouted.

'I don't know! I don't know! What's happened? What's all this water?'

'The pool! Hold on tight! Don't let yourself get dragged under!'

The water in the living-room was almost nine feet deep, and

it was churning around and around in a violent whirlpool. Jim could reach up with one hand and actually touch the ceiling, and the water showed no sign of going down.

'Stay here! I have to find Washington!'

'Don't leave me, please!'

'I have to!'

Jim took a huge breath and dived down under the water. In the racing whirlpool, everything was weightless: chairs, lamps, books, ornaments. He saw a dark shape on the far side of the room and he swam toward it, even though the water kept rolling him over sideways and forcing him violently toward the walls.

He managed to swim up to an overturned sofa and climb on to it, kicking himself up to the ceiling for more air. Above the surface, the noise in the living-room was thunderous, and it looked as if even more waves were gushing into the broken windows from the pool. Jim took another breath and went back down.

At first he couldn't see Washington anywhere, and he was afraid that the current had whirled him back around the room. But then he saw a leg kicking behind the immense wide-screen television, which had been slewed around and into the corner. He swam nearer and heaved the television aside, and there was Washington, with the television cable twisted around his ankle, struggling to get himself free. Jim tried to unwind it, but it was tied so tightly that his fingers couldn't get a grip and he was unable to budge it. Washington grabbed wildly at his sleeves. Bubbles came flooding out of his mouth and Jim heard him let out a muffled cry of desperation. He tugged at the cable again and again but he still couldn't work it free.

He wrenched Washington's hands away from his sleeves and propelled himself off to one side, kicking against the wall to give himself more momentum. He could see Washington staring at him wide-eyed in panic, but there was nothing else he could do. He swam toward the side of the room where he had last seen Gabriel's table overturned, and there it was, lying on its side. He groped all the way around it until he found the drawer, and tugged it open. Sheets of paper were dragged out into the whirling water, as well as pencils and envelopes. But Jim saw the fish-like gleam of Gabriel's scissors and that was all that he wanted. He picked them up, dropped them, picked them up again, and half stumbled and half swam back to Washington against a current that battered him even harder than it had before.

Washington's head had fallen back, although his eyes were still open and a fine trail of bubbles was still pouring from his mouth. Jim dug the point of the scissors under the television cable and cut through it in three quick snips. Then he pulled Washington out from the corner, and dragged him toward the broken windows, walking across the floor with the slow dancing gait of a deep-sea diver. He knew that he simply didn't have the strength to take Washington up to the surface and he could only pray that the water gushing in through the windows had begun to subside.

He reached the windows, treading on sodden carpet and broken glass, heaving Washington's inert body after him. The air in his lungs was almost exhausted and he felt as if his eardrums were going to burst. Then – with one last effort – he staggered out through the window and found himself standing in the back yard with the water only knee-deep.

He lifted Washington's head out of the water and managed to manhandle him across to the side of the loggia, above the waterline, his arms and his legs dragging. The living-room behind him was filled with raging foam, like the wake of a ship. By now the swimming pool was almost completely drained, and water was still gushing *upward* out of the pool and across the yard, as if it were eager to fill the living-room right up to the ceiling.

Jim dropped Washington into the recovery position and started to massage his chest, but it was only a few seconds before Washington suddenly retched, and regurgitated half a gallon of swimming-pool water.

'Washington? Can you hear me?' Jim shouted at him.

'I can hear you, man,' Washington coughed. 'I can hear you.'

'Are you okay? I have to get Laura out of there.'

'Go get her, man. I'll be all right.'

'You're sure about that?'

'Just be careful, man. Somebody tied that cable around my ankle. Somebody did it deliberate.'

'Did you see who it was?'

'I didn't see nobody, man. I only felt them. There was somebody in the water with me, but I never saw who it was.'

'Well, just take it easy, okay?'

Jim waded through the water outside the living-room windows and stood for a moment looking at the dark, foaming whirlpool in front of him. It looked as if it were defying all the forces of nature . . . but supposing there were forces of nature that were far greater than the ones we understand?

He filled his lungs with air, and then he plunged without any more hesitation straight into the wall of water that filled the space where the window had been. It was like being hit by a water-cannon: he was instantly knocked off his feet, and thrown against the corner of a large white display cabinet, in which smashed-up ornaments and silverware were jangling and bobbing.

His hip was bruised, but he managed an ungainly upward swimming motion until he reached the gap between the surface of the water and the ceiling. There was less than a foot of air-space remaining, and he was so close to the ceiling that he could hold on to the chandelier to keep him afloat. Two of the chandelier's bulbs still burned, giving him enough light to see Laura at the other end of the room. She had managed to keep her grip on the top of the door, and he shouted to her, 'Laura!' and waved. 'Do you think you can swim over here?'

'I don't know! I can try!'

'You haven't seen Gabriel, have you?'

She shook her head. 'I think I heard him shouting, but I don't know where he is!'

'Okay . . . just start swimming toward me! Watch out for the current, it's running every which way!'

Laura hesitated for a moment, and then she launched herself away from the door. Immediately she was swept around to the left side of the room, screaming, her arms frantically thrashing to keep herself from going under.

'It's okay! It's okay! Just keep trying to swim toward me!'

'I can't, I'm going to – *blllggghhhbbllee*! I can't!'

'You can! Come on, Washington's okay! We're going to get you out of here too!'

Laura steadied herself for a moment by placing her hand against the wall. Then she called out, 'I'm coming! It's okay, I'm going to make it!'

She plunged back into the whirlpool and this time she managed to strike out toward him, using the powerful current to help her rather than trying to struggle against it. She was carried toward him so quickly that he didn't know whether he was going to be able to catch her or not, and when he lunged out to snatch her arm he felt the chandelier lurch in his hand. He caught her wrist, but his hand slipped, and he only just managed to grip her fingers.

'You're going to be fine!' he reassured her. 'All we have to do now is dive down and swim out through the back window!'

'I don't understand!'

'There's no water in the yard – only in the house!'

She still couldn't grasp what he was saying, but that wasn't important. They had to escape from the living-room now before the water rose any higher. They could worry about scientific impossibilities later.

Jim held her hand as tight as he could. 'Ready?' he asked her. 'Take a real deep breath!'

But before they could dive, the water exploded in between them and a gray head reared out, its eyes bulging, its mouth gushing like an ornamental fountain.

Laura screamed and let go of Jim's hand. The whirlpool instantly washed her away, so that she struck the opposite wall. The gray head stared at Jim for one hideous moment, gargled, and then disappeared under the water again.

Eleven

'Gabriel!' Jim shouted. He thrust one hand under the water to see if he could reach him, but Gabriel was gone.

Jim called over to Laura, 'Hold on! I have to go down and see what's happened to Gabriel!'

'Don't leave me again!' Laura shrieked at him. 'The water's getting higher!'

'Hold on – I have to go down just one more time!'

It wasn't that he believed there was any chance that Gabriel was still breathing: he had been under the water far too long. But the way that he had plunged back beneath the surface had suggested to Jim that he had been dragged by something more than the current. He had to see for himself. He had to know. In the end, he was the only one who could save the people around him from being drowned, one after the other, and that was too great a responsibility for him to shirk.

He wanted more than anything else to grab hold of Laura and swim right out of that room. He hated the idea of being a martyr. But there was nothing else he could do.

He released his grip on the chandelier and dived beneath the surface. Only one light bulb was still glowing, and it was much darker under the water now. Not only that, the whirling current had filled the water with thousands of fragments of soggy paper, so that it was like swimming through a dense snowstorm.

He touched Gabriel before he saw him: the medium's cold dead fingers trailed across his cheek like crabs' claws and he couldn't stop himself from letting out a small belch of bubbles. There was no doubt that Gabriel was drowned. He stared at

Jim as he rolled and tumbled through the paper snowflakes and his eyes were completely blind.

Jim looked urgently right and left. Maybe he was mistaken, and Gabriel had sunk so quickly because his stomach was full of water. But then he saw a shadowy shape, only nine or ten feet away from him, circling with the current. He saw two legs flickering, and hair waving.

He was short of breath, but he pushed himself one more time, swimming wildly across the room. When he reached the opposite wall, however, there was nobody there. He turned around and around, dog-paddling hard to keep himself stabilized.

No – if the Swimmer were here, she wasn't showing herself. He had to get out of here now, and make sure that Laura was safe. The Swimmer would have to wait for another time.

He started to kick for the surface, but as he did so he felt something scrabble at his ankles and then catch hold of them tight. Not something – *somebody*. He tried to struggle free, but he could feel two strong-fingered hands pulling him back down to the bottom again.

He looked up. Only three feet above him he could see the single remaining light bulb, wavering and dipping through the turbulent water. He tried to kick again, but he was being dragged down too strongly. He looked down, and through the chaos of paper he saw the watery, glistening head of Jane Tullett, with her transparent face and her waving hair and her shadowy eyes. She was staring at him with intense hatred, and deliberately drowning him.

For a split second he thought, Maybe, if she takes me, she'll leave my students and my friends alone.

But he knew that he couldn't deliberately allow himself to be drowned. Apart from the fact that his instinct for self-survival was overwhelming, what guarantee could he possibly have that the Swimmer would consider his death was revenge enough?

The Swimmer's hands climbed up his ankles until she was clasping him around his knees, and then his thighs. Although she was so transparent, she was overwhelmingly strong, and no matter how much he struggled he couldn't break free. She felt extraordinary – as slippery as if she had been oiled all over, so that when he tried to pull her hands away he couldn't get any grip.

God, he thought, she's really going to drown me. I'm really going to die, in somebody's flooded living-room, and nobody will ever believe it. He thought of Karen, dressed in black, coming to his funeral.

He twisted himself over on to his hands and knees. The Swimmer slid around behind him, and slipped her hands around his throat. She didn't squeeze him hard enough to choke him, but the pressure on his Adam's apple made him feel that he desperately needed to inhale.

With all the strength he could summon up, he started to crawl across the living-room floor, with the Swimmer floating above him, her hands still clasping his throat. He didn't know if he was capable of making it all the way across the room, but at least he had to try. The Swimmer tried to pull him back, but he kept on crawling forward, his lungs aching for lack of oxygen, but refusing to breathe in. With every step he dug his fingers into the wet shagpile carpet to give him purchase; or seized the side of one of the sofas; or gripped the legs of the tipped-over table.

As he neared the end of the room, the Swimmer tried to strangle him even harder, until his vision was misted with scarlet. But he reached the broken window, where the water was still pouring in, and he crawled over the broken glass until dozens of tiny fragments were sticking into his hands and knees and the foaming water turned pink with blood.

The Swimmer clutched his throat in one last terrible squeeze and for a moment he was convinced that he couldn't make it. But then he felt the sharp edge of the window-frame beneath his knees, and he toppled out into the back yard, where the water level had dropped to nothing but a few inches, and the Swimmer toppled out with him.

Instantly she released her grip, and all he felt was water gushing over his back, as she lost her physical shape. He fell sideways and looked up, and she was crouching down beside him – at least her spirit was, the insubstantial, glistening spirit that only *he* could see.

'No more,' he croaked at her. 'Don't drown anybody else.'

But the hatred on her face was undiminished. She stared at him with her shadowy eyes for a little while longer, and then she stood up and walked into the darkness. The only sign of her going was the way her invisible feet made quick, pattering splashes in the water.

'Mr Rook!' called Washington. 'Are you okay, Mr Rook? Where's Laura?'

Washington came over and knelt down beside him. 'Where's Laura, Mr Rook? What went down in there?'

Jim didn't have the chance to answer. As the Swimmer's spirit vanished from sight, all of the swimming-pool water in the living-room came roaring out of the window as violently as it had roared in. Jim and Washington were swept across the yard, along with sunbeds and parasols, couches, tables and books. They were tossed into the half-empty pool while thousands of gallons cascaded over their heads. The water foamed and churned until it was all frothed up and Jim began to think that the torrent was never going to end.

He heard screaming from the house and then Laura was swept through the doors and across the loggia, and tossed into the pool like a disjointed doll. She disappeared from sight for a moment, but Washington immediately waded toward her, his head bowed down against the water that was still hammering down on top of them. He helped her to struggle to her feet, and then the three of them made their way toward the shallow end while water crashed all around them like the worst rainstorm in human history.

Lieutenant Harris stood in the middle of the dripping living-room and said, '*This*' – and he lifted his hand and gave little choppy gestures as if he were a bishop giving benediction – 'this is not normal.'

'No,' said Jim.

A bald, businesslike medical examiner came up to them,

snapping off his latex gloves. 'This is a weird one. Never seen anything like it.'

'Cause of death, at a rough guess?' asked Lieutenant Harris.

'No rough guess about it. Asphyxiation caused by drowning.'

Lieutenant Harris did some exaggerated pacing around, his feet squelching rhythmically on the sodden carpet. The whole living-room reeked so strongly of chlorine that everybody's eyes were watering. 'Any evidence of foul play?'

'Bruising to both ankles and left calf-muscle consistent with being forcibly pulled or dragged.'

'I see. Pulled or dragged by whom – or by what?'

'A young woman, I'd say, judging by the finger marks.'

Lieutenant Harris rubbed the back of his neck. 'I don't get it. How can you be drowned in your living-room?'

'Look around you, lieutenant. There must have been thousands of gallons of water in here. Judging by the tidemark, it came within three or four inches of the ceiling.'

'So how did that happen?' Lieutenant Harris asked Jim. 'How did thousands of gallons of water pour out of the swimming pool and into the living-room? Didn't I learn at grade school that water never runs uphill?'

'It can do, under exceptional circumstances. You can get a siphon effect, like when you suck gasoline out of an automobile. Or a flash flood. Or a major seismic disturbance, which creates a *tsunami*, or tidal wave.'

'There were no earthquakes tonight, Mr Rook – not that I know of. No dams collapsed, no water mains burst, and it wasn't raining either.'

Jim shrugged. 'Then your guess is as good as anybody's. All I know is that the water came out of the swimming pool and flooded the living-room.'

'Do you know something?' said Lieutenant Harris. 'Whenever you and I get to meet, which must be more often than the law of averages dictates, there's always something unnatural going on. Something spooky. Something that defies the natural order of things.'

'This is Los Angeles,' said Jim. 'The whole city defies the natural order of things.'

Jim drove Washington and Laura back to their homes. Before he let Laura out of the car, he said, 'Listen, Laura. I think it's better if you call this one quits. I can't take the risk of anything happening to you.'

'But I want to help you, Mr Rook. And I want to help everyone else in Special Class II. Supposing I quit now and somebody else drowns? How am I going to feel about that?'

'Laura, I'm responsible for you. And it's not responsible to expose you to this kind of danger. We could have *all* drowned in that room tonight – and then what good could we have been to anybody?'

'I'm sorry,' said Laura. 'I'm going to stick with this, and there's nothing you can do to stop me, even if I have to do it on my own. I have some ideas about this water thing, okay, and I want to look through some of my witch books and see if I'm right.'

Jim was damp and exhausted and he didn't want to argue any more. So he opened the car door for her and said, 'Okay . . . you go look through your witch books and give me a call tomorrow. Not too early.'

As he drove Washington home, he said, 'You got any theories about what happened tonight?'

'I don't know, sir. It was totally unreal. But I got the feeling that the water was more than just water, if you can understand what I mean. It was almost like the water was out to get us.'

'That's interesting. That was my feeling too. It wasn't just the Swimmer . . . it was like the actual water was trying to get its revenge on us.'

He pulled up outside Washington's apartment building. Two pretty girls in hotpants were sitting on the wall outside swinging their legs. 'Hey, Washington! Coming down to the Ice Club tonight?'

Washington climbed out of the car. 'I'll give you a call in the morning, Mr Rook. Don't try to turn me off this thing. I want to find this sucker just as much as you do.'

Jim gave him a weary wave of acceptance and drove off.

Back at his apartment, TT immediately scurried into the kitchen and started mewling for food and milk, but Jim went to the icebox first and took out a beer. He popped the top and swallowed a huge mouthful that made his cheeks bulge. 'Owners before pets,' he told TT, after an eye-watering swallow. 'It's called the pecking order.'

He went through to the bedroom and dragged off his damp shirt and pants. His linen jacket was so crumpled that he hung it up on the back of the bathroom door, in the hope that the steam from his shower would help some of the creases to fall out.

Wearing a clean T-shirt and jeans, he went back into the living-room and switched on the television. He was just in time to see the tail end of a report on what had happened at Gabriel Dragonard's house. 'Police are still baffled by the huge surge of water that apparently filled the mystic's home and drowned him. Three survivors from the incident said they were lucky to be alive but could offer no explanation as to how thousands of gallons of water had suddenly gone on the rampage – flying in the face of all the known laws of physics. And now this . . .'

He was emptying cat food into TT's dish when the doorbell chimed. He went to the door still carrying a spoon and the half-empty can, and peered through the spyhole. It was Susan Silverstone, and Michael. 'Hold on!' he said, and opened the door. Susan came sweeping past him, silvery-faced, her black hair drawn up into an elaborate braid, wrapped in a long black dress with a deeply plunging neckline, and wearing five assorted silver crosses on five silver chains. Michael followed closely behind her, wearing an old cotton hat that made him look like a cross between a baby and a senior citizen, and petulant enough for both.

'I'm sorry,' said Susan. 'I didn't mean to interrupt your supper.'

Jim looked down at the can of cat food. 'Oh . . . that's okay. I was almost finished anyhow. Come on in.'

'We just caught the news,' said Susan, and it was more of a question than a statement.

Michael repeated, 'Yes . . . we just caught the news.'

'We saw you,' Susan added, accusingly. 'You and your two students. You held a seance, didn't you?'

'We held a seance, yes, and it ended very badly. We were lucky we didn't all drown.'

'Don't you realize how irresponsible that was?'

'I don't think we had much choice. *You* didn't want to contact the Swimmer, did you? In fact, Michael expressly told you not to, didn't you?'

'Come on, Jim,' said Michael. 'Didn't I say that I'd do everything I could to find another medium?'

'Sure you did. But *have* you found another medium?'

Michael looked defensive. 'No, I haven't, not yet.'

'No, you haven't, and I don't believe you were even going to try. What's going on here, Michael? We have to hunt this Swimmer down. It's critical. My whole class is in danger, not to mention anybody else who tries to help me. More than that, I don't want Gabriel Dragonard to have drowned for nothing, just like Mikey and Dennis. And I don't want Dottie to have suffered for nothing, either.'

'Look, there's a whole lot more to this than you can possibly know,' said Michael.

'Yes, I think you're right. And that's why I'm doing my damndest to discover what.'

Michael was obviously agitated. He kept tugging at his earlobes and running his hands through his hair. 'I told Susan that she shouldn't try to contact the Swimmer because I really care about her, and I didn't want to see her hurt. For God's sake, Jim, we're not just dealing with one or two vengeful spirits here, we're interfering with the elemental forces of the millennial world.'

'The which of the what?'

'Listen, Jim, the last time Susan tried to do anything like this, it practically took her apart, physically as well as mentally. She almost died – even though she's one of the strongest sensitives I've ever met. Like I told you, it's taken over a year to get her back together again, and she's still very vulnerable. I don't want that to happen again.'

'If you find another medium it *won't* happen again.'

'That's my whole point. *Any* medium who tries to fight these forces is in just as much danger – no matter how good they are. Look what happened to Gabriel Dragonard. Jesus – if only I'd known what you were planning to do, I'd have stopped you.'

'Gabriel knew that there were risks.'

'He knew that he could be drowned in his own house? I don't think so. Nobody really understands these forces yet. We don't have the technical knowledge or the psychological strength to control them. Besides that, they're constantly evolving from day to day, so we can never know what to be prepared for.'

Jim said, 'I see. So when you promised that you were going to look for another medium, you were just stalling me. You were just trying to stop me from persuading Susan to do it.'

'All right, yes, I admit it. I might have let you do it before we talked to David DuQuesne. But when we went to meet him, I really began to understand what we're up against. Let's put it this way: Swimmers have only appeared in the past hundred and fifty years, haven't they? And why?'

'Search me,' said Jim. 'But you obviously have some kind of a theory.'

Michael said, 'Water has always had powerful spirits of its own . . . you only have to read Ancient Greek sea stories and Native American legends to know that. But a hundred and fifty years ago, the water was too pure for a stray spirit like Jane Tullett to use it as a way of getting her revenge.'

'So what's happened since?'

'These days the water's polluted. That means that the supernatural forces in the water are polluted, too. You give people contaminated water to drink, what happens to them? Cholera, dysentery, liver disease . . . freak pregnancies like they had in Japan. That's exactly what's happened to the spirits in the water. They're sick, Jim. The spirits themselves are sick.'

Michael lifted four fingers. 'In the ancient world, okay, there were four basic elements . . . air, fire, water and earth.

Out of those four basic elements we developed medicine, religion, astrology, spiritualism and magic ritual. The elements were true and they were pure. The air was unpolluted . . . fires came from the burning of natural combustibles like wood and coal . . . the waters were clean enough for fish to thrive in them . . . and the only fertilizers in the soil were organic composts and animal manure.

'But now the air is full of lead and sulfur and carbon monoxide and God knows what else; fire comes from burning plastics and all kinds of disgusting trash; the rivers are full of industrial effluent; and the soil is full of chemical fertilizers and seepage from landfill sites. Every time you drink a glass of water in Los Angeles, you can guarantee that it's passed through the bodies of eight other people before it's reached your lips. If you poison your natural environment, don't you think you're going to poison your supernatural environment too?'

Jim swallowed some more beer. 'It's an interesting theory. But what kind of proof do you have?'

'Susan. What happened to Susan, that's the proof. That's why – when David DuQuesne started to explain about urban legends – I suddenly realized what we were really up against.'

'So are you going to tell me exactly what it was that happened to Susan – or is Susan going to tell me what happened to Susan, or don't either of you want to talk about it?'

'She doesn't want it all raked over again. It's taken her so long to come to terms with it.'

But Susan said, 'No . . . I think Jim has the right to know.'

'You're sure?' said Michael. 'You know what could happen if you do.'

'I'm sure.' Susan walked over to the window and looked out over the sparkling lights of Venice. Her silvery-white face was reflected in the glass, suspended there like the moon. 'It happened just over a year ago. A seventeen-year-old girl called Mary came for a consultation because she'd been having persistent nightmares about somebody coming into her bedroom at night – a young boy, as far as she could tell. He would sit on the end of her bed with his back turned and cry, very quietly. She said the nightmares were so vivid that it was hard for her to believe it wasn't really happening.'

She paused for a while, and in the kitchen Jim could hear TT rattling her dish against the floor as she lapped up the last of her food. 'Is that all?' he asked. 'He just sat on the end of the bed crying?'

'At first that was all. But after three or four nightmares, she was sure she could smell burning, like scorching wool; and one night, when the boy was sitting on the end of her bed, she saw smoke pouring out of his sweater. Night after night the boy came back, and each time the smell of burning grew stronger and the smoke grew thicker.'

'Didn't she tell anybody about these nightmares?'

'Her father was away on a six-month business trip and her mother was a very nervous type, so she didn't like to. But one night the boy came into her room, and the smoke grew so thick that she felt as if she was being choked. Smoke was even coming out of his *hair*.

'It was then that he turned around to look at her, and she saw his face for the first time. And it was then that he burst into flames. All of his clothes were on fire, his hands were on fire, his legs were on fire. He was screaming and screaming at her, kicking and struggling as if he was trapped, and couldn't move.

'She got out of bed and tried to beat out the fire with a blanket, but the boy was charred black and there was nothing she could do to save him. She woke up sweating and struggling and badly shocked. And when she switched on the light, the room was still filled with smoke and there was a faint scorch mark on her bedcover.

'It happened again the next night, and the next night, and the night after that. Each time the boy came into her room, sat on her bed and caught fire. And each night the heat was more intense, and the smoke thicker, and her bedcovers more badly burned. She hid the scorches from her mother, in case she thought she had done it herself, but on the third night the cover actually caught fire. She managed to escape but the nightmares went on, and even when she was locked alone in her bedroom with no access to matches the fires continued, until one night her hands were badly burned.

'That's when her mother first brought Mary to see me. She was desperate, like most of my clients. Ordinary people don't find it easy to ask a sensitive for help, believe me.'

'So did you manage to help her?' asked Jim.

'Yes, I did. I held a seance and talked to the boy's spirit and asked him what had happened to him and why he kept appearing in Mary's bedroom. It took five or six confrontations before I managed to get some kind of sensible answer out of him. His spirit was very distressed, as well as vengeful. He was very angry and very bewildered and he was *hurting*.

'He told me his name was Peter. It turned out that he had been a passenger in his mother's car. She had been taking him to a football game when an oil-tanker overturned in front of them on the San Diego Freeway and his mother hadn't been able to stop in time. There was a multiple collision and his mother was killed instantly. He was trapped in the car with his seat-belt jammed.

'There was a fire . . . and even though there were several other drivers standing around, none of them was brave enough to rescue him. He was burned alive, screaming.

'One of the drivers who left him to burn was Mary's father. So when he kept appearing in Mary's bedroom he was punishing her father for allowing him to die. If his appearances had carried on, he probably would have set fire to Mary's bed and burned her alive, too.'

Michael said, 'Usually, when somebody burns to death, their spirit finds perfect peace. That's why we cremate people. But the fire that burned this boy was poisonous with plastics and diesel . . . an impure fire. A sick fire. Your spirit can never find any rest if you've been burned in a fire like that.'

'So how did you stop him?' asked Jim.

'She did a very stupid thing,' said Michael.

Susan turned away from the window. 'There was no other way. He would have gone on visiting her every night for the rest of her life if I hadn't . . . and her life would have been very short indeed.

'I did what we call a spirit-transference. That means that I obliged Peter's spirit to enter *me*. I was older than him, mentally stronger than him, and so he had no choice. It's a very difficult thing to do, spirit-transference. It was originally devised in the 1920s by the Irish medium Kate Goligher. She took the spirits of young children who had been killed in accidents, and transferred them into her own mind so that she could calm them down and help them to accept the fact that they had died. She called it "spirit-cradling", and she said it was the most rewarding thing she ever did – but also the most exhausting. Sometimes it made her very ill. Once she cradled the spirit of a ten-year-old boy who had been crushed by a farm cart and it almost killed her. She used to wake up in the morning with her chest all bruised, hardly able to breathe.'

'Peter almost killed *her*,' said Michael. 'She used to feel unbelievable pain, as if she was burning from the inside. She suffered it in silence. What choice did she have? If she let his spirit go free, it would go after Mary and burn her alive. Her moods changed, she lost weight, but none of her friends seemed to care. When I first met her she was suffering so much pain she was seriously thinking of taking an overdose and ending it all.'

Susan laid her hand on Michael's shoulder. 'Michael nursed me through it. He sat with me every night and he helped me to deal with the pain. He looked through every book and every research paper on spirit-transference that he could find. In the end he found a way in which he could put Peter's spirit into a kind of hypnotic coma, so that he wouldn't feel the burning any more.' She touched her forehead with her silver-ringed fingers. 'Peter's still inside me, he's still inside my mind. But it's like he's asleep.'

'That's why I wouldn't allow her to hold a seance to confront the Swimmer,' said Michael. 'From what David DuQuesne told us, it looks like the Swimmer is to water what Peter's spirit is to fire – a spirit which uses one of the basic elements to give itself a physical form, and take its revenge on the people who allowed it to die. If Susan gets spiritually weakened, even a little, there's a serious danger that Peter's spirit is going to come out of his coma and burn her alive from the inside out.'

'Why didn't you tell me this earlier?' said Jim.

'I didn't make the connection until we talked to David DuQuesne. Even now I'm only guessing. But the way I see it, the risk is far too great. Susan doesn't like to talk about Peter, or even think about him, in case she disturbs him and wakes him up. You should have seen her, Jim, when she was going through the worst of it. She used to cry for hours because of the pain.'

Jim took hold of Susan's hands. 'I'm glad you told me why you didn't want to hold a seance, I really am. But we still have to find a way of stopping the Swimmer.'

'I could *try* to find another medium,' Michael suggested. 'But after what happened to Gabriel Dragonard, I don't know if I could persuade anybody else to hold a seance.'

'I wouldn't even dare to ask them,' said Jim. 'Besides, it seems to me that when we try to raise up the Swimmer's spirit all we're doing is giving her an opportunity to drown even more people. It was sheer luck that she didn't drown me and Laura and Washington, too.'

'We'll have to look for another way,' said Susan. 'But let's remember that we have one critical advantage . . . you can *see* her, Jim, even when she's not in physical form.'

'I'm going to have to find her first.'

Next morning he was woken up by his doorbell repeatedly chiming. He lifted his head off the pillow and stared at the digital clock beside his bed. When he got it into focus he saw that it was 9.17. God, it must be Mervyn, making his daily call to collect the trash. He squinted down to the end of the bed where TT was still asleep, and threw a box of tissues at her.

'What's your problem? Some alarm cat you are . . . I told you to wake me up at eight!'

The doorbell rang again and he called out, 'Keep your hair on, Mervyn, I'm coming!'

He swung his legs out of bed and picked the T-shirt up from the back of the chair. Then, yawning and scratching himself, he went to answer the front door. He opened it without looking through the spyhole, and turned back toward the bedroom.

'Mervyn – there's a whole lot of boxes and bubble-wrap in the kitchen closet . . . if you can take those, too.'

But then a girl's voice said, 'Good-morning, Mr Rook!' And a whole chorus of voices said, 'Happy Thursday morning, sir!'

He looked around and there was every member of Special Class II, standing in the corridor outside his apartment, all twenty of them, including Laura and Washington and Christophe and Nestor and the Karakatsanis twins and Jack Hubbard and Katie Untermeyer and Stella Kopalski.

'I don't believe this,' he said. He was overwhelmed. 'I never thought I was going to see you guys again. Come on in, find yourselves someplace to sit. I think I'd better find myself some pants.'

The class crowded into his apartment, jostling and giggling and 'sshh'ing. Jim went back to the bedroom and hopped into his jeans. Then he splashed his face with cold water and tugged a comb through his hair. His face still had wrinkle marks on it from his pillow, but there was nothing he could do about those.

When he came back into the living-room, the class were all sprawled on chairs and packing cases and sitting on the floor.

'Everybody comfortable?'

'Saw you on the news last night, Mr Rook,' Christophe volunteered. 'You and Washington and Laura. That was unreal, that old guy drowning in his own house. Laura said that you guys nearly drowned, too.'

Jim said, 'You remember I warned you about staying away from water. We were trying to track down the spirit that drowned Dennis and scalded Dottie. Well, we found out last night just how dangerous it can be. We were lucky . . . but we haven't beaten it yet, and you could still be in danger.'

'Don't you worry, Mr Rook. After what Washington said, we take the point. With a capital P.'

'Anyhow,' said Jim. 'To what do I owe the honor of your all coming here today?'

Arlene Carollo stood up. She was a very tall, thin brunette, with freckles and a wide smile crowded with shining white teeth. 'We couldn't let you leave without a leaving party, sir. We couldn't have it on Tuesday because of what happened to Dottie, but when we heard that you were still in LA . . . Well, the e-mails started flying and we decided to hold it today.'

David Baliga stood up, too – a stocky boy with a handsome, square-jawed face, but a slow, monotonous way of talking. 'The whole class owes you, Mr Rook. What you did for us nobody else could have done and nobody else was ever bothered. So that's why we came. And also to hand in our assignment.'

'Your assignment?'

'Sure,' said Jewel Karakatsanis. 'You asked us to write a four-line poem, remember, about the way we felt?'

'You wrote it? You didn't have to write it.'

'Sure we did. We know what kind of a blue fit you get into if we don't turn in our work on time.'

Washington produced two clanking brown-paper sacks from behind his back, and said, 'Champagne! Well, sparkling wine, anyhow! Let's have a party!'

Roberta Szredinski came forward with a large red box. Roberta was a plump, russet-haired girl who had struggled particularly hard with her reading during the year, because she had been desperate to qualify for a catering course. When Jim had first started to teach her she had scarcely been able to read the ingredients for a recipe. Now she was capable of writing ten-page essays on ethnic foods. She opened the box and displayed a huge white frosted cake with flowers and birds on it, and the message *I thank you for your voices, thank you – your most sweet voices.* TO MR ROOK FROM SPECIAL CLASS II.

'You remembered your *Coriolanus*,' said Jim.

'I think we remembered most everything, Mr Rook,' said Marcette Griffith, a pretty black girl with her hair threaded with thousands of colored beads, and a scarlet ruffled blouse. 'You gave us the power.'

Jim went into the kitchen and managed to assemble a motley collection of glasses, while Washington opened the sparkling wine and Roberta cut the cake.

'How you going to beat this water-thing, Mr Rook?' asked Nestor.

'I don't know. I'm not too sure that I can, but I'm going to have a damned good try.'

'Does this mean you won't be going to Washington?'

'I don't know. I'm supposed to be there on Monday morning at the latest. But there's one thing you can count on, I won't leave you guys in any kind of danger.'

'You can't put a hold on your whole career because of us,' said Joyce. 'We can take care of ourselves.'

'I wish I could be certain of that. If you'd seen the water rearing up out of that swimming pool . . .'

'It was *truly* frightening, man,' said Washington.

They filled their glasses and David called for a toast. 'To Mr Rook, who introduced us to William Shakespeare and William Faulkner and Tennessee Williams and William Carlos Williams . . . in fact more Bills than a pondful of ducks. But more than anything else, he introduced us to ourselves. Up until the day we walked into Special Class II, we didn't believe that we could do nothing and we didn't think that we were worth nothing.'

'Double negative, stupid!' called out Jewel.

'Whatever, Mr Rook showed us that we had ability, and that we had value; and that's what I want us to drink a toast to today.'

They clinked their glasses, and drank; and if Jim hadn't been so worried about them he would have been happier than he had ever been. But he couldn't stop thinking about Jane Tullett's watery face, and her voice whispering, '*What happened in the pool that day?*'

One by one they stood up and read their poems. Shannon Karakatsanis' poem was one of the tenderest.

'The sunshine moves around the class
And brightly measures out our hours.

Today will be tomorrow's past
These seeds will be tomorrow's flowers.'

Nestor Fawkes read his poem with a deep frown.

'I'm not too sure that I'm really ready
To walk out of these doors and into the street.
I can hear people outside there, laughing
I hope at jokes and not at me.'

When each student had finished reading, they all clapped – not just as a compliment, but with a feeling of mutual pride. When they had all finished, Jim stood up and said, 'I didn't think that I would be reciting anything to you ever again. But I'd like to leave you with one poem by Conrad Aiken that will give you all something to think about, and maybe something to guide you, too.'

He took a book out of one of his packing cases and opened it.

' . . . The mirage of spring
shatters about us in a broken prism of rainbows
never to be assembled again, or to be assembled
only in the ironic despair of a dream;
the false sunset has vanished under more than the sea:
the stage is suddenly vaster, there are no wings
for the off-stage voice of the pseudo-god – *that's me* –
instead, the silence and loneliness of self
become a new world, of which the shores
are faintly audible, faintly visible.'

Jim paused and looked up, and took in one face after another. '*We will go there*,' he said, and closed the book.

Twelve

Jim drove back to West Grove Community College later that morning, and parked his Cadillac, as usual, in Dr Friendly's personal space – even though Dr Friendly had already taken his wife and two children to Oahu for their summer vacation and the gesture was only symbolic. The campus was deserted except for a team of pool-maintenance men emptying out the swimming pool and cleaners sweeping and polishing the corridors.

He walked through to the library, where he found Clarence the caretaker up a stepladder, replacing the fluorescent tubes.

'Hi there, Mr Rook! Thought you'd taken off to Washington, D.C.!'

'Hi there, Clarence. One or two loose ends to tidy up.'

'You should have seen my cousin Hattie. She had the loosest end I ever saw! Hey, caught you on the TV news last night – that guy who drowned in his living-room. Soon as I saw it was you, I said to Charlene, "You can guarantee it . . . anything weird happens around here, Mr Jim Rook's got his thumb in the pie someplace."' He climbed down the stepladder and said, 'What was the story on that – drowning in his living-room?'

'Kind of a psychic phenomenon, Clarence. Hard to explain.'

'Hard to pronounce, too.'

Jim found the serried ranks of West Grove Community College yearbooks, bound in green leather with gold lettering, and took one down from the shelf. 'Tell me, Clarence, do you remember that first summer I was here, that girl who drowned? Jane Tullett?'

'For sure, Mr Rook. How could I ever forget it? That was a sad, sad business.'

'You were there, Clarence. Do you think we could have done any more than we did? Do you think that we could have been more vigilant?'

Clarence took out another fluorescent tube. 'Nobody saw what happened, Mr Rook. She dove off of the diving board, but there was more students in that pool than a bucketful of shrimp, wasn't there, and when she didn't come up – well, nobody took no notice.'

'So you don't think we were to blame?'

'Mr Rook – that poor young girl took a heck of a chance diving into all of those people. She was showing off. It wasn't your fault and it wasn't nobody's fault. She struck her head on the bottom of the pool and nobody saw her and that was all there was to it.'

'I don't know,' said Jim. 'Somehow I'm not convinced. When you think about it, she must have hit the water with one hell of a splash – how come nobody saw her floating at the bottom? How come nobody realized what had happened to her?'

'What you trying to say, Mr Rook?'

'I'm trying to say that maybe somebody *did* see her – and, whoever it was, that somebody was negligent, at the very least. Or actually wanted her to die.'

'Oh, come on now, Mr Rook. Some of these students have blood-feuds against each other, that's for sure – and we've had two guns confiscated this semester, haven't we? – but I can't believe that nobody would have seen Jane Tullett drowning and not done nothing about it, do you?'

Jim opened the West Grove College Yearbook for 1990 and flicked through it until he found Special Class II. There – right in the center of the page – was a smiling photograph of Jane Tullett, her long blond hair swept back, her eyes sparkling. On her left was George Opal, the captain of the college football team – wavy hair, modest smile and a deeply-cleft chin. He looked like a young Jack Kennedy, but he had never had anything like the young Jack Kennedy's brains. He hadn't been quite illiterate enough to rate a place in Special Class II, but Jim had given him one or two private-tuition sessions.

One of his knottiest problems had been telling the difference between 'of' and 'have', as in, 'we could of gone to the football game, last Saturday'.

'Come here, Clarence,' said Jim. 'Look at these two, Jane Tullett and George Opal. Didn't they go steady for a while?'

Clarence took his wire-rimmed eyeglasses out of his dungarees pocket and squinted at the yearbook intently. 'Sure. I remember George because his old man was Carson Opal, who used to play football for the Bears. George looked the spitting image of his old man. He was always walking around campus arm-in-arm with Jane. She was a beauty, wasn't she? They was always talking about getting engaged, but George had kind of a restless eye, if you know what I mean. He was always messing around with other girls, especially the sophomores, and then he and Jane would have a heck of a scrap, and then they made up and it was all quiet for a while. Until next year's intake of pretty young trouble, anyhow.'

'George wasn't in the pool when Jane drowned, was he?'

'No, he wasn't. He was over on the basketball court. I remember that because Dr Ehrlichman had to send a student to run tell him what had happened.'

'So . . . that rules *him* out, doesn't it?'

'I don't get it. What makes you think that Jane was drowned on purpose?'

'I've talked to her.'

'You've *talked* to her? Come on, Mr Rook. She's ten years dead.'

'That guy who drowned in his living-room was a medium, a psychic, somebody who can talk to people who have passed over to the other side. Or not quite passed over, in this particular case. We held a seance . . . and Jane appeared and I talked to her.'

'No shit. And she told you that she was drowned on purpose?'

'Not in so many words. But she kept asking me what happened in the swimming pool that day – like there was something that I'd missed.'

Clarence slowly shook his head. 'I don't know, Mr Rook.

I was there just like you were that morning and I never saw nothing untoward.'

Jim looked at all the faces in the yearbook. Eager, expectant, all on the very edge of adult life. Except for Jane, who had never grown to be an adult, and seemed to be taking out her bitterness on those she had left behind.

He sat down at one of the library desks and wrote out the names of everybody in Special Class II. 'What you doing?' Clarence asked him, as he climbed back up his stepladder.

'I'm doing the only thing I can do: finding witnesses. If Jane was really drowned deliberately, somebody must have seen something, even if they didn't understand what they were looking at. It's like being a passer-by, and seeing some guy walk into a building. What you saw isn't important unless you know that somebody was killed in that building only a few minutes later.'

'If you say so, Mr Rook. I just hope you ain't barking up some blind alley.'

He found Piper McConnell working in a bar called the Black Velvet Alligator, on San Vicente. The bar was pitch-dark after the glare outside and the air-conditioning was set to 'igloo'. A worn-out sound system was playing syrupy orchestrated versions of old Monkees hits. 'Well, hey-hey-hey . . . I'm a believer . . . couldn't leave her if I tried . . .'

Piper looked so different from her yearbook picture that he hardly recognized her. The neat brunette hair had been replaced by masses of highlighted blond curls. Her nose had obviously been surgically bobbed and given a little tilt, and her lips were so plump with collagen that she seemed to be permanently pressing them up against an imaginary toy-store window. She was wearing a black velvet *bustier* to match the dusty life-size alligator which was suspended on the wall behind her.

Jim sat up on a bar stool and she came over and asked him, in a deeply bored voice, 'What's it to be?'

'Draft Bud would be good, thanks, Piper.'

She frowned at him through her sooty eyelashes. 'Do I *know* you?'

'You should do. You and I spent nearly a whole year together once, bickering with each other.'

She peered at him even more intently. 'We weren't *married*, were we?'

'No, we never had the time. We were too busy arguing about the relevance of *Paradise Lost* to a career in the modern catering trade. You said you never saw the point of learning Milton if you were going to work for Burger King.'

'Say what?'

'"Embryos and idiots, eremites and friars – white, black, and gray, with all their trumpery" – and two double cheese-burgers to go.'

Piper clapped her hands to her mouth. 'Mr *Rook*! I can't believe it! This is amazing! What are you *doing* here? It's so good to *see* you! I never had the chance to say sorry for the way I was always talking in class and saying what's the use of English and all. You taught me so *much*! Do you know I can still remember some of that *Paradise Lost*! "My fairest, my espoused, my latest found, Heaven's last best gift, my ever new delight." That sends *chills* down me, these days! Mind you, my husband thinks I'm talking, like, Korean or something.'

'So you're married?'

'Number four, would you believe? I always found it difficult to stick at anything for long. My psychiatrist said I have the lowest boredom threshold of anybody he ever knew. I can get bored crossing the street.'

'I remember. So what's your name now?'

'Mrs Piper Bogdanovich. No – not *that* Bogdanovich! I wish! But I'm very happy. Well, I'm not *unhappy*. Ray's into audio-visual. He sets up public-address systems for weddings, business meetings, stuff like that. You know – "Testing, testing, one two three . . ."'

'How about kids?'

'Only one. He was a little boy. Stillborn. Well, you know. But I can still remember *Paradise Lost*. Don't ask me why. He would have been five next Tuesday.'

'I'm sorry.'

'Well . . . you can't be sorry for ever. I don't even remember who his father was. But I was going to call him Kenny, if he'd lived. After *my* father.'

Jim took hold of her hand. 'Piper . . . can you remember when Jane Tullett drowned?'

'Jane Tullett? How could I forget it? That was so *awful*! That was the last day of the summer semester, wasn't it? I liked Jane. We weren't close or anything, but I liked her.' She blinked at Jim, and said, 'Are you asking me all of this stuff for a *reason*?'

'That day when Jane drowned, I wonder if you saw anything unusual, that's all.'

'Like what? The pool was so crowded and everybody was splashing.'

'Were you close to Jane when her body was discovered?'

'Sure, pretty close. Me and Rachel Mendosky were splashing water at Dick Ramon and some other guy.'

'Who else was around you?'

'I don't know . . . I can't really remember. I know it was Jennie Bauer who first saw Jane lying under the water. She was screaming like you couldn't believe.'

'Who was Jane's closest friend at college, would you say?'

'Oh, Mary Weiland, of course. Do you remember Mary? Very frizzy hair, like one of those big tumbleweed things you see rolling around in cowboy movies. They were so close, though, she and Jane. They even shared lip gloss. Yeuch! I wouldn't share my lip gloss with *anybody*.'

'Me neither,' said Jim. 'You don't know where she is these days, do you, Mary?'

'No, I don't. But Rachel would know. I'll give you her number.'

At that moment, a fat man in dark glasses came out of the rear of the bar and said, 'Come on, Piper! Quit gassing! You got work to do!'

Jim turned on his stool and looked around the bar. Apart from him, there were only three people in there, two men and a blowsy woman in a leopard-spotted leotard who was smoking a cigarette in a long cigarette holder and arguing with one of the men in a voice as harsh as a nutmeg grater.

Piper picked up a ballpen and wrote Rachel's number on the palm of Jim's hand. The fat man said, 'Hey! Dates you can fix up after hours!'

'He's my teacher, not my date,' Piper retorted. 'He taught me all about Milton.'

'*Milton?* You mean Milton, North Dakota? What the hell for?'

As Jim left the Black Velvet Alligator he was almost blinded by the bright sunlight. But as he unhooked his sunglasses from the front of his polo-shirt he noticed a quick, semi-transparent flicker on the far side of San Vicente – like the wavering heat from a midsummer barbecue.

The sidewalk opposite was jostling with people, which made it difficult for him to distinguish what he had seen. But as his eyes became more accustomed to the glare, he picked out a barely visible figure moving through the crowds. It was no more substantial than a bending of the light, but as it passed it created a ripple in the air that Jim found that he could just about follow, if he shaded his eyes.

He kept pace with the figure as it made its way eastward; and then he crossed San Vicente at the next intersection and kept it in sight as it made its way northward on Hauser. The sidewalk here was almost deserted, so he could follow it much more easily. As it walked by a restaurant window, it appeared to distort the glass; and when it passed in front of a mailbox the letters US MAIL wavered as if he were looking at them through running water.

He began to catch up with it, and now there was no question in his mind who and what it was: Jane Tullett, in her spirit form. But what was she doing here? She must be following him, because the odds of him catching sight of her by accident were far too remote. Yet what did she want? And if she wanted to know where he was going, why was she hurrying away from him?

At the intersection of Hauser and Olympic Boulevard she stopped and turned around. Jim slowed up. He was close enough now to see that she was glistening, as if she were wet, and her hair was stuck to her scalp. He could see right through her to the opposite side of Olympic. He could see automobiles passing to and fro, and a man walking a brindled dog – yet he could see Jane quite distinctly too.

As he came nearer, he saw that she had an expression of terrible coldness on her face. He glanced around to see if there were any readily accessible sources of water close by. A few yards further down Olympic there was a flower shop, Blooming Miracle, with large green buckets of fresh flowers outside; and there was a man outside a Mexican restaurant hosing down the sidewalk, but that was all. Cautiously, he walked right up to Jane until he could have touched her with his outstretched arm, if she had possessed any physical substance. Her expression didn't change. She continued to stare at him as if she were willing him to drop dead on the spot.

'Jane?' he said. 'Jane – I'm trying to find out what happened to you in the pool that day. But you have to help me.'

Jane said nothing, but didn't take her glassy, empty eyes off him.

'Jane, listen – I need to know if somebody drowned you deliberately, or if it was an accident. If somebody did drown you, I can put things right. I can make sure that they're punished. I can settle your spirit and give you peace.'

A convertible Mustang drew up alongside him, with two young women in it. As they waited for the red traffic signal to change, they gradually became aware that Jim was talking to thin air.

'Jane, I know you're angry and I know you feel that I let you down. But you can't go on taking your anger out on other people. Tell me what happened, please.'

One of the girls in the car called out, 'Looks like she left you already, buddy, or hadn't you noticed?'

Jim looked around. 'I'm an actor,' he lied. 'I'm, you know, rehearsing my lines.'

But when he turned back, Jane's spirit had flickered away across Olympic. She walked diagonally across the intersection and passed through a huge red refrigerated truck as if it had no substance at all. Jim called out, '*Hey!*' and immediately ran after her, dodging his way through the traffic. A taxi driver blew his horn at him and yelled out, 'You lunatic! You got some kind of a death wish?'

Jim reached the other side of the avenue, looking desperately left and right to see which way Jane had gone. There seemed to be no sign of her anywhere – and he had to face the possibility that she could have simply walked through a wall and disappeared, like she had in the showers at college. He was just about to turn westward when he saw the hose-water that was running across the sidewalk outside the Mexican restaurant. For a split second, it formed into two bare disembodied feet, one of them with half an ankle. The man who was holding the hose didn't even notice as the feet splashed across the water and then vanished – although they left six or seven footprints on the hot dry concrete on the other side.

Jim went running after her. He saw the briefest quiver of light and then she disappeared around the next corner. '*Jane!*' he shouted. 'Jane, you have to help me!' A telephone engineer perched up on a utility pole stared at him, mystified. There was nobody else in the street at all. 'Jane!' he called again. But now she was walking very fast, as if she had suddenly made up her mind to do something important. She reached the end of the street and turned right. Jim went jogging after her. He was already out of breath and sweaty, and his polo shirt was clinging to him.

At the end of the next street there was an Amoco gas station. Jane walked toward it and crossed the forecourt between the pumps. She headed right for the drive-through car-wash, which was already halfway through sudsing a large green Lincoln.

Oh Christ. Water – gallons of it. And who knew what kind of murderous intent she had on her mind. Jim yelled out, '*Jane!*' and sprinted across the gas station as fast as he could, trying to catch up with her before she disappeared into the spray.

She stood for a second beside the car-wash, motionless, almost as if she were waiting for him to catch up with her. The warm breeze blew the water into clouds, and the clouds settled on her, so that Jim could gradually see her physical outline appearing, shimmering with rainbows.

'Jane,' he said, coming closer. He could feel the water prickling softly against his cheek. 'I don't know what you want. I don't know what you're trying to do. But this isn't the way. Drowning other people isn't going to bring you back. You have to move on. You've lived out your life. It's over, even though it was short. Now you have to dream the dream. That's your future . . . someplace out there.'

The figure stayed still, staring at him. Only a few feet away the car-wash started to shoot out detergent, and flecks of foam blew between them like dirty snow.

'Jane . . . you were one of my favorite students. I loved you. I love you still. But I'm begging you. Don't hurt anybody else.'

Jane moved toward him. Her face was iridescent; her hair shone like diamonds. She reached out with watery hands and took hold of his arms, and he could actually feel her, slippery and cold.

'Jane . . . make me a promise. Don't hurt anybody else.'

She looked up at him with her colorless eyes, and she could have been smiling at him, smiling indulgently.

'Jane . . . remember what we talked about in Special Class II. We talked about showing our feelings, didn't we? We talked about explaining ourselves. That's what the English language is all about, isn't it? It gives us the power to ask for what we want. You learned all of those lessons, like everybody else. Tell me why you're drowning people. Tell me why you tried to drown *me*.'

Jane lowered her head, and for a moment Jim thought that she was going to answer him. But then, without warning, she gripped both of his wrists and twisted him sideways, so that he lost his balance. The next thing he knew, he was toppling into the car-wash, with soapy water blasting into his face, and nylon brushes whirling toward him. He hit his head against the side of the Lincoln, and dropped to his knees, and then a huge brush assembly knocked him to the ground, stunned.

He tried to stand up, but he was battered again by the brushes, which whipped his face and his arms, and then he was deluged with stinking, recycled water. Coughing and spluttering, he clung to the side of the car, but then he was battered by another torrent of soapy water and a second row of brushes, which lashed his cheeks and stung his eyes and set his ears on fire.

He dropped to the ground and managed to roll underneath the car. But as he did so, he felt a hand seizing one of his ankles, and then the other. He turned his head and saw that Jane was down on her knees, trying to drag him out into the open again.

He kicked at her, but she twisted her watery hand around the cuff of his pants and pulled him even harder. Her strength was unbelievable, but then it wasn't simply the strength of a twenty-year-old girl – it was the unimaginable strength of a natural element. Jane wasn't just Jane any more; she was the full malevolent power of polluted water. She was the Swimmer.

Grunting with effort, Jim tried to get a grip on anything he could. The Lincoln's exhaust pipe was far too hot, and he scorched his knuckles – but he snatched at the parking-brake cable and held on to that.

Inch by inch, however, the Swimmer managed to pull him out. The brake cable cut deeply into his fingers and when she gave him a final, violent wrench he tore the skin off the palm of his hand and he had to let go. She climbed on to him and pinned him down against the concrete, staring down into his face with chilling intensity.

'*What happened in the pool that day?*' she demanded. Her face kept shifting and changing as the water-spray traveled along the length of the car. '*Everybody was there . . . everybody must have seen what happened. . . but none of you lifted a finger to save me. I was drowning, and all you did was laugh!*'

Jim tried to speak but the car-wash gantry was almost directly above him now, and high-pressure water was cascading into his face. He thrashed his head from side to side, spitting and snorting, but the Swimmer seized his hair with one hand and forced his head back so that the water poured directly into his mouth and up his nose. At the same time, she reached out with her other hand and held on to the gantry to stop it from moving any further along.

God, thought Jim, *I'm drowning*. No matter how hard he struggled, the Swimmer had him locked hard against the ground, and the water kept gushing into his face, gallons and gallons of it, stinking and thick with wax. He kept his eyes closed and his mouth tight shut, but he knew that he was going to have to take a breath before long – and all he could breathe was water.

Suddenly, however, he heard somebody shouting. He half opened one eye and saw two men in red Amoco overalls kneeling down beside the car-wash. 'Hey, you two! What do you think you're doing in there? You want to get yourselves killed?'

Almost at the same time, the car-wash abruptly stopped pumping, and the water was shut off. He looked up at the Swimmer and for a split second she was shining and perfectly formed, even though she was made out of nothing but filthy water. He thought he saw her smile at him. Not a smile of forgiveness or of understanding, but a smile of mockery. Then with a clatter she collapsed, and vanished.

Jim saw her spirit rise like nothing more substantial than a sunlit reflection and walk away from the gas station, but of course he was the only one who did. The two Amoco attendants came over and helped him up and then they looked around in bewilderment.

'Hey, man – what happened to the girl?'

'What girl?' he said. He reached up and tore off a sheet of paper towel so that he could press it over his injured hand. The graze wasn't serious, but it was bleeding all down his wrist and it stung.

'You was in there with a girl. Where the hell did she go?'

'I tripped, that's all. Fell into the car-wash. The brushes caught me, almost knocked me out.'

'You was in there with a girl. If you want to know the truth, we thought you was doing it.'

'In a car-wash? What do you think I am, some kind of pervert?'

The attendant bent down and looked under the car. Then he walked around the car-wash to the other side. 'I swear to God I saw a girl. I swear it. You saw a girl, didn't you, Freddie?'

The other attendant didn't say anything, but kept on looking around the gas station in stupefaction.

At that moment, the Lincoln's door opened and the driver managed to struggle out.

'What's going on? Do I get my car washed, or what?'

'I totally and utterly saw a girl,' the attendant persisted. 'You saw her, Freddie, didn't you?'

'Girl?' said the driver. 'I didn't see no girl.'

'Don't worry about it,' said Jim. 'Sometimes things aren't all they appear to be.'

With that he limped out of the gas station and back toward Olympic. His hand hurt, his knees were bruised and his head was thumping, but he was all the more determined to find out what had happened to Jane Tullett on the day that she drowned.

He met Mary Weiland on the boardwalk at Venice Beach. She had set up a little folding card table to sell hand-made silver earrings and bracelets. She hadn't changed as much as Piper, except that she had cut her frizzy hair very short and covered it with a blue silk bandanna. She was a petite girl with a round, doll-like face and big round sunglasses with yellow plastic frames. She wore a pink bikini top, blue Daisy Dukes and high cork-heeled sandals.

'Mary . . . how are things with you?'

'Hi, Mr Rook. Pretty good.' She had a high, piping voice that went with her looks. 'Hey – did you have a fight with somebody?'

Jim tenderly touched the bruise on his forehead, and winced. 'I had a disagreement with a car-wash, and lost.'

'A *car-wash*? You were always a true original, Mr Rook, I'll give you that.'

'These yours?' he said, picking up one of her bracelets.

'You like them? I make them myself. They're not exactly Cartier, but they help to pay the rent.'

'They're good. They're dangly. I like dangly.'

'You said you wanted to talk about Jane.'

'That's right. You and she were very close, weren't you?'

'Like sisters. I still miss her, even now.'

'Did she ever have a serious argument with anybody at college? Was there anybody at West Grove who really didn't like her?'

'What's this about?'

'I need to know what happened the day she drowned. The coroner said it was an accident. It sure looked like an accident. But now I'm beginning to think that maybe it wasn't.'

'You mean somebody drowned her?'

'I don't know for sure. Did Jane ever argue with her boyfriend?'

'George? For sure, she was *always* arguing with George. Well, he was a great-looking guy, wasn't he? Even *I* liked him, and I never normally went for jocks. He was always dating other girls and then Jane would find out and she would throw books at him and stuff. But they always got back together. I think they would've gotten married, if she hadn't died.'

'Was she involved with any other boys?'

'Not really. But there was this real creepy dude who used to follow her around all the time and send her notes saying how much he adored her. What was his name? He had so much acne we used to call him the Human Pizza. I know – Chris Bayless. I shudder even now. He was always sniffing and wiping his hands together like they were wet, which they probably were.'

'I remember Chris,' Jim nodded. 'Poor guy's mother contracted MS and his father ran off with another woman. He had to do everything at home – cook, clean, take his mother to the bathroom. Then he had to study too.'

'Now you've made me feel so *mean*.'

'Well, you weren't to know. But I can see why a guy like Chris was attracted to Jane. She was always so full of life, wasn't she?'

'There were a couple of girls that Jane didn't particularly get along with.'

'Oh, yes?'

'Vickie Albertyn was one. They had some argument about a dress that Jane had lent her, and which she never gave back. And, like, Vickie always denied that she still had it. And there was another girl, I never found out who it was, but Jane said that she was always flirting with George. Apparently this girl told George all kinds of lies about Jane – like she was incredibly promiscuous and that she had two abortions before she was sixteen. Real nasty stuff, none of it true.'

'Jane didn't give you any idea who she was?'

'Unh-hunh. She only told me about it the morning before she died. When I asked her, all she said was something like "Can't you guess?" and then George came over and whisked her off and she didn't have the chance to tell me. But she was real mad about it, I can tell you that.'

'Hmm . . . I wonder who that was.'

'I guess you could ask George. He'd know, wouldn't he?'

'Good idea. Meanwhile, how about selling me a pair of those dangly earrings? I know somebody who'd really go for those.'

He chatted to Mary a little longer and then walked back to his car. As he unlocked the door, he paused for a moment to watch two girls who were roller-blading in figures of eight. In between them, he was sure he could see an unnatural shimmer of light – a shimmer that could have been another girl, in another existence.

He climbed into his car and backed out of his parking-space. After all, he was only a hundred yards from the seashore here, and, if the shimmer of light was Jane Tullett's spirit, the ocean would give her all the water she needed to drown him and half the people on the boardwalk.

Thirteen

Karen was pleased with her silver-and-amethyst earrings, and with the huge bunch of lilies he bought to go with them. 'You're not trying to bribe me now, are you?'

'I'm just trying to show you that I'm a reformed character. I'm no longer a slob. My sock drawer is still ship-shape, I've hoovered the car, and I haven't eaten anything directly out of a can since yesterday morning.'

'When do you think you'll be going to Washington?' she said. They were sitting at a sidewalk table outside the Hungry Harlequin, drinking coffee and eating cinnamon donuts. Karen was wearing tiny sunglasses with very dark lenses so it was difficult for Jim to read her expression.

'I'm still aiming for Sunday evening . . . my flight's booked and everything. But I'm not going to go until I've exorcized this water spirit, or whatever I have to do to put her to rest. She might try to drown *you*.'

'I think I can look after myself.'

'Unh-hunh. Not against this thing you can't. I only wish I could find a way to give her some peace.'

'She wants justice, doesn't she?'

'Sure. But there's justice and justice. Somebody might be a murderer, but you don't punish him by killing his friends and relatives, do you?'

'Did you talk to George Opal?'

Jim shook his head. 'He's in Tokyo, at some business conference. I might be able to catch him tonight, when he's having breakfast.'

'What if Jane's making a mistake? What if she *did* drown by accident? How are you going to convince her that it was nobody's fault but her own?'

'I don't know. If I can't persuade her to stop drowning people – you know, voluntarily – I'll have to find some other way to get rid of her.'

'Such as?'

'Search me. But Susan Silverstone's doing some research into vengeful elemental spirits, and so is Laura.'

'You'll be careful, won't you?'

'Sure I'll be careful. I want to live long enough to twist your arm into coming to Washington with me.'

Karen smiled, and held his hand. 'You never give up, do you?'

He was paying the check when his mobile phone warbled. It was David DuQuesne. 'Jim – I hope I'm not disturbing you, but after we talked about the Swimmer I started to think that it might be worthwhile doing a little research into it. I've come up with something that you'll be very interested to see.'

'Okay . . . give me a half-hour, and I'll be up there.'

Karen said, 'Don't tell me, you have to rush off.'

'I'm sorry – but after I've sorted out the Swimmer we can spend a whole day together. Two whole days. A lifetime, if you want.'

'Jim – there'll always be a Swimmer. Well, maybe not a Swimmer, but some other spirit that you have to deal with.'

'I told you: when I go to Washington I'm going to be through with all that. I don't care if spirits come knocking on my door all night, I'm not going to answer any more. I can't accept the responsibility for every supernatural manifestation I see – even if I *am* the only one who can see it.'

'And if they threaten your friends and the people you love, like the Swimmer?'

'Well, that's different.'

'No, Jim, it's not different. It's just more of the same. Don't you realize why I can't go with you? It's not really your untidiness or your taste in music. It's your gift. Or your curse, or whatever you want to call it. How can I live with somebody who feels he constantly has to fight against dangers the rest of us can't even see? You were almost drowned today. What happens if you come up against a spirit that's much too powerful for you to cope with?'

'Karen, you have to trust me.'

'I do trust you. But not to ignore ghosts and demons when you see them.'

The car-hop drove up in Karen's Saab convertible, and she climbed into it. Jim gave her a kiss and said, 'I'll call you later. Watch out for anything watery, won't you?'

She drove away and he stood outside the café watching her go.

'Sir?' said the car-hop, after a while.

'What? Yes, sure, you can bring my car around.'

'I'd like to, sir, but the muffler's fallen off.'

It cost $27 for a taxi to take him up to David DuQuesne's house in Hidden Valley. The air-conditioning wasn't working properly and by the time they arrived he was slithery with sweat.

'You want me to wait?' asked the taxi driver.

'No, but next time I feel like a Turkish bath I'll know who to call.'

David DuQuesne came out on to the verandah to greet him, his dogs scrabbling on the deck as bloodthirstily as they had before. 'You look hot,' he remarked. 'I'll have Amy bring you a beer.'

He released the dogs and for a split second Jim thought they were going to pounce on him, but they tore straight past him, almost knocking him over, and bounded off into the grounds. 'They smell rabbit,' said David DuQuesne. 'Much more exciting than cat.'

He ushered Jim inside and through to a cool and elegant study with a large desk of limed oak and a collection of twisted sculptures made from driftwood. On the desk were arranged about a dozen color prints, five-by-fours, and six or seven black-and-whites.

'Whenever I'm investigating an urban legend, I always find that one photograph is worth a million words. What do we all remember about Bigfoot? Not the sworn testimony of the men who saw him walking through the woods, but that one blurry picture.'

Jim picked up one of the black-and-white photographs. It showed a crowd of young people in a swimming-pool, waving their arms. At the foot of the photograph was the typed caption: `June 9, 1991: Hi-jinks in the pool at West Grove Community College to celebrate the year's end.`

'A friend of mine works in the photo library at the *Los Angeles Times*,' said David DuQuesne. 'I asked her to dig up every picture she could find of the day when Jane Tullett was drowned.'

'And? Do they tell you anything?'

'I think they do, yes. I've placed them in chronological sequence. Here – look: this shows Jane being lifted out of the water after she was drowned. She's wearing this distinctive navy-and-white swimsuit with diagonal stripes. That's how I was able to identify her in this first picture in the sequence. Here – in picture one – we have a general view of the pool, with everybody jumping around and splashing . . . but in the background Jane is making her way toward the diving boards. You can't see her face but there's no mistaking that costume.

'In this second picture we can see her climbing the ladder to the top board . . . and there she is, that's a very good shot of her just before she dived . . . arms spread, back straight – excellent posture.'

Jim picked up the fourth picture. 'I can't see her in this one . . . there's just a whole crowd of students.'

'Ah, but you can see her if you magnify it. I put it through my computer scanner and zoomed it up. Here . . . those look like nothing but waving arms underneath the diving board, but right *there* you can see Jane's legs as she disappeared into the water.' He drew a circle with a red marker. 'As you can see, it's a clean dive, and she doesn't appear to have struck anybody else.'

'The coroner said that she could have hit her head on the bottom.'

'I don't think that's likely, when you consider that she went into the water at the proper angle, and the water was certainly deep enough to prevent her from striking the floor of the pool.'

'What am I looking at in this next picture?'

'This is the most interesting picture of all. Again, I had to enlarge it to make sense of it. But if you look right down here in the bottom left-hand corner you can just make out a swimming cap and a pair of eyes breaking the surface of the water, close to the side. That's Jane, coming up after her dive . . . and you can see from her eyes that she doesn't look at all concussed.

'Now look at all the students around her. They're wildly splashing each other, and so many of them have their eyes closed or half closed, it's not surprising that they didn't see Jane coming up.'

Jim examined the photograph carefully. He recognized Piper and Mary, not far away from Jane's emerging head, but they were facing the opposite direction. However, there was another girl, much nearer to Jane, and she actually had her face turned toward her . . . so she must have seen her.

'Do you know who that is?' asked David DuQuesne.

Jim took off his glasses and peered at the photograph even more closely. 'She looks blonde, doesn't she . . . but all you can see is the back of her head.'

'I've located her in four other pictures, but you can't see her clearly in any of them. But look at this.'

The next picture showed the same girl even closer to the side of the pool, holding on to the rail with her right hand. Her left hand was out of sight below the water. The water was so churned up that it was impossible to see clearly below the surface, but David DuQuesne produced an enormous blow-up of the area where the girl's left hand would probably have been. And just below it, there was a distorted pattern of diagonal stripes.

'This isn't conclusive proof, by any means,' said David DuQuesne. 'But it looks to me as if Jane executed a perfect dive and came up safely. But this girl in the photograph struck Jane's head against the side of the pool and then deliberately held her under water until she drowned.'

David DuQuesne showed Jim the next and last picture,

which showed Jane lying at the poolside while the swimming coach was trying to revive her. Jim recognized a much younger version of himself, in sunglasses, and most of the rest of Special Class II.

'I think these pictures are unique,' said David DuQuesne. 'They show the actual moment when an urban legend came into being. I've made my whole living out of urban legends, but there's rarely any incontrovertible proof that they actually happened. But this one, my friend – this is something special. Not only that – if you can identify the young lady who's holding Jane underwater, then you've got yourself a halfway decent chance of appeasing Jane's spirit, and putting her to rest for ever.'

'Why do you think Jane herself didn't tell me who it was, at Gabriel Dragonard's seance?'

'My guess is that she doesn't know. She came to the surface – *bang*! – her head was knocked against the side of the pool, and she was pushed back under before she had the chance to catch her breath. It's obvious from the random way that the Swimmer is drowning your friends and your students that she blames *all* of you . . . and especially you. She considers that you were ultimately responsible for her safety, and that you let her down. Or even that you and your class were actually part of a conspiracy to drown her.'

'That's crazy, why should she ever think that?'

'Vengeful spirits get some pretty strange ideas into their heads, Jim. Especially when they died so young.'

'Can you make me some copies of these pictures? I can show them to Piper and Mary and some of the other students who were there at the time.'

'Sure. I'll print some off now. There's one important thing you have to think about, though.'

'Oh, yes?'

'What are you going to do when you *do* identify the girl who drowned her? Are you going to report her to the police; or summon up Jane's spirit and have her confess to her, and apologize; or what?'

'I don't know. I was hoping you were going to tell me

that. I don't have a whole lot of experience when it comes to exorcizing urban legends.'

'I don't either, I'm afraid. You think I wouldn't have gone back and exorcized Mad Frank Butler if I knew how to do it? Jane Tullett's spirit deserves some rest in heaven, but Mad Frank Butler deserves to go to hell.'

'You still think about your brother, huh?'

David DuQuesne's face was momentarily illuminated by the light from his photocopier. 'Every day, Jim. Every single day. It's what gives my life purpose.'

Laura Killmeyer was waiting for him when he got home, sitting on the steps outside his apartment building with Mervyn, who was entertaining her with his notorious alternative version of 'Strawberry Fields'.

'How's it going, Mr Rook?' she asked him, one eye screwed up tight against the sunshine. She was looking a little more like her old sorceress self this afternoon, in a purple T-shirt with gold stars sewn on it, a pair of black satin pedal pushers and gold-painted Nike shoes.

Jim tiredly rubbed the back of his neck. 'I think I'm making some progress . . . but I had another run-in with the Swimmer.'

'Hey – are you okay?' asked Mervyn. 'I thought you were looking a little under the weather.'

'Under the car-wash, more like,' Jim said, and told him what had happened.

Mervyn said, 'It's unbelievable. You're not going to be safe anywhere at all until you get rid of this thing. You won't even be able to leave the faucet running while you wash your teeth.'

They went up to Jim's apartment. Tibbles Two was sleeping outside on the balcony, although he saw her ear prick up and swivel around to follow what they were saying. Jim laid out the photographs of the West Grove College swimming pool on the table and showed Laura and Mervyn how Jane Tullett had been drowned.

'It shouldn't be too hard to find out who this girl is,' said

Mervyn. 'Her swimsuit's not particularly distinctive, but she does have some kind of dolphin motif on it, see?'

Laura said, 'I can't believe that she managed to drown Jane in front of all of those people and nobody saw her do it.'

'It's the old trick of doing something in plain sight,' said Jim. 'If people don't expect to see you drowning somebody right in front of them, they won't. Anyhow – Laura, what did you manage to dig out of those old books of yours?'

'I looked up water spirits in every single one of them, and there's a whole lot of stuff about kelpies and shellybacks and all kinds of horrible spirits that can drag you into the sea and drown you. And there's something about Swimmers, too. I don't think David DuQuesne was completely right . . . Swimmers appeared in the seventeenth century, so they're not just a modern phenomenon. The Puritans wrote about them as far back as 1659. But what you said Michael told you about polluted water, *that* was right. As far as I can make out, the only times when Swimmers appeared was when people were drowned in slimy stagnant ponds or wells tainted with sewage. So, like he said, the water itself was sick, so the spirits in the water were sick.'

'Good work. But did any of your books suggest how to get rid of water spirits?'

'Not really. In the seventeenth century people tried to have them exorcized by a priest, but that never seemed to do any good. The Swimmers only appeared to be satisfied once they had drowned everybody who had taken part in drowning *them*, and their friends, and their children, and sometimes their livestock too. Sixty-five head of cattle walked into the ocean off Providence in 1789, and all of them were pulled under, one by one, and drowned.'

'Well, that's reassuring – not,' said Mervyn. 'From now on I'm going to take an aqualung into the tub.'

'There was only one mention of a Swimmer being completely exorcized,' said Laura. She rummaged in her bag and brought out a tatty old book with a broken spine. 'It's in this book . . . *De La Demonomanie des Sorciers*, by Jean Bodin. Look, I've marked the page. It was in Newbury Old Town,

Massachusetts, in 1659. A woman called Biddy Morley was ducked in the town pond for being a scold. They kept her under for too long and she drowned, but five years later, on the anniversary of her death, she came back, "the verrie image of her, but fashion'd from water".

'According to this, she dragged her husband into the pond and drowned him. And anybody in Newbury Old Town who had witnessed her drowning, or given evidence against her for being a scold, they were drowned, too – either in the pond or in a water-butt – and one man drowned while walking on the seashore.'

'So what did they do to get rid of her?' asked Jim.

'They could never catch her, because she was made of nothing but water. But one day they persuaded one of the local wives to act as bait. She was bathing in a wooden tub in front of the fire when the Swimmer appeared right out of the water in front of her and tried to drown her . . . just the way Mervyn was almost drowned. But her husband and two other men had been hiding in the next room. As soon as the woman screamed, they pulled her out of the tub and threw bucketfuls of blazing pitch over the Swimmer. Her spirit had no time to escape, and her physical form was evaporated, *pfff*, into a cloud of steam. Bodin says here, "There was such screaming and exhalation of steam that they thought they had conjur'd up all the demons from hell."'

'So that's it,' said Mervyn. 'You have to fry the bastards.'

'I don't know whether we can be sure of that,' Jim told him. 'I mean, how old is this *De La Demonomanie des Sorciers*? You wouldn't trust a road map published in 1778, would you?'

Laura said, 'I'm not making any recommendations, Mr Rook. I'm just saying that the only authority on vengeful water spirits that I could find was Jean Bodin; and he says that using another element is the only answer. Fire to fight water, just like water fights fire. He calls it "the evaporation and the sterilization of the evil spirit".'

Jim went to the icebox and came back with his last two beers, which he popped open and shared between the three of them. 'The problem is – even if setting fire to this spirit is going to work – how are we going to trap it and put it into a position where we *can* set fire to it? Jesus, I tried to boil a live lobster once. Getting that monster into the pot was like going three rounds with Jesse Ventura.'

'I had a dream about Jesse Ventura once,' mused Mervyn. 'He was rubbing maple syrup all over my back.'

'Mervyn . . . if this fire thing is the only way to get rid of Jane Tullett's spirit, then we're going to need somebody to act as bait. A Judas goat, that's what they call it, isn't it, when you tie up a goat as bait for a lion.'

'Well, don't look at me. I was almost drowned the last time.'

'I don't even know if using fire against the Swimmer is going to work,' said Laura. 'Like you said, these are very old books. I know that the kids in all of these television shows like *Buffy* and *Charmed* find old magic books and they discover the secret spell and everything's okay, but this isn't television, is it? This is real life, and the Swimmer today could be something way different from what it was in 1659.'

'That's true. But so far we don't have any alternative, do we?'

'I might remind you of something else,' put in Mervyn. 'According to that necklace you bought at the psychic fair, you only have six more days to live. So if I were you, Jim, I'd try to torch this Swimmer as soon as you possibly can.'

'You don't believe in that, do you?' asked Laura. 'I mean, spirits are one thing . . . but telling the future? I do tea-leaf readings and I look in mirrors to tell people who they're going to marry. But that's just fun, most of it. I wouldn't ever dare to predict when somebody's going to *die*.'

'Who knows?' said Jim. 'After the Swimmer, I'm beginning to think that anything's possible.'

He took a taxi back down to the Black Velvet Alligator. It was six o'clock before he managed to get there, and Piper was just finishing her shift, wiping the tabletops and emptying the ashtrays. 'Give you a ride home?' he suggested.

'No, sorry. Ray always comes by to pick me up. He's the possessive type.'

'I'm your teacher, Piper. I'm nearly old enough to be your father. Well, I could have been, if I'd have had a willing girlfriend when I was eleven.'

'I know. But you're still a man, and Ray wouldn't see it that way.'

'Okay . . . no problem. But how about taking a quick look at these photographs for me? They were taken by a freelance news photographer the day that Jane drowned. There's somebody I need to identify.'

Piper folded a stick of chewing-gum into her mouth. 'It's so weird to see all of these people again . . . Look, there's *me*! Wasn't I *frumpy*! I'm amazed I ever had any boyfriends at all!'

'You weren't frumpy – you were gorgeous.'

'Don't tell Ray that. Please. He'll go ape.'

Jim pointed to the girl in the plain swimsuit with the dolphin motif. 'Her – do you recognize her?'

Piper squinted closely at the photograph, chewing noisily with her mouth open. 'Yeah . . . I think I know who that is. There's only one person it could be, judging from the way we're all standing and all. That's Jennie Bauer. Like I told you, she was the first person to find out that Jane was drowned.'

'You're sure about that?'

'One hundred and ten per cent. Look at this picture here, that's her . . . she always wore these love-bracelets around her wrist. One for every boyfriend, she said. Well, that's what she *said*.'

Jim collected up the photographs and shuffled them straight. 'Thanks, Piper. You'll get your reward in heaven for this.'

'What did I do?'

'I can't tell you yet. But you've been a fantastic help.'

'Hey – you're not saying that it was Jennie Bauer who drowned Jane, are you?'

'I'm not saying anything yet. But I have to know exactly what happened that morning, and this is a very good start.'

At that moment the bar door opened and a bull-necked young

man in a tight white T-shirt and jeans pushed his way in, his hair cropped to less than a millimeter. He waded across the room as if he were up to his hips in water. As soon as he reached Piper, he threw one arm around her and squeezed her in close, and looked Jim up and down with eyes like steel nailheads.

'Hi,' he said, aggressively.

'You must be Ray,' said Jim, extending his hand. 'I'm . . . Jim.'

Ray ignored his hand and turned to Piper. 'What did I tell you about coming on to these dorks? What did I say?'

Jim said, 'I hope you said, "My fairest, my espoused, my latest found, Heaven's last best gift, my ever new delight".'

Ray turned to him and his mouth was nothing more than a narrow slit. 'What are you, some faggot? Leave my wife alone. She's mine.'

Jim couldn't help smiling. He remembered Piper in class, dreamy and inattentive but always imagining things: castles and princes, wars and coronations.

'Let me give you a word of advice, Ray,' he said as he tucked away his photographs and stood up. 'Piper will never be yours, not in the way you mean it, ever, for as long as she lives. And you won't be doing yourself any favors if you think that she will.'

'Hey, you!' Ray yelled at him, as he walked toward the door. 'Who do you think you are? Who the hell do you think you're talking to? Hey – you come back here, man, nobody talks about my wife like that!'

Jim walked out of the bar and back on to San Vicente, wishing he had kept his mouth shut. But as he turned back, the door swung open for a moment and he glimpsed Piper sitting at the table in the corner. The look on her face reminded him so much of the days when she had sat fiddling and daydreaming in class. She half raised her hand, a kind of weak goodbye. He was really pleased that she had remembered fragments of Milton, even if they were sentimental, and even if they were only fragments. But when things go bad, and you're married to Ray, and you work behind the bar in the Black Velvet Alligator, who wants to be reminded of *Paradise Lost*?

Fourteen

That evening thunder began to grumble over the Santa Monica Mountains, and lightning flashed behind the clouds. Jim picked up his Eldorado from Mr Muffler, under the San Diego Freeway on National, and he was delighted by the understated burble that came out of the engine. Mr Muffler wiped his greasy hands on a rag that was even greasier, and told him that his entire exhaust assembly had been rusting away for months, and that he had been forced to replace the whole length of it, from manifold back to tailpipe, $565 plus tax.

'I've just had to pay $250 for a seance,' Jim protested.

'There you go,' said Mr Muffler, licking his thumb to count out the cash. 'Personally, I never trusted those foreign cars.'

Jim drove to Washington Freeman III's house, pleased by the soft, luxurious whistling of a properly silenced engine, but still irritated by the cost of it. At this rate he wouldn't be able to afford to pay for his air fare to D.C., let alone furnish his apartment, and stock up on groceries, and buy himself the three-piece charcoal-gray suit that he thought his new position in the Department of Education demanded.

Washington was wearing a black T-shirt and baggy khaki combat pants with dozens of pockets all the way down the legs. 'What do you keep in those?' Jim asked him as they pulled away from the curb.

'Essentials,' said Washington, and he sounded offended.

'Essentials? You mean like grenades and stuff? Extra ammunition?'

Washington muttered something under his breath.

'What did you say?' Jim demanded. 'Bombs?'

'I said, condoms.'

'I see. Well, good for you. Better safe than not safe, huh?'

There was a long pause as they drove along Santa Monica. Then Jim said, 'They flavored, or what?'

'What?'

'The condoms. You can get them in strawberry, piña colada, melon flavor, anything.'

'Man, you supposed to be my teacher. I'm not supposed to discuss things like that with my teacher.'

'I was just curious. I was just wondering who you were expecting to jump tonight? Or should I say hump? Would that be more accurate?'

'They're just a precaution.'

'A precaution against humping and jumping?'

'Don't razz me, Mr Rook.'

'You're embarrassed. You cried in class when I read you Emily Dickinson. Were you ever embarrassed about that?'

Washington sniffed and said, 'No. Absolutely not. That was poetry. That wasn't personal.'

'So Emily Dickinson is less embarrassing than condoms?'

'Man,' said Washington, turning around in his seat, 'you always knew how to mess with my mind. I left college Tuesday . . . I ain't never going back. But you're still doing it to me, aintcha? Flavored condoms! You're still messing with my mind.'

'No, I'm not, Washington. You're messing with your *own* mind, nobody else's. And most of all, you mustn't let the Swimmer take control of you. She has all the power of the ocean behind her, all the power of every rancid river and every polluted stream and every acid rainstorm. I don't think we've even started to realize what we're dealing with here. We haven't even scratched the surface! We have to think clearly and logically and never let her twist our imagination.'

They collected Laura and then drove to Jennie Oppenheimer's house. On the way, Jim steered with one hand and showed them the photographs of Jane drowning.

'How come the cops never looked at these?' said Washington.

'They probably did. But what can you really see, unless you *know* that Jane was drowned on purpose – unless she'd told you herself? A wobbly image of a striped swimsuit? A girl clinging on to a handrail? It's not exactly *prima facie* evidence, is it?'

'What if Jennie denies doing it?' asked Laura.

'That's a risk we'll have to take. But if she's got anything like a guilty conscience about it, she'll probably be relieved that we've found out.'

They parked right outside the Oppenheimer house and climbed out of the car. In the distance it was still thundering, but so far there was no sign of rain. Jim rang the doorbell and Jennie answered almost at once. She was wearing a white blouse and a plain black skirt and she was looking flushed, as if she had been baking.

'Mr Rook – Jim – what a surprise!'

'I hope you don't mind us dropping in like this. By the way, these are two former students of mine – Washington Freeman and Laura Killmeyer. They've been helping me to look into what happened to Mikey.'

'Oh, sure. Come on in. Would you like some lemonade? It's awfully hot, isn't it? I wish this weather would break.'

They followed her into the house. Outside in the yard, the pool had been covered over with a blue plastic sheet. Jennie noticed Jim looking at it and said, with a twitchy little smile, 'It's been drained. The house is up for sale, as a matter of fact. Doug and I have decided to go our separate ways. After Mikey died, there didn't seem to be very much left of our marriage.'

'I'm sorry,' said Jim. 'Death takes different people in different ways. Sometimes it brings you closer. Other times – well.'

'Are you sure you won't have some lemonade? I made it fresh – Tracey will be home soon.'

'No, no thanks. I just came to talk to you about something. About Jane Tullett, as a matter of fact, and the way that she drowned.'

Jennie looked blank. 'What about it? She dived, she

hit her head. It was an accident, and it was such a long time ago.'

'The fact is, Jennie, she didn't hit her head. Somebody else hit it for her. And after she'd hit her head, that somebody deliberately held her under the water until she drowned.'

Jennie still looked blank. 'I thought the coroner was satisfied that it was an accident.'

'He was. But the coroner didn't have the advantage of talking to Jane in person. So – even though he had all the evidence – he wasn't able to draw the right inferences from it.'

'What do you mean, the "right inferences"?'

Jim spread the photographs on Jennie's coffee table, next to the copies of *Redbook* and *Architectural Digest*. 'This was the moment that Jane drowned . . . and these are pictures of the girl who drowned her.'

Jennie's expression stiffened. Jim pointed his finger directly to the picture of Jennie clinging on to the handrail, but she wouldn't look at it.

'Recognize yourself?' he asked her. 'The proof is here, Jennie. The proof has been lying in the files of the *Los Angeles Times* for ten years, ever since you did it. The trouble was, the only person who could interpret these photographs was Jane, and she was dead. Nobody would have known about it even now, if Jane hadn't decided to make her presence felt.'

Jennie said, '*Jane* drowned Mikey.'

'Yes, she did. She also drowned Dennis Pease and Gabriel Dragonard and seriously injured Dottie Osias and almost drowned my friend Mervyn, Washington and Laura and me. And so far there's no sign that she's going to stop drowning people, and all because of you.'

'She drowned Mikey,' Jennie repeated, with tears streaming down her face.

'She drowned Mikey because *you* drowned *her*. And the way things are going, she'll probably drown you too, and God knows how many more people besides.'

Jennie lowered her head and covered her eyes with both hands. When she spoke, it was in a low, hurried whisper, as if she were speaking in a confessional. 'Jane had everything that I never had. She was beautiful, she was popular, she was always good at basketball and track. And she had George, and I *adored* George. I adored him! The very first day I walked into college and saw George I knew I had to have him for myself. I did everything I could to win him. I brought him home-made candies, I always dressed in my best. I flirted with him whenever I had the chance. But he never noticed me. I might as well have been transparent, made out of water, like Jane is now.

'Every time he dated some pretty young sophomore, he and Jane would have a fight, and I always prayed that she would leave him and that finally – *finally* – he would turn around and see me standing right next to him and fall in love.

'But it never happened, no matter what I did. And then it was the very last day of college and I knew I had to do something, or else Jane and George would go off together and I would lose him for ever. They were talking about marriage already.'

She paused, took her hands away from her eyes and lifted her head. 'I didn't plan it. It just happened. I was splashing in the pool with everybody else, and I looked up, and there was Jane, just about to dive off the top board. She entered the water only a couple of feet away from me, and under the water I could see her turn and swim toward the side.

'Her head came up. I turned around and nobody was looking in our direction. I grabbed her swimming cap and hit her head against the rail, as hard as I could. Then I pushed her under, and twisted my legs around her neck, and held her under. It was horrible. She seemed to take for ever to drown . . . struggling and hitting and even biting my knee. But in the end she stopped struggling. I counted to a hundred, and then I let her go. That's when I pretended that I had found her. I screamed, and I couldn't stop screaming. It was the shock, I guess . . . and the realization that I had actually killed her.'

There was a long silence. Jennie took a crumpled tissue out

of her sleeve and wiped her eyes. Then she said, 'Now what? Are you going to call Lieutenant Harris?'

'It depends,' said Jim. 'I think we have a choice here.'

'A choice? What kind of a choice? I drowned Jane Tullett. I've just admitted it.'

'Jennie, we need your help. I'm not trying to take the law into my own hands here, but my most urgent priority is to stop Jane from drowning or hurting any more of my students. As far as I can see, you've already suffered the worst punishment that anybody could have inflicted on you: you've lost your son. I could take you to Lieutenant Harris, for sure. But it's far more important that we put Jane's spirit to rest.'

Jennie hesitated for a moment, then she nodded. 'All right. I suppose it's my fault that she's come back, anyhow.'

'What do you mean?'

'I always made a point of being Jane's best friend, so that I could get close to George. I lent her my dresses, I even lent her money once. I took her home to see my parents one weekend. The day before I drowned her we were sitting on the grassy knoll outside of the physics block and she said, "You've been so good to me . . . I promise you that, wherever you are, I'll come back in ten years' time and pay you back for everything you've done for me."

'The next day, she found out what I'd been saying to George – that she'd had dozens of boyfriends, and two abortions. It was all lies, of course. But I was so much in love with George that I thought I had the moral right to win him in any way I could.'

Jennie paused, and then she said, 'She promised she'd come and find me, and pay me back, and she sure did, didn't she?'

Jim said, 'We're going to have to lure Jane's spirit into a trap. The only way we can do that is to use somebody as bait. Somebody that she really wants to hurt. I can't expect Washington or Laura to do it, so I'm asking you. I won't pretend that it's not going to be dangerous. It will be. But maybe you'll think that it's a way of redeeming yourself. If we can exorcize the Swimmer, we won't say any more about these photographs, or what you confessed to us today, and you'll be free to put your life back together again.'

'I never would have taken you for a blackmailer, Jim.'

'Sometimes we have to use whatever methods we have at our disposal. I need to catch the Swimmer, Jennie. Otherwise, God alone knows what's going to happen to us.'

They went round to see Susan Silverstone. She had just returned from a long natural-therapy session in somebody's back yard, and she was looking tired. Michael was in his Medlar Tree ensemble, his face painted chalky white, his eyes painted with black circles, so that it almost looked as if he had two large holes where his eyes should be and his head was empty.

'That was so-o-o exhausting,' said Susan, draping herself on to her brown brocade daybed. 'Every plant in that yard was hysterical. You could feel it the moment you walked out there. It was like they were screaming at me.'

'What was the problem?' asked Laura.

'The owner was the problem. He's so uptight about his career that he goes out every evening and takes all his anger out on his plants. The whole place was shivering with terror.'

'Excuse me, but how do you take your anger out on a plant?' asked Washington.

'The same way you take your anger out on a person. You yell at it. Didn't you know that plants grow better when you talk nicely to them, and play them soothing music? It works the other way around, too. I never saw such a neurotic bougainvillaea in my life.'

Jim said, 'We think we've found a way to put the Swimmer's spirit to rest. We use fire. We trap it, and then we burn it.'

'Talking of burning, I could really use a cup of herbal tea,' said Susan. 'Medlar Tree, would you mind putting on the kettle?'

Medlar Tree nodded, and went through an elaborate mime of pouring out a cup of tea. Then he went through to the kitchen.

'Why does he *do* that?' asked Washington. 'Act like he's dumb and all?'

Susan gave him a weary smile. 'He says that if he puts a mask on his face and doesn't speak for twenty-four hours it purifies his mind. Like drinking mineral water after you've been drinking too much alcohol. It subjugates his identity. Recharges his humility. If you can't speak you can't boast, that's what he says.'

'Oh yeah? How come he can still be such a pain?'

'You'll have to forgive Washington,' said Jim. 'He was one of Special Class II, where eloquence was considered to have a price beyond rubies, and anybody who was dumb was considered to be – well, dumb.'

'Oh, believe me, Michael's far from stupid, even when he puts on his Medlar Tree motley. He's very loyal, too. I couldn't survive without him – and I'm not the only one.'

Jim said, 'Listen – we have to summon up Jane Tullett's spirit, and the only person I can ask to do that is you. I know what the risks are, raising up a manifestation as vengeful as hers, but you won't be alone.'

'You know that Michael won't allow it.'

'This time, I don't care what Michael thinks. I only care what *you* think . . . and I think that *you* think that this situation is right on the edge of being desperate. People are going to die, Susan, and you know it.'

'He won't let me.'

'Can't you decide for yourself? The only reason he won't let you is because he's in love with you and he doesn't want anything to happen to you. But if none of us ever took risks, what the hell kind of a world would this be?'

Susan smoothed back her shiny black hair. Her eyes told him nothing. 'What do you want me to do?' she asked him.

'First of all, we have to have a seance, to bring Jane's spirit through to the place where we want to trap her. Once we've done that, we have to tempt her into taking on the shape of the Swimmer. I don't think that's going to be difficult, because we can make sure that there's plenty of water around, and we can give her somebody that she's more than anxious to drown.'

'Like who?'

'The woman who pushed her under the water at West Grove College, and killed her. It was Jennie Oppenheimer . . . Mikey's mother.'

Susan nodded, and kept on nodding. 'Of course. Jennie Oppenheimer. That doesn't surprise me at all. Do you know something, I had such a strange feeling about her when we first went to her house to do the spirit-trace. She had such a disconnected aura, like she was trying to hide something from me. And it seemed really unusual for anyone to come to the conclusion so quickly that their son was drowned by a vengeful spirit – even if she *did* see footprints beside the pool, and the bushes moving like somebody had just walked through them. I mean, a vengeful spirit: that's the very last thing that most people would be prepared to believe.'

'Jennie has a real bad conscience about what she did to Jane all those years ago and she's prepared to help. In return – well, I've agreed not to report her to the police.'

'I hope she realizes how dangerous it could be.'

'She does, yes. I've warned her. But she says she's still prepared to do it. She's grief-stricken about Mikey, of course she is. But I think she's still genuinely guilty about what she did to Jane . . . and what Jane's spirit has been doing to get her revenge.'

'So, what's your plan?'

'You raise up Jane's spirit. Once you've done that, I'll be able to see her – so we'll know where she is and what she's going to do next. We'll fill the bathtub, which will give her all the water she needs to turn herself into the Swimmer – and Jennie will be in the bathroom too.'

'Then what?'

'Once she takes shape as the Swimmer, we pull Jennie clear, and then we throw gasoline all over her, and set her alight. We have to fight one element with another – at least as far as Laura's old occult books tell us.'

'And where are you planning on doing this? Not here, I hope? I don't want you burning the whole place down!'

'No . . . we'll do it back at my apartment in Venice. Everything's packed up and ready for me to move. The bathroom's all tiled, so there won't be much of a risk of the fire getting out of control. And just to be doubly safe, I'll borrow a couple of fire extinguishers from college.'

'I don't know,' said Susan. 'I'd be willing to do it, but I don't think Michael is going to approve.'

'Can't you make your own decision?'

'You still don't understand, do you? Michael saved my life, and every minute of every day he goes on saving my life. I'm carrying a time-bomb inside me, Jim. A time-bomb that could explode at any second, and kill me. I have to be grateful to Michael for every breath that I take.'

She hadn't even finished speaking when they heard a high-pitched gargle from the kitchen, followed by the crash of crockery. It was Medlar Tree. Washington jumped and said, 'Jesus! I thought that guy was dumb!' But all the same he barged his way through to the kitchen, Jim and Susan and Laura following close behind him.

Medlar Tree was standing over the sink with his back to them. He had stopped gargling but he was quivering violently, as if he had just been electrocuted. He had dropped a large Chinese teapot on to the floor, where it was lying broken in three pieces. He was making an odd grunting noise, '*Unh, unh, unh*,' as if he were finding it difficult to breathe. Jim and Washington cautiously approached him.

'Michael – Medlar Tree – what's happening? What's wrong?'

Michael still didn't answer. Maybe he didn't want to talk to them. Either that or he still refused to break his vow of silence.

'Michael, come on – tell me what's wrong.'

Jim came closer, and it was only then that he saw that Medlar Tree was being gripped by the throat by a transparent arm reaching out of the sink . . . an arm that was made of nothing but steaming water. His white make-up was dripping and his cheeks were streaked with black. The watery fingers had a tight grip around his Adam's apple and his whole neck was scalded scarlet.

'Holy shit,' said Washington. He reached out toward the arm, to pull it away from Medlar Tree's throat, but Jim said, 'Don't! That's boiling hot water!'

'Then what?'

Jim wildly looked around. 'Then – then – turn on the Insinkerator.'

'Say what?'

'The Insinkerator! Turn it on!'

Washington flicked down the switch of the sink disposal unit, and there was a sudden blurt of noise. The arm twisted around and around, still clinging on to Medlar Tree's throat, and then suddenly it spun faster and faster and was whipped away down the drain. Within seconds it had vanished.

Jim soaked a dishcloth in icy cold water and clapped it over Medlar Tree's face and held it there. Washington guided him back to the kitchen table and helped him to sit down.

'Michael, are you okay? Come on, Michael, tell me what happened.'

'I was warming the teapot,' Medlar Tree whispered, still trembling . . . 'I filled it with boiling water, swilled it around and threw it down the sink. Then *wham*. It came back up at me and tried to strangle me.'

'How do you feel now?'

'Better, thanks. My face is still burning.'

'Why don't you go take that make-up off? Then we can see if you need to go to hospital.'

'I'm okay, I'm fine. I'm just shocked, that's all. That water came up and grabbed me like a goddamned conger eel. I couldn't breathe. Couldn't even move . . . it was pressing my nerve.'

'All right, now, take it easy.'

Susan was standing in the doorway, looking fraught. 'Michael, are you okay? If anything ever happened to you . . .'

'I'm okay, I'm fine. Let my get my breath back, that's all.'

'It was *her*, wasn't it?' said Susan. 'It was the Swimmer.'

'I'm afraid so,' Jim told her. 'It's just like I told you. Anybody I know . . . anybody who's been helping me . . . she's going to try to drown them all.'

'In that case, we have to do something about her,' said Michael. 'We have to summon her up, like you said, and we have to burn her.'

'You heard us talking about that?'

Michael nodded. 'Taking care of Susan . . . that involves keeping my eyes open and my ears pricked up.'

'Then you'll allow her to hold a seance?'

'If we're going to be chancing death every time we go near water, then I don't see that we have very much alternative, do you? All I want you to promise is that you won't expose Susan to any more danger than you have to.'

'I can't promise you that there won't be *some* risk involved.'

'Well, that's something we'll have to face up to when the time comes, isn't it? God, my throat hurts. If you guys hadn't been here, that thing would have strangled me for sure.'

'Okay,' said Jim, 'if you're really prepared to go ahead with this, I'll fix my apartment up for tomorrow evening. I'll get the gasoline and the fire extinguishers. All you have to do is bring Susan.'

Michael gingerly rubbed his throat. 'I'll never forgive you for bringing this on us, you know that.'

'I didn't bring it on you. It was Susan who approached *me*, remember?'

'So what are you trying to tell me? That it was *our* fault?'

'No . . . I'm just saying that fate moves in very logical ways, and that maybe Susan was *meant* to approach me. It could be the answer to her problems, as well as ours.'

Michael went into a spasm of coughing. When he had finished, he said, 'Let me tell you one thing, Mr Rook. If this goes wrong – if anything happens to Susan – then you won't just have the Swimmer to watch out for. You'll have me, too.'

Fifteen

Mervyn said, 'This is incredibly risky. You could burn the whole building down to the ground.'

'I don't think we have any alternative,' said Jim, as he carried two two-gallon cans of gasoline into the bathroom and set them down beside the washbasin.

'Can't you do it outside? By a lake? By a pond? By the sea, even?'

'Too much water there. Water gives the Swimmer strength. We wouldn't be able to produce enough fire to overwhelm it.'

'Well I'm warning you, Jim, if anything happens to my apartment . . . I've got some very precious stuff in there, quite apart from *moi*.' Mervyn was wearing a black-leather biker's jacket, a short red skirt and fishnet stockings, and Judy Garland-type ruby slippers. He was carrying Tibbles Two under one arm, so that her legs dangled, and it was obvious from the expression on TT's face that she was mortified.

'You really shouldn't carry her around like that,' Jim remarked. 'She's not a purse.'

Mervyn tickled the top of TT's head. 'I know . . . but she's such a darling. She and I are going to get on *famously*, aren't we, Tibbles? Don't you love your new daddy, then, sweetcheeks?'

Jim took a final look around the apartment. All of the cardboard boxes containing his books, clothes and sound equipment were pushed well away from the bathroom door, right on the opposite side of the room. Most of the furniture was stacked in the bedroom, including his blue-painted rocking horse and his half-packed statue of Hanuman the ape-god. He had managed to borrow three red-painted fire extinguishers from college, and they were resting against the wall where he could quickly reach them if the flames got out of control.

It was almost nine o'clock. Three times three. There was a knock at the door and Washington came in, wearing a black T-shirt and black jeans, followed by Laura, who was dressed all in white, with a white silk scarf tied around her head.

'Susan not here yet?' asked Washington.

'She called about ten minutes ago. She's on her way.'

'I wish you could think of some other way of doing this,' said Mervyn. He tried to change TT from one arm to the other, but TT took advantage of him loosening his grip and struggled herself free. 'Ow, you beastly creature, you scratched me! There's cats for you – same as women, no gratitude.'

Laura said, 'I tried to find out more about Swimmers, but I pretty much drew a blank. There's a mention of them on one of those urban-legend websites, but it doesn't tell you anything we don't already know.'

Jim put his arm around her shoulders. 'If there's one thing I've learned about dealing with supernatural threats, Laura, it's that you have to play it as it comes. It's no use relying on myth or legend or anecdotal accounts. Each spirit is an individual, and each spirit is looking for something different, even if it's nothing more than frightening the pants off the people they left behind.'

'How about a cup of coffee while we're waiting?' Mervyn suggested.

'No – I don't want any water in here apart from the water in the bathtub. I've tightened up all of the faucets with a spanner and I've strapped down the lid of the toilet with packing tape. I've even emptied out TT's water bowl.'

They waited a few minutes more and then Jennie appeared, followed by Susan and Michael. Jennie was wearing a simple black dress with a black pearl necklace. Susan was dressed in a padded jerkin of dark crimson velvet that made her look like a medieval page-boy, and black leggings. Michael was out of his Medlar Tree ensemble, and wearing a sweatshirt and tatty embroidered jeans. His neck and one side of his face were still red from where the water-hand had tried to strangle him.

'Well, this is it,' said Jim. 'We're all here, so we might as well get started. Nine o'clock is supposed to be an auspicious time for spirits, isn't it?'

'For *vengeful* spirits, yes,' Susan agreed. 'Are you going to show me your bathroom? I need to make sure that we can do this safely.'

Jim took her into the bathroom. It was small and L-shaped, with the tub on the left-hand side and the washbasin opposite, in the alcove. There was a small high window with a stained-glass fleur-de-lis in it.

'Can that window be opened?' she asked.

Jim shook his head. 'You don't think the Swimmer could get out of *there*, do you?'

'You never know. You have to take all the precautions you can think of, and then some. If we summon this spirit today, and don't succeed in getting rid of her for good, then the likelihood is that she's going to come after us, only ten times more vengeful than she was before. Like I explained to you, spirits usually feel resentful because they think we've forgotten them – because they feel we don't love them any more. On top of that, if they get the idea that we actively want to get rid of them . . . well, that's trouble with an upper-case T.'

'What do you want to do?' Jim asked her. 'You don't need us to sit around a table or anything, do you?'

'No, that's not necessary. Besides, there isn't enough space. All we have to do is fill the tub with water. Then we'll stand around it and hold hands together to increase the strength of our spiritual link. I'll be able to talk to the spirit even before she appears . . . but of course I won't be able to see her. Only you can do that, Jim.

'We're counting on her entering the water and taking on the shape of the Swimmer. The instant she comes out of the bath, Michael and Washington will pour gasoline on top of her.'

'Just one hefty splash,' Jim warned them. 'We don't want to blow up the whole apartment building.'

Susan said, 'When you've done that, you take your gasoline cans and you get out of the bathroom double-quick. That's when Jim will throw his cigarette lighter into the bathtub and set the Swimmer alight. Hopefully, the fire will be more than enough to evaporate her.'

'And if it isn't?' asked Jennie.

'I said "hopefully". This is a big risk – not just physically, but spiritually too.'

Jim said, 'The most important thing is to think and act quickly and clearly. Whatever you see – no matter how strange and frightening it is – try to keep your cool. Your survival may depend on it.'

'Hey, man, I'm cool,' said Washington. 'I'm *always* cool. You know that.'

'Okay then, let's get started. Michael – you want to bring those jerry-cans over here by the side of the bath? I'll start running the water.'

The plumbing in Jim's apartment building dated from the 1930s, and it took nearly five minutes for the bath to be filled up to the halfway mark, with the pipes shuddering and groaning in protest. All the time, Washington talked quietly to Laura, and Laura kept on nodding, but the rest of them were too tense to say anything.

Eventually, Jim turned the faucets off, and tightened them as hard as he could. He didn't want Jane to have more water than she needed to form herself into the Swimmer. Water, after all, was the element which gave her spirit its power to take on a human shape, and drown them – and the more water she had at her disposal, the more powerful she would be.

'That's it. Let's take the lids off those jerry-cans and have them ready. Don't forget – as soon as the Swimmer rises out of the water, splash your gasoline and run. And whatever you do, don't drop your can.'

'We got you.'

They shuffled themselves into a semi-circle around the side of the bath. Jim caught sight of himself in the mirror beside the bath and thought how ridiculous they all looked, five grown people standing around a tub of water, holding hands.

Anybody who accidentally walked in would have thought they belonged to some nutty sect – Druids or Culdees or the Ancient Order of Bath Worshippers.

Susan closed her eyes and said, 'Jane Tullett, I am calling you through from the spirit world. I am calling you to meet us where death and life converge. I have people here who wish to talk to you; and a very special person who needs to tell you how deeply remorseful she is about the way you died.

'Listen to me, Jane. I know that you're angry. I know that your spirit never seems to be able to find the repose that it seeks. But I am offering you a way out. I am offering you rest and contentment. Come through, Jane. I know that you can hear me. Come through and meet us face to face, so that we can give you the peace you so desperately crave.'

There was a long silence, during which the only sound was the swish of traffic from the streets outside and the deep, dyspeptic grumblings of the waterpipes. Then Jim heard a noise like nothing he had ever heard before. It was soft and high and incredibly unsettling, like somebody running their moistened finger around the rim of a brandy glass. Only it was much eerier than that: it had elements of the wind in it, blowing under a doorway in a deserted house. It had elements of the sea in it, churning in the darkness of a winter's night. It had elements of crying, and pain, and utter loneliness.

'I can hear you, Jane,' said Susan. Jim felt Susan's thin, silver-ringed fingers closing tightly around his. 'I can hear you coming closer. Come on, Jane, don't be afraid. We're here to help you, not to harm you.'

'*You could have saved me . . .*' breathed an unearthly voice. It sounded so close that Jim jolted in shock. Not only was it close – it was close *behind* him.

'*. . . You let the water take me, and you didn't do anything . . . you stood by and let me drown . . .*'

Jim could actually feel Jane's freezing cold breath on the side of his neck. He turned around, and there she was, only just visible, standing less than two feet away, a faintly shuddering outline. He could see her wet hair sticking to her scalp. The water ran in a constant cascade from her nose and her lips, and the droplets coursed down between her bare thighs and ran between her toes. She had been drowned: so she would always be wet, until she found her release.

'She's here,' said Jim, clutching Susan's hand even tighter. 'For Christ's sake, she's right behind us. Breathing down our necks.'

'I can't feel her,' said Susan, twisting her head around in a panic. 'I can't feel her – tell me where she is!' Jim grappled her hand and laid it on Jane's almost-transparent shoulder. 'She's here . . . can't you feel her? She's standing right here.'

Susan kept her hand where it was. 'I can feel . . . coldness,' she whispered. 'I can feel *wet*.'

'That's right. Until she can find somebody to release her, she's always going to be the same way she was the morning she died.'

Jane's spirit figure glided around them like the dancing reflection from a swimming pool, until she stood close behind Jennie, and touched her hair with her invisible fingertips.

'*Didn't any of you like me?*' she whispered, turning and looking at Jim with her watery, transparent eyes. '*Don't tell me there wasn't one single person in that whole college who liked me?*'

'I can hear her,' said Jennie. 'I can hear her talking!'

'Jennie . . . stay calm,' said Jim. He squeezed her hand to reassure her. Then he turned to Jane and said, 'Of course people liked you. You were one of the best students I ever had. You were bright, you were popular, you were always laughing.'

'Yes, and every other girl was jealous because I was going steady with George.'

Jennie looked blindly around her, trying to see where Jane was standing. 'You're right, Jane, we *were* jealous, and I was the most jealous of all. But that was a long time ago, Jane, and we were all very much younger then, and the things that seemed to be important when we were nineteen . . . well, they don't seem to matter very much, not today.'

'Not to you, maybe. But then you didn't lose your life, did you?'

'I've said I'm sorry. It was more of an act of passion than anything else.'

'What was? What was an act of passion?'

'I was angry, Jane. George always wanted you, instead of me, and I could never understand why. I thought that I was much prettier than you, my folks were better off. But George always came back to you – even after he'd been flirting with all of those sophomores. He should have been mine, Jane. Couldn't you see? He should have been mine.'

'So what are you telling me?' asked the spirit, in a voice like a chilly draft.

'So I pushed you under. You don't know how often I confessed it. I confessed it in dreams. I confessed it when I was praying at church. I drowned you, Jane, because I believed that if you were dead George would suddenly realize how much he didn't miss you and how much he really loved *me*.'

'And did he?'

'Did who what?' asked Jennie. She was growing increasingly flustered and frightened.

'Did George realize how much he didn't miss me, and how much he loved you?'

Jennie hesitated, and two large tears rolled down her cheeks. 'No. He missed you very, very badly, and he never noticed me, ever.'

Jim said, 'Jane . . . you can see how much Jennie regrets what she did. I'm asking you now to forgive her. I'm asking you to forgive all of us. We failed you, I can see that now. But don't take it out on innocent people like Mikey and Dennis and Dottie. They never did anything to you.'

Jane moved further around, to the end of the bathtub. '*Water*,' she said. '*Were you thinking of taking a bath?*'

'We were thinking of nothing else but you, and how we could put you to rest.'

'Oh, you'd like that, wouldn't you, to put me to rest? Then you could conveniently forget that Jennie deliberately

drowned me, and the rest of you stood around and watched me while they broke my breastbone, and still didn't manage to save my life? You wouldn't have to worry any more about what I could have been, if I had lived.'

'Jane . . . nobody's trying to evade their responsibilities. But it's all over; and it was ten years ago; and little kids like Mikey don't deserve to drown because of something that happened to you.'

'*You may be right,*' said Jane, in a voice that sounded like somebody speaking into an empty washing machine. '*But who am I to judge? Once the water takes you, you become water. And nothing on earth can ever exist without water. Water can take your life away in a matter of seconds – look at me. But it gives life, too. It's the greatest single force in the world.*'

'Jennie here wants you to know that she's truly sorry for what she did to you. She hopes that she can make it up to you somehow.'

'*She wants to make it up to me, for drowning me, when I was only nineteen years old? With my whole life in front of me?*'

'Jane – listen to me, I'm begging you. If there's anything that we can do, please tell me what it is. But I can't see any more of my students hurt – nor my friends, either.'

'*You should have thought of that on the day you drowned me.*'

Without another word, Jane's spirit figure shimmered down to the end of the bathtub. Jim could see her, but nobody else could, and they all turned their heads warily from one side to the other. Washington looked even more wildly around than the rest of them and kept silently mouthing, 'Where? Where is that sucker, Mr Rook?'

'You guys ready?' Jim asked them in a matter-of-fact voice. At the same time, he could see Jane's spirit climbing over the back of the tub and into the water. She disappeared from sight almost immediately, as if she had melted.

'She's in the water!' Jim shouted out. 'Get that gasoline ready!'

Michael and Washington hefted up their jerry-cans. They all stared down at the bathwater. It lolled and slopped, but it didn't look as if it had anything in it.

'Are you *sure* she's in there?' asked Michael.

'Oh, you bet. I saw her climb in, and I expect Susan can feel her aura.'

'She's there all right,' said Susan. 'I can sense these very, very emotional vibrations. She's feeling angry and sad, both at the same time, but mostly angry.'

'Supposing she doesn't come out?' asked Jennie, still hysterical. 'What happens if she doesn't come out?'

'Oh, she'll come out,' said Jim. 'And if by any remote chance she doesn't – well, we'll have to do what Mervyn did, and pull out the plug.'

'Well, *you* can put your hand in the water and pull it out,' said Mervyn, 'because I'm certainly not going to.'

They waited and waited, while the surface of the water gently stirred.

'I don't think there's nobody in there, man,' said Washington, after almost three minutes had passed. 'I mean, I can't see nothing.'

'Wait . . . don't get impatient.'

'I'm not impatient. I just don't want to be fooled, that's all . . . standing here all evening staring at some bathtub with nobody in it.'

'Ssh,' said Jim. 'She's probably thinking what to do next.'

'I can't stand it,' said Jennie. 'I really can't stand it any longer. She won't forgive me, will she? She's going to go on haunting me for the rest of my life.'

'Not if this works.'

But another three minutes went by, and still the Swimmer didn't appear.

'She gone, man,' said Washington, shifting his jerry-can from one hand to the other.

'I can feel her,' said Laura. 'It's like Susan says . . . she's sad and bitter, both at the same time. She wants us to love her but she hates us for what we've done to her.'

'I think you imagining all of this,' Washington protested. 'Her spirit was here for sure, I heard her like the rest of you. But she ain't in that bathtub, not now. She long gone. She probably watching us from some other dimension, laughing her butt off.'

He laid down his jerry-can and prodded the surface of the water with his finger.

'Washington – don't!' Jim warned him.

But Washington prodded the water again and again, and caused no more disturbance than a pattern of ripples. 'See . . . there ain't nothing here, man. We all standing around here scared of nothing.'

To emphasize his contempt, he swept his arm into the water from one end of the bath to the other. 'What did I tell you? There's nothing in here but – *sheee-it!*'

With a shattering splash, a watery figure reared out of the bath and seized Washington's arm, dragging him over the side of the tub and into the water. It pushed him right down to the bottom, kicking and wrestling, and the surface of the bath was a froth of bubbles.

'Get him out of there!' Susan shouted. 'Jim – quick! Get him out of there!'

Jim tried to grip the Swimmer's shoulders, but even though the Swimmer was so strong, she was only water, and his hands went right through. He swung his arms and punched at the Swimmer's head, again and again, but it was just like punching the water that comes streaming out of a faucet. Her head splashed, and then went back to its original shape.

All the time, Washington was pinned down on the bottom of the tub, and Jim could see his eyes wide with terror.

'Pull the plug out!' said Michael.

But Susan said, '*No!* If we lose her now, she'll only want to drown us all the more!'

Jim grabbed one of Washington's arms and tried to heave him out, but the Swimmer pushed him away, soaking his shirt and his pants. He tried again, but this time the Swimmer hit him across the side of the head and sent him staggering back across the bathroom. He stumbled, lost his footing and fell against the towel rail, bruising his back.

Jennie started to scream, the way she must have screamed when she pretended to find Jane's body in the college pool. Laura tried to be more practical, and distract the Swimmer by slapping at her back with a wet towel, but the Swimmer ignored her, and kept Washington's head under the water, no matter how ferociously he fought back at her. The bath was only six or seven inches deep, because most of the water had been used by the Swimmer herself to take on her physical form, but it was enough for Washington to drown.

'You have to pull out the plug!' said Michael. 'She's going to kill him if you don't!'

Jim made his way back to the edge of the bathtub on his knees. The Swimmer didn't even bother to look at him. Her watery shape kept shifting and changing, so that it looked as if it were made out of melting glass – but one thing that didn't alter was the expression on her face. An expression of total, almost maniacal hatred.

Jim thrust his hand into the water and tried to find the plug. But the Swimmer shoved him away with another burst of spray, and when he tried again she shifted Washington sideways so that his head was jammed right on top of the wastepipe. Washington was panicking now. He had run out of air and his arms and legs were jerking convulsively.

'Get him out of there!' screamed Jennie. 'Can't you get him out of there?'

Mervyn said, 'What if we all pull him together? Come on, let's all pull him together!'

But at that moment, something extraordinary happened. Tibbles Two came running into the bathroom – really running, faster than Jim had ever seen her running before. Without any hesitation she jumped up on to the top of the laundry basket and then on to the rim of the bathtub.

'TT?' Jim called her. 'What the hell are you—?'

TT flattened her ears back and bared her teeth and let out a vicious, cackling hiss. Her fur stood up on end until she looked as if she were twice her normal size . . . a hellcat, with glaring yellow eyes. She leaped on to the Swimmer's back, plunging straight into her, her claws scrabbling and scratching at the water as if she thought she could tear it to pieces.

The Swimmer twisted around and lashed out at her – obviously surprised and upset. TT danced around the bathtub, her fur completely drenched, but unstoppably vicious, clawing at the Swimmer's face and arms.

Jim shouted, 'Michael – Mervyn! Give me a hand here!'

While the Swimmer tried to fend off Tibbles Two, the three of them grabbed hold of Washington's arms and T-shirt and heaved him out of the water on to the bathroom floor. He coughed and coughed and sicked up almost a quart of water, but Jim didn't give him time to lie on the floor and recover.

'Out of here! *Out!* All of you! *Quick!*'

Michael and Mervyn dragged Washington along the floor and out to the living-room. Jennie, Laura and Susan followed behind.

Susan took hold of Jim's sleeve and said, 'For God's sake be careful.'

But Jim had already lifted up one of the jerry-cans and was swinging it backward and forward.

In the bathtub, the Swimmer was still furiously struggling with TT. Jim couldn't guess why she was so distressed by a cat, but then TT had never been an ordinary cat, and if cats had a natural antipathy for water, then maybe water felt the same way about cats.

'TT!' he called at her, and whistled. 'TT, get out of there – now!'

Usually TT took no notice of anything he said, and he had to throw sneakers at her to stop her from jumping up on the table and sniffing at his dinner. But now she lifted her head and looked at him, and she must have understood how serious he was because she ducked underneath the Swimmer's arm and sprang up on to the edge of the bathtub again, and dropped to the floor. She was so wet that she looked like a skinny kind of rat instead of a cat. Jim gave her a kick and she scurried out of the bathroom door.

Now he didn't hesitate. He turned toward the bathtub. The Swimmer had already half risen out of it, glistening in the colored light that came through the stained-glass window. She smoothed back her hair and then she stood up straight.

Jim knew that he could close the bathroom door and run off and she wouldn't be able to catch up with him. But she would catch him one day, when he wasn't expecting it, and neither he nor his former students could spend the rest of their lives staying away from showers, swimming pools and lakes.

He swung the jerry-can back behind him.

'*Think what you're doing*,' said the Swimmer.

'I'm thinking, all right. I'm sorry it has to end this way, but I can't think how else to give you any peace.'

'THINK WHAT YOU'RE DOING!' roared the Swimmer, and took one fluid step out of the bathtub, and then another.

Jim sloshed gasoline all over her. She lifted her hands to protect her face, and staggered for a moment as if she couldn't see. But the gas immediately ran off her watery skin like scores of rainbow-colored snakes, and puddled on the floor.

He threw more gasoline over her, and this time he took his Zippo lighter out of his shirt pocket and flicked it into flame.

The Swimmer lowered her hands and stared at him. He had been frightened more than once, especially when he had seen spirits and ghosts and supernatural manifestations that he couldn't even begin to describe. But the expression on the Swimmer's face was the expression of death itself. He had never seen anybody who looked so utterly determined to kill him.

The Swimmer took one step toward him and he threw the lighter at her. It fell right through her and clattered on to the floor.

For a fraction of a second, he thought that nothing was going to happen. But then there was a deep, subdued *whooommmphhh!* and a huge ball of orange fire rolled up off the floor and engulfed the Swimmer in flames. The heat was enormous, and Jim had to shield his face with his hand and step back toward the door.

Michael looked around the doorway and said excitedly, 'You did it, Mr Rook! You did it!'

The Swimmer was standing in the center of the bathroom, both arms raised, while the fire roared all around her with a soft, fierce, funneling sound. Steam began to pour out of her, adding a high, intense hiss. She was evaporating . . . and Jane's spirit was evaporating with her.

Susan appeared in the doorway too. She watched in silence, with orange flames reflected in her eyes. The Swimmer didn't scream or cry or try to escape. She just stood amidst the flames with steam gushing from her shoulders and the top of her head.

Beneath her feet, the bathroom tiles began to crack with the heat, and there was a sudden snap as the mirror broke. But then there was another crack, and another. Pieces of plaster dropped from the ceiling – tiny fragments at first, but then a large triangular lump, and then another.

'What the hell's happening?' asked Michael. 'That's not just the heat, that's—'

This time – with a deafening crash – an immense section of plaster dropped on to the floor, followed by a thumping, tumbling, banging cascade of joists, floorboards and crossbeams.

'The whole building is falling down!' screamed Mervyn. 'I told you this was too dangerous! I told you!'

'Michael – get me one of those fire extinguishers,' said Jim.

'You're not going to put her out yet?' said Susan. 'Look at her – she still has her physical shape. If you put her out now Jane's spirit will be able to escape!'

Another section of timber fell on to the bathroom floor. It bounced off the side of the tub and almost hit the Swimmer's legs. Immediately it caught alight, and started to burn almost as fiercely as the Swimmer herself. The whole bathroom was filled with steam and black oily smoke and plaster dust.

'She's diminishing,' said Susan. 'Look at her now –

she's going down on her knees. We've done it, Jim. We've beaten her.'

But then – from directly above them – they heard an extraordinary splitting, ringing noise. It sounded like an immense church bell cracking. Jim looked at Susan with a frown, but all Susan could do was shake her head.

It was only when hundreds of gallons of water abruptly dropped into the bathroom that they realized what had happened. It crashed on to the Swimmer and instantly extinguished her flames. It surged across the floor, almost waist-deep, and forced Jim and Susan and Michael to stagger back into the living-room. There, it flowed quickly and relentlessly across the carpet.

'Goddam water tank burst!'

'How could it burst, just like that?'

'It's water, isn't it? It's a thinking, evolving, spiritual element! It was protecting its own!'

The bathroom door opened and the Swimmer appeared, as glassy and as perfect as she had been before. She glided across the living-room and out through the open front door, her feet splashing in the inch-deep water that had spread across most of Jim's apartment. She walked out of the open front door and along the corridor. There was no point in trying to stop her. As she walked, she gradually drifted apart, like a passing rainshower, and by the time she reached the head of the stairs there was nothing to show that she had been there except for a trail of wet footprints. Nothing except Jane Tüllett's spirit, which only Jim could see.

She stood for a moment at the top of the stairs, staring back at him.

'*Now I know how you really feel about me*,' she said. '*You're not interested in finding me peace. You're only interested in killing my spirit, just like you killed my body*.'

'Jane, turning yourself into the Swimmer – drowning people – that's never going to bring you peace.'

'*Maybe it won't. But it'll bring me satisfaction*.'

With that she vanished down the stairs, no more substantial than a blink of light.

Susan came out. 'What's happened? She's got away, hasn't she?'

Jim nodded.

'That's terrible. That was the last thing I wanted to happen.'

'How's Washington?' asked Jim.

'He's okay,' said Mervyn. 'I'm going to take him across to my place and let him lie down.'

'Thanks, Mervyn.'

'So what are you going to do?' asked Susan.

'I'm going to go after Jane. I'm going to try to make a deal with her.'

'A deal? What kind of a deal?'

'I'm going to ask her if she'll stop drowning my friends and my students if I let her drown me.'

'You're out of your mind. You can't do that.'

'Why not? I've brought nothing but death and pain and grief to everybody who's ever met me. My girlfriend doesn't want to marry me, my head of department is glad to see the back of me, even my *cat* doesn't like me.'

'Come on, Jim. You're all stressed out, that's all.'

But Jim shook his head. 'This has to end, Susan. I can't allow any more people to die . . . not for me, anyhow. I'm going after Jane and that's the proposition I'm going to put to her.'

'In that case, I'm coming with you.'

'Why? You don't owe me anything.'

'I can help, that's why. I'm a sensitive. I know what I'm doing when it comes to spirits.'

Michael came out of the door too. 'If Susan's going then I'm going.'

Jim took a deep breath. 'All right. But if we're all going, we'd better go now.'

Sixteen

At first he thought he'd lost her, but as they crossed Rialto Avenue, looking right and left, Jim saw the faintest distortion in a drugstore window only fifty yards away, and then a rippling effect along the shiny side of a highly polished black Lincoln.

'She's there,' he told Susan. 'She's headed toward Riviera.'

'Do you think she knows that we're following her?'

'I haven't a clue. Who knows what spirits think about?'

Whether Jane was aware that they were following her or not, they kept their distance, as far as they could. Sometimes, when she was walking along a darker section of the street, Jim could see her quite distinctly – her wet hair shining in the streetlights. At other times, when she was passing a brightly lit store, he could barely make her out at all.

They turned down Windward Avenue toward the oceanfront. Although it was a warm summer night, there was a thin, edgy breeze blowing from the sea. Jim couldn't help shivering, and Susan reached out and took hold of his hand.

'You don't have to do this, you know. There must be other ways to get rid of the Swimmer.'

'Like what? It's a myth, it's an urban legend, hardly anybody has ever encountered a Swimmer, or knows what to do about it when they do.'

'You could try to talk to some more spiritualists.'

'Are you kidding me? The last spiritualist I talked to wound up drowned. I shouldn't even be talking to you . . . I'm exposing you to just as much danger as me or any of my students.'

'That's down to me, Jim. I know how dangerous this is.

Don't you understand? When you can feel things, like I can – when you can *see* things, like you can – you don't have any choice. You have a gift and you have to use it, whether you want to or not.'

'Listen,' said Jim, keeping his eye on Jane's flickering image as she crossed Speedway toward Ocean Front Walk. 'I never wanted any gift. I never wanted anything except to be normal, like other kids. I didn't want to be a teacher, I wanted to be a pilot. But I saw demons; and I saw people's dead relatives; and what kind of a pilot do you think you can be when you walk into an Air Force recruitment center and you can see the sergeant's grandmother standing behind him, smiling at you like a goddamn Cheshire Cat?'

He wiped his forehead with the back of his hand. They had walked more than seven blocks now, and he was beginning to sweat. 'Besides, I had an astigmatism in my left eye. No Tomcats for me.'

'Do you know what amazes me about you?' said Susan. 'You can help all those kids to deal with the world. You can teach them how to think for themselves, how to communicate. And yet you can't do the same for Jim Rook.'

'What's this? "Physician, heal thyself"?'

'No . . . it's "Teacher, learn your own lessons."'

Jim stopped, and Michael almost bumped into them. He looked at Susan, and for the first time he recognized what it was that made her so attractive. Her face was silvery-pale and her eyes were full of magic. Apart from her figure – full-breasted, narrow-waisted – she had the same quality as the moon, when you look at it through binoculars or a telescope. Shining, unreachable, strange. The moon gives you no answers at all, yet you can never take your eyes off her.

All of a sudden, it didn't seem to matter so much that Karen wasn't coming to Washington with him. All of a sudden, it seemed that life could have new possibilities.

'So what are we doing?' asked Michael. 'Are we going after this swimming-person or what?'

Jim raked his hand through his hair. 'Yes . . . we're going

after her. There she is . . . I can see her on the corner. Let's go.'

They reached Ocean Front Walk. The boardwalk was still blazing with light and blaring with rap music and dreamy long-legged roller-bladers were still making circles around the strollers and the talkers and the hawkers and the buyers. Jim almost lost sight of Jane's spirit; but then he saw her cross over the boardwalk like the last flickering flame of a candle before it dies out. She was making her way across the sand toward the ocean, where it was dark, except for the pale luminescence of the foam.

'She's headed for the beach,' he told Susan. 'I think she's aware that we've been following her. She wants to get her revenge on us for setting fire to her, and she's looking for all the strength she can get.'

'Jim . . . if she gets close to the ocean, and she turns into the Swimmer, you won't stand a chance.'

'I still have to talk to her. I still have to try to make a deal.'

'Jim, I haven't known you very long, but there's one thing I know about you. You're definitely not the suicidal type.'

'I'm not talking about suicide. I'm a teacher. I'm talking about taking responsibility, making amends.'

'Being a martyr.'

'Jane Tullett is suffering, Susan, and she's been suffering for ten years. I don't excuse what she's done to get her revenge. But I understand how she feels – how her spirit feels, in any case; and I also understand that I have to try and stop her.'

'All right,' said Susan, 'but I'm coming with you.'

'No,' said Michael. 'Absolutely, totally not.'

'You're afraid of what might happen?' Susan asked him.

'Of course I'm afraid. It's not just you.'

'Well, I'm sorry . . . this had to happen sooner or later, didn't it? One day we had to make a decision. And this is it. This is the day.'

'You'll die,' said Michael miserably.

'Michael, everybody's going to die someday.'

But Michael wouldn't be appeased. 'You'll die, and *he'll* die with you, and what will be the good of that?'

Jim looked out toward the ocean, where the sun had long since disappeared, leaving a last blood-colored smear across the horizon. He saw a slight judder of light, and he knew that it was Jane. She was leading him on, like a will-o'-the-wisp . . . leading him out to the greatest body of water on the planet, where her strength would be unsurpassed.

'One last appeal,' said Susan. 'This isn't your responsibility: you didn't drown Jane and you don't have to take the blame for it, let alone die for it.'

'I know,' said Jim. In actual fact he was deeply frightened, but he couldn't see any other way out of it. What if Washington had been drowned today, and Laura? What if Tarquin and Joyce and Christophe were killed? He couldn't allow it. So long as there was any chance that he could protect them, he would. In a remedial class like Special Class II, you always had to be very much more than a teacher. You had to be a surrogate parent, and a friend.

They crossed the sands, which were soft and surprisingly hot, even so long after the sun had gone down.

'Can you still see her?' asked Susan.

Jim could make out an attenuated figure standing at the water's edge. She appeared to be looking out toward the black, swelling breast of the ocean. The sea grumbled and seethed and sucked at her feet, yet she remained where she was, staring westward. Jim wondered if she were still thinking about the days when she was alive, and missing them so badly that she could hardly bear it.

Susan said, 'Jim – please don't—' but he walked up to Jane's spirit and stood beside her. He didn't say anything at first. He noticed that the wind blew *his* hair while hers remained perfectly untouched.

'Maybe we could come to a compromise,' he said.

She turned and looked at him contemptuously. '*A compromise? Jennie Bauer drowned me and you stood by and let her do it. Now you've tried to burn me, so that I can never walk in this world again.*'

'Jane . . . no matter what you think . . . what happened to you was the result of one person's malice, Jennie Bauer's. Nobody stood around and laughed when you were drowning. We didn't even know it was happening . . . and up until yesterday, we didn't even know that you hadn't drowned by accident. I swear it. Everybody at West Grove was so cut up about it. You should have seen your funeral. They were crying buckets.'

'*You're lying to me. You're trying to make me go back to the spirit world. Well, I happen to hate the spirit world. It's so claustrophobic. Nothing but seniors with no eyes talking about golf, and hospital procedures, and how they found their husbands lying dead in bed, right next to them.*

'*I was so young, Mr Rook. Nobody should have taken my life away from me. How can I ever get any of those years back again? Living, learning, falling in love. If only people knew how precious life is.*'

'That's my point, Jane. That's why I followed you here tonight. Life is so precious, and there are no more precious lives than those of my students, like you once were. So I'm going to try to make a very special deal with you. I'm going to ask you to take my life, mine alone, in full and final settlement of all of the grudges you hold against me and the students of West Grove Community College, and all of their friends, and their mentors.

'In other words, Jane, if I give you my soul, and my memories, and everything that makes up Jim Rook, will you swear to leave my friends and my former students well enough alone?'

Jane laughed. Even out here on the beach, it sounded like somebody laughing in another room. And of course, metaphorically, she *was* in another room. She didn't exist here and now, like Jim did, but *then* and *there*.

'*You want me to take you, Mr Rook? I'll take you, gladly. Come on . . . let's go down to the ocean . . . let's go down to the water's edge.*'

Jane's spirit held out her hand and Jim took it. It felt prickly and electrical, as if it were charged with static. His heart was beating in long, slow thumps, and he could scarcely hear the noise of the surf as Jane's spirit led him right to the very edge of the ocean.

'*Take off your clothes*,' she told him.

'What?'

'*Take your clothes off. You won't be needing them any more.*'

'Come on, Jane, I'm your teacher. I can't do things like that.'

'*You* were *my teacher, in another age. But now you're Jim Rook, who allowed me to drown. Take off your clothes.*'

Reluctantly, Jim unbuttoned his shirt and tossed it on to the sand. Then he struggled out of his pants and tossed them away too.

'*Everything*,' Jane insisted.

Jim glanced back toward Susan, who was standing on the sand only seventy-five feet away, with Michael close beside her.

'Listen—'

'*As you came into this world, so you will go out, into the next.*'

'But—'

'*No.*' Jane wouldn't take 'but's. So, as deftly as he could, Jim pulled down his red Hawaiian undershorts and threw them back across the beach, too.

'*Now*,' said Jane, taking hold of his hand. Her fingers were as cold and wet as half-melted ice cubes. '*Let's take a walk in the water, shall we?*'

'I need to know for sure,' asked Jim, as he waded into the water up to his knees. 'Does this mean that you're going to leave my friends and my students alone?' Jane's spirit kept on tugging him on, tugging him deeper. Soon the water splashed up between his legs and he gasped, feeling very naked and very vulnerable.

'*This means that you've decided to take the blame for what you did, that's all*,' said Jane, pulling him deeper, and even deeper. '*Once you've paid the price, all of the others will have to pay the price, too – the same as you.*'

Jim wrenched his arm free. The water was almost up to his armpits, and every wave made him surge up higher. 'This was supposed to be a deal – you were supposed to take me, instead of them!'

'*Do you really think that I could forgive you all so easily?*' said Jane. '*I will never forgive you – any of you – till hell freezes over.*'

With that, she sank down below the surface. For one moment Jim was left on his own, treading water to keep himself afloat. Ahead of him, the Pacific rollers surged and grumbled. Behind him, the lights twinkled all along Ocean Front Walk, and beyond. He suddenly began to wonder what he had got himself into. He turned around and began to struggle back toward the beach, as fast as he could.

'*Jim!*' Susan shouted. He could only just hear her calling him over the endless seething of the surf and the fluffing of the wind and the distant, intermittent sound of rap music. '*Jim, look out behind you!*'

He was only waist-deep in the water now, and he was wading up the beach with an extravagant, hip-swiveling walk. But he turned around and looked behind him, and it was then that he saw a dim green phosphorescent glow approaching him, at speed. It was like an illuminated *Jaws*.

'*Jim, she's right behind you! Get out of there!*'

Jim was splashing through the shallows now, panting with effort. He turned around – and to his horror the Swimmer was less than twenty feet behind him: a figure made of foam and phosphorescent spray, with a face contorted by the hunger for revenge.

'*Get out of the water, Jim!*' Susan screamed at him, and came hurrying across the sand with Michael right beside her.

'Susan!' Michael shouted. 'Susan, for God's sake be careful!'

Jim had nearly reached the beach. But as he splashed through the last few yards, he heard a deep sucking sound and the water was suddenly dragged backward, beneath his feet, as if the tide were going out. He found himself running on flat wet sand, and he knew that if he could reach the boardwalk he would be safe. The Swimmer couldn't run across a hundred yards of dry sand without her physical shape being simply *absorbed.*

He turned around again. The Swimmer had reached the water's edge, and now she was standing still, although her stare of hatred was unrelenting. Susan and Michael came jogging up to Jim and Michael gave him his pants, which he had picked up from the beach.

'Thanks, Michael.'

'No problem. She didn't accept your offer, then?'

'Oh, she gladly would've drowned me,' said Jim, struggling to force his wet sandy legs into his pants. 'But she still wants her revenge on everybody else. There's no stopping her – she's going to go on drowning people until she's punished everybody who was standing around the pool that day, and a few more besides. And the trouble is, who's going to believe us?'

The water slid further and further out, and the sucking sound grew deeper and harsher. Jim looked along the shoreline, right and left, and he began to realize that the tide was going out much further than he had ever seen it before. The Swimmer stayed where she was, but behind her, the ocean was beginning to rise, higher and higher, and a massive wave was beginning to form.

'Jesus,' said Michael. It was bigger than any wave that Jim had ever seen before. It was dark and tumultuous, and it made a rumbling noise that was already beginning to shake the beach beneath their feet like an earthquake. Still it grew higher – millions and millions of gallons of ocean, piling itself up.

'I have the distinct feeling that we ought to be getting out of here.'

'I have the distinct feeling that you're right. Let's go.'

As they started to hurry toward the boardwalk, however, Jim heard a cataclysmic thundering sound. He glanced over his shoulder and saw that the giant wave was racing toward the shore – a boiling, churning avalanche of water that was already higher than the buildings along Ocean Front Walk.

'*Run!*' Jim shouted, and seized hold of Susan's hand. Ahead of them they could see people on the boardwalk looking around in bewilderment, wondering what the thundering sound was.

They ran, tripping and stumbling, their feet sinking into the sand. But they were only halfway across the beach when Jim felt a blizzard of sand and spray against the back of his neck. He glanced around again and saw that the wave was almost on top of them. It rushed toward them like a mountain on wheels.

'Hold on tight!' he yelled, gripping Susan's hand even harder. 'Whatever you do, don't let go!'

'*Michael!*' Susan shouted, reaching out for his hand too. But the next thing they knew the wave had collapsed on top of them, tons and tons of furiously seething water. It felt to Jim as if a building had fallen on top of him. He was driven to his knees, and then he was dragged up the beach, rolling over and over, hitting his shoulder against a volleyball post, colliding with a low concrete wall, and then being swept right across the boardwalk. His hand was snatched away from Susan's and he found himself fighting alone to keep himself from being drowned.

The wave was so huge that he was completely disoriented. One second he was being washed against the window of a swimwear store, the next he was being whirled around and tangling with a row of bicycles. He was bruised and battered and his ribs hurt like splintered glass, and the noise all around him was shattering.

Almost as quickly as the wave had rolled over the beach, however, it began to draw back. Jim felt an overwhelming suction. His glasses were pulled off his face and he grabbed the cast-iron leg of a bench to try to stop himself from being dragged out to sea. But then a girl tumbled into him, and another, all arms and legs, followed by a heavy, wet Labrador dog, and he lost his hold. Immediately the water pulled him away from the boardwalk and back across the beach toward the ocean. He was swirled into deeper water, his lungs aching, his eyes tight shut, just praying for the maelstrom to stop.

Gradually, however, the waters began to calm down. He doggy-paddled up to the surface, his ribs giving him agonizing stabs with every paddle. When he emerged, blinking and spitting, he saw that he was less than thirty yards from the shoreline. People on the boardwalk were screaming and shouting and running around, and he could hear the warbling sound of sirens. He looked around for Susan and Michael, but although there were twenty or thirty other people in the water, he couldn't see them anywhere.

Slowly, painfully, he paddled his way toward the shore. As soon as his feet touched the bottom he was able to wade. He was still up to his knees in water when he heard Susan calling him. 'Jim! Is that you? I thought you were drowned!'

He tried to cough but it hurt too much. 'Think I've broken a couple of ribs. But it didn't get me this time.'

Susan came splashing through the shallows to help him. 'Here,' she said, holding out her hand. 'Michael and I held on to a telephone booth. He's sprained his ankle, but otherwise he's fine.'

Michael was sitting on a wastebin that had been washed right down to the water's edge. He raised his hand and called out, 'You okay, Mr Rook?'

'I've felt better.'

Susan said, 'We'd better go back to my place and try to decide what we're going to do next. This thing is far too powerful for us to fight it without any help.'

The night was clamorous with the noise of fire sirens wailing and car horns honking and people shouting and crying. Jim stopped for a moment, and looked back at the ocean. 'You know something, I never really understood until today that we're nothing but guests on this planet. Look at it. All that strength. All that secrecy. All those millions of years of nurturing life.'

Michael called, 'Jim!'

Jim took hold of Susan's hand and together they started to walk along the waterline. The waves had receded now, and did nothing more than lap at their feet.

'*Jim!*' shouted Michael, more urgently.

'What is it?' said Jim, turning around.

'I can't be sure, but – there! Look!'

Jim peered short-sightedly along the beach. He couldn't see anything at first, because of all the people milling around on the sands and the flashing of red emergency lights. But then he saw a shining figure running toward them through the surf . . . the Swimmer, and she was approaching them fast.

'You go that way!' Jim told Susan, and pointed toward the boardwalk. 'I'll try to lead her someplace dry!'

He pushed Susan away from him and then he started to run. His ribs were hurting him so much that he could only manage a kind of limping trot, as if he were taking part in a one-man three-legged race. But he had to coax the Swimmer away from Susan and Michael, and if he could take her well away from the ocean and into the sand, *he* might stand a chance of getting away from her too.

As he ran, he could hear himself gasping, as if somebody else were jogging beside him. The ocean seethed softly on his right; the lights of Marina Del Rey sparkled up ahead of him. He could hear footsteps splish-splashing in the water close behind him, but he was determined not to turn around, not yet.

He was about to veer off to the left, toward a wide stretch of bone-dry sand, and a volleyball court, when the Swimmer suddenly jumped on his back and brought him thumping to the ground. It was like being knocked down by a high-pressure hose, and his broken ribs jabbed into him so painfully that he screamed out loud.

Without any hesitation, the Swimmer took hold of his legs and began to drag him into the water. A wave splashed directly into his face, forcing salt water into his nose; and then she dragged him even deeper and he swallowed a mouthful of it. He tried to kick out against her but he was far too weak, and she, in the ocean, was immeasurably strong.

He took in another mouthful of water and tried to spit it out, but he only succeeded in swallowing more. The Swimmer kept dragging him deeper and deeper until he was completely submerged. His eyes were wide open, but he couldn't see anything except darkness and criss-cross patterns of foam.

This is it, he thought. This is really it. He even wondered if it was worth trying to hold his breath any longer. 'To die would be an awfully big adventure.'

At that second, though, the Swimmer released him. He kicked his legs, expecting her to grab him again, but she had definitely let him go. He kicked again, and rolled himself over, and managed to stand up. The water was only waist-deep – even though that would have been more than enough for him to drown in.

'Fffgghh! God almighty!' he spluttered.

The Swimmer was less than ten feet away, but to his surprise she wasn't paying any attention to him at all. She wasn't even looking his way. She was staring toward the shoreline, where Susan was standing, her arms upraised, her damp white dress clinging close to her body.

'It's time for you to find peace, Jane!' Susan called, in an oddly sing-song voice. 'It's time for you to stop taking your revenge on innocent people, and go through to the other side!'

Michael, a few yards further away, shouted out, 'No, Susan! You can't!'

'I have to,' sang Susan. 'It was always my fate. I knew that it was going to end this way as soon as I saw Jim Rook. Like a real rook, he came and perched on the shoulder of my destiny, and I knew that he was bringing me the answer to everything.'

'Susan! This isn't the way! I need you, Susan!'

'The *world* needs me, Michael. Remember that I love you, and remember that I'll always be grateful for the years you gave me, when nobody else cared.'

Jim began to wade back toward the shoreline. 'Susan – what are you doing? What's going on?'

Susan stepped into the surf and slowly approached the Swimmer, with her arms still outstretched. Her expression was almost beatific, as if she were experiencing a holy vision. The Swimmer stayed where she was, transfixed, her watery outline reflecting the flashing red lights from the fire trucks as if they were blood cells coursing around her arteries. But of course she had no arteries, only the ocean.

'I call on the child within me to awake,' Susan chanted. 'When I count to three, I want him to open his eyes and come back to life. Peter – can you hear me? Peter?'

'No!' screamed Michael. 'No, Susan, you can't!'

He stumbled into the water and tried to pull her back toward the beach. 'Listen to me, Susan, you can't do it! You can't!'

But Susan lifted one hand and touched him on the forehead as if she were giving him a blessing. 'I have to, Michael. You know I do. It had to happen one day.'

The Swimmer slowly started to wade toward them. Michael hesitated, not knowing what to do.

'Go on, Michael,' Susan smiled at him. 'For all of our sakes.'

Michael reluctantly retreated. Jim circled around behind Susan and joined him on the sand.

'What's she doing?' he asked.

'Showdown,' said Michael.

'*Showdown?*'

'The battle of the elements. Fire against water.'

'Fire? What fire?'

'Peter!' cried Susan, almost in a shriek. 'Peter! You have to wake up now! One – two – three!'

The Swimmer was approaching Susan even faster. Her hair was running down her back like a waterfall. Her eyes shone liquidly, empty as jellyfish.

Susan stayed where she was, her arms wide. 'Time to wake up now, Peter! Time to go to heaven!'

To Jim's alarm, smoke began to billow all around Susan, and he suddenly caught the smell of burning hair.

'Michael – what the hell is she doing?'

'She's bringing Peter back – the boy who was burned in the car crash. She's had him cradled in her mind all this time.'

'But you said that she'd die, if she tried to wake him out of his hypnosis.'

Michael clamped his hand tightly over his mouth. His eyes filled up with tears.

'Susan!' Jim shouted, hurrying toward her. 'Susan, you mustn't!'

But it was too late. As he came nearer, the smoke poured out thicker and thicker. It spiraled out from the top of her head and twisted off into the night sky like a flag. Suddenly, she screamed at the top of her voice – a scream so dreadful that it nearly made Jim lose his balance. The Swimmer was wading toward her, faster and faster, but even before Jane could reach her, her whole body burst into flame.

She took a lurching step forward, stiff-legged, and then another. The Swimmer, illuminated by the leaping fire, seemed confused. But Susan didn't give her a chance. She strode forward three more paces and embraced the Swimmer in her blazing arms.

There was a piercing hiss of steam. The Swimmer tried to struggle free, but Susan kept her arms tightly clenched around her waist. The fire blazed hotter and brighter, until it began to roar, and the louder it roared, the faster the steam began to blast out of the Swimmer's body.

Jim and Michael couldn't do anything but stand on the shoreline and watch in horror.

Susan burned even more fiercely. Jim could see her skull through the flames, and her ribcage. Yet somehow she still managed to keep the Swimmer locked in her embrace, and the Swimmer began to collapse, and shrink.

Susan literally exploded. Her head tumbled into the sea, with her hair on fire. Her arms flew end-over-end like blazing drum-major's batons. Her pelvis dropped into the surf, leaving nothing but two burning legs standing for a moment on their own, a vision of hell by Salvador Dali. But the Swimmer herself had evaporated. Her substance had been boiled into superheated steam, and carried away by the wind.

Jim took two more steps into the water. In the darkness, he could see the faintest outline of Jane Tullett. She was no longer glistening with wet: she looked now as if she were wearing a white veil over her head, the way she had looked in her casket, when he had attended her funeral.

'Jane,' said Jim.

'Hello, Mr Rook.'

'Jane – I hope you can rest now. I really do.'

Jane smiled behind her veil, and nodded. Then she half turned, and held out her hand. Out of the shadows came the barely visible figure of a young boy, wearing a simple white nightshirt. He stood for a moment, blinking, unsure of himself.

'Are you Peter?' Jim asked him.

'I've been sleeping,' whispered Peter, in a small, haunted voice. 'I dreamed that I was burning, but I wasn't.'

'You can go back to sleep now,' said Jim. 'Don't forget that everybody still thinks about you.'

'Thank you,' said Peter.

Jim stood and watched as the two young spirits turned and walked away, hand in hand, out on to the black wallowing breast of the ocean, and beyond. Their lights flickered briefly in the darkness, and then they were gone. He turned and trudged back to join Michael.

'I told her not to,' said Michael, wiping his eyes with the backs of his hands. 'What more could I do? I loved her. I always wanted to keep her safe.'

Jim laid his hand around Michael's shoulders. 'You can't protect people from their destiny, Michael, no matter how much you may want to. Life is a risk. Death is a risk. Sometimes we just have to be brave, and take what's coming to us.'

'I don't think you understand. Peter was my younger brother.'

'What?'

'Peter was my younger brother and Mary was my cousin. The driver who stood by and watched Peter burn was my uncle Ted, who was driving to the football game right behind my mother and Peter. That's why I went to look for Susan . . . that's why I took care of her. That's why I helped to put Peter into a state of spiritual hypnosis. I felt responsible for him and

I felt responsible for her, too. After all, she risked her life, helping Mary.'

Together they walked across the sand toward Ocean Front Walk. They didn't need to talk to each other any more. They had both loved Susan Silverstone, in their different ways, and grief is often better borne in silence.

Mervyn said, 'You're going off to Washington, then? You're really going?'

'You didn't think I would?'

'I thought you'd find any excuse to stay. I thought you'd dream up yet another supernatural threat, just to make sure that you had to stick by Special Class II.'

They were lounging around Mervyn's apartment, drinking sake and nibbling tiny Japanese snacks, like raw tuna on shreds of seaweed, sesame prawns and *chirasizushi*. In the far corner, Tibbles Two was devouring all the offcuts of salmon and mackerel from a rectangular lacquered dish.

Washington had his leg hooked over the end of the couch, and was swinging his foot. 'I should have been there, man, when you blew up the Swimmer.'

'You supported me, Washington, all the way along the line, you and Laura both, and the rest of the class. I couldn't have made it if it hadn't been for you.'

'Still and all, we weren't there, were we?'

'No, you weren't. You have your own lives to make, from now on. You can never go back. Jane could think of nothing else but going back, but all it ever brings you is disillusionment, resentment, and grief. Look ahead, Washington: there's a great new life out there, just waiting for you to live it.'

Washington took off his sunglasses. Without them, he looked very young. 'I hate to tell you this, sir. It's not supposed to be any kind of reflection on how you taught us or anything. You taught us good. But I don't feel like I'm ready for a new life yet – you know, not *really* ready.'

Jim couldn't help smiling. 'Nobody is ever really ready, Washington. Just fake it if you think you can't make it. The most important lesson to learn in life is that everybody else is just as scared as you are.'

'But you ain't scared of *nothing*, man.'

'You don't think so? I'm leaving LA, I'm leaving my friends. I'm leaving behind me a job that I love and a woman that I almost think I probably love.'

'I never thought of it that way. But least you ain't taking that cat.'

'That's true. But TT's got a good home now . . . better than *I* could ever have given her.'

'Yes,' said Mervyn. 'And maybe she'll learn some discipline now.'

'I'll give you a word of advice, Mervyn,' said Jim. 'Don't try to be too authoritarian. TT has a way of getting her own back.'

'She protected *you*, though, you can't deny it. When she thought you were in trouble, she came hurtling into that bathroom like the Cannonball Run.'

Jim stroked TT under the chin, and she closed her eyes and purred like a rattlesnake.

'I don't know,' he said. 'Sometimes I don't think she's a cat at all.'

They said their goodbyes – Washington, Laura and Jim. They had only been a year together, but it seemed as if they had known each other all their lives.

'You don't have to feel obligated to write me on a regular basis, or send me e-mails,' said Jim. 'But I would like to hear from you just once how you're getting on – what job you've managed to land, and how the world is treating you in general. And if you do ever marry and have children . . . well, I'm a pretty good godfather. I've had enough practice. My sister's kids, my cousin's kids. Always the god and never the father.'

'One day,' said Laura, and kissed him on the cheek.

He sat with Karen on the front porch, gently swinging the rocker with his foot. It was one of those weird nights when the sky looks unnaturally orange, and lightning crackles on the Santa Monica Mountains. One of those nights when you can almost convince yourself that it's going to rain within a couple of hours, except that it never does.

Karen said, 'I don't know what you need, Jim. A trip to Hawaii? A lobotomy? Your old job back at Special Class II?'

'Maybe you're right,' said Jim. He still hadn't replaced his glasses and his eyes looked unfocused. 'Maybe I'm falling apart.'

Karen picked up the empty bottle of Sutter Home Chardonnay that had dropped on the deck beside his chair. 'This has got to stop, Jim. If you and I are ever going to have any kind of meaningful relationship, you have to tell me the truth.'

'The truth, Karen? You don't want to know the truth. The truth is nothing but ashes on the ocean.'

'Now you're being really obscure.'

'And that's the trouble, isn't it? You can't handle anything obscure.'

She leaned across the couch and gave him a long, lingering kiss.

He looked intently into her eyes for a moment, as if he were capable of reading anything that anybody would ask him. Then he stood up, and picked up his bag. 'Oh, well . . . just thought you'd like to know how all this turned out. It should help you to sleep easier, knowing that the Swimmer was evaporated . . . boiled dry, whatever.'

Karen was about to say something, but both of them knew that it was time to let go. He kissed her once on top of her fresh-washed hair and then she walked out of the apartment and closed the door.

He called David DuQuesne. The phone rang for a long time and then his Chinese maid answered. 'Mr DuQuesne's residence.'

'It's Jim Rook. I just wanted a word with Mr DuQuesne.'

'I'm sorry. You haven't heard the news.'

'The news? What news?'

'Mr DuQuesne go to Pennsylvania.'

'I see. Did he say when he was going to be back in LA?'

'He never back.'

'Excuse me? He's left LA for good?'

'He never back. He die.'

'Mr DuQuesne is *dead*? I can't believe it.'

'You Mr Rook, yes? He left a message for you. Hold on. No hang up.'

Jim waited for two or three minutes, and eventually she came back. 'You want I should read?'

'Of course, yes, sure – if you can.'

'I good read English. It say, "Dear Jim, if you are reading this then I am dead. I was inspired by your hunt for the Swimmer, and so I am going to do something that I have been promising myself for many years that I would do, but have never summoned up the nerve. I am leaving tomorrow for Pennsylvania to find Mad Frank Butler – or whatever it was that murdered my brother. This time I am going to lay this urban legend once and for all. I want you to wish me luck."'

'And?' asked Jim. 'What happened to him?'

'Very sorry to say, Pennsylvania police find Mr DuQuesne dead yesterday afternoon in the woods. Bits and pieces all over.'

'Did they find his feet?'

'Excuse me?'

'It doesn't matter. I'm very sorry to hear that. I hope you'll accept my condolences.'

Jim hung up, and sat back in his chair. The sun was going down and the apartment was filled with warm amber light. In his hand he was holding the necklace that he had bought at the psychic fair at De Longpre Park, the Sunday morning that he had first met Susan. It had predicted that he would die tomorrow, on the thirteenth day of the month.

But what was death? Leaving your life behind, and going someplace new? Ending a chapter, or starting something fresh? Was it a blessing, or a torment?

He took the necklace and dropped it into the wastebin. Then he went into the bathroom and furiously brushed his teeth, with tears streaming down his cheeks.